Guardians Of The Round Table 8

Bard's Hollow

Guardians Of The Round Table 8
Bard's Hollow

Avril Sabine, Storm Petersen and Rhys Petersen

Cracked Acorn Productions
Australia

Guardians Of The Round Table 8: Bard's Hollow

Published by
Cracked Acorn Productions
PO Box 1365
Gympie, Queensland 4570
Australia
email: office@crackedacornproductions.com

978-1-923031-09-8 (Ebook)
978-1-923031-10-4 (Paperback)
978-1-923031-11-1 (Digitally Narrated Audiobook)
Genre: Young Adult Fantasy LitRPG

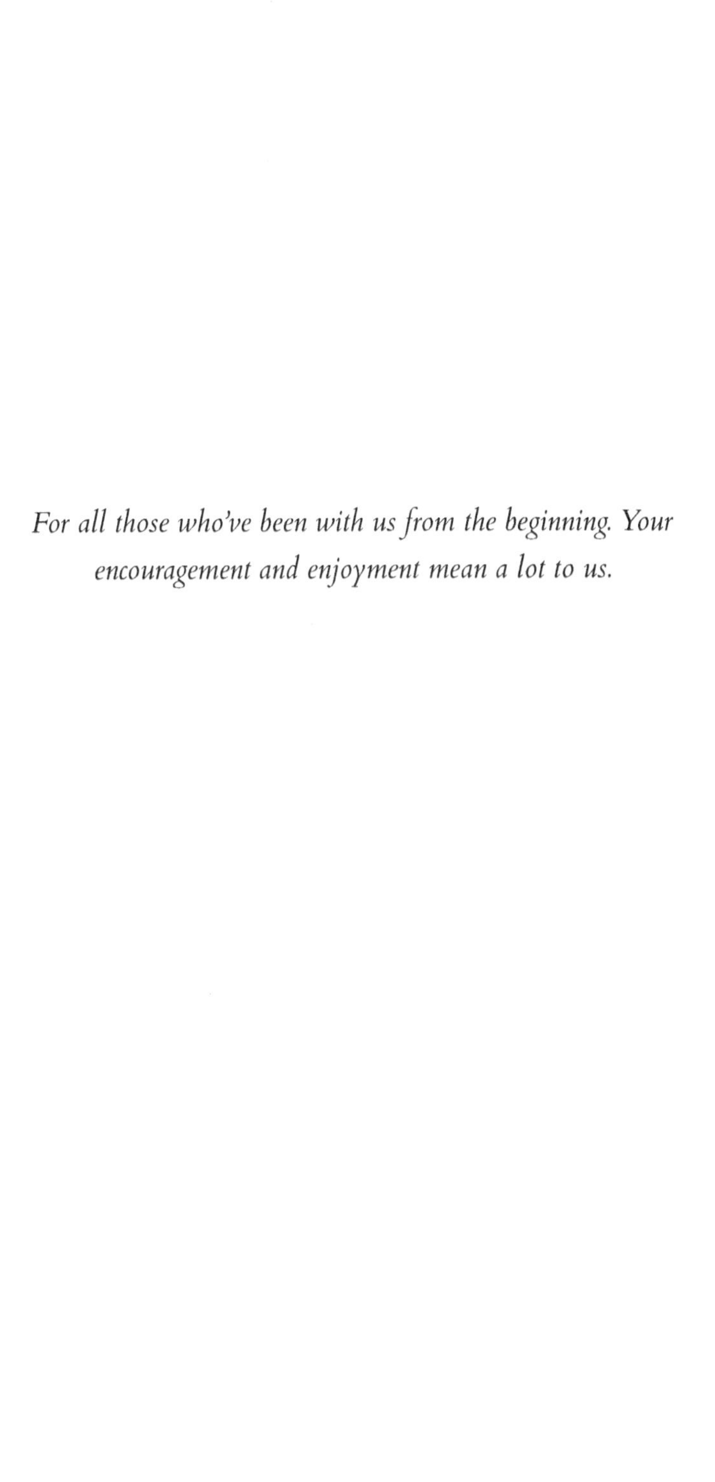

For all those who've been with us from the beginning. Your encouragement and enjoyment mean a lot to us.

Book Description

After spending more time than she'd prefer in her own world, Mallory is determined to complete some of the quests they've wanted to do for a while. But obstacles keep getting in their way. While her brother is convinced they can complete the harder quests too, she isn't so certain. Maybe they should take some time to level up, rather than risk losing what few revives they still have.

*

This story was written by Australian authors using Australian spelling.

Name Pronunciation

Like many names there is more than one way to pronounce the following ones. These are the pronunciations used in this story.

Characters

Ahron (ah-ron)

Danae (da-nay)

Darwil (darr-will)

Deneg (den-eg)

Drohgolrik (dro-gol-rick)

Emica (em-e-cah)

Esben (es-ben)

Goswin (goz-win)

Hisoki (hiss-oh-key)

Jofren Flintah (joff-wren flin-taa)

Jorgen (jaw-gen)

Lialanore (lee-ah-lah-nor)

Morth Helden (more-th Hell-den)

Ninette (nin-et)

Relmir (rel-mer)
Rodina (row-dean-uh)
Sarisa (sa-risa)
Sarnla (sarn-la)
Welby (well-bee)

Places
Buckneth (buck-neth)
Donris Island (don-riss)
Estwater (est-water)
Eswen (es-when)
Inadon (in-ah-don)
Maregan (mare-eh-gan)
Merrow (mare-row)
Shadhurst (shad-hurst)
Simria (sim-re-ah)
Surith (soo-rith)
Ursen (ur-sen)
Velkden (velk-den)
Wildebay (wild-bay)

Foreword

Opening stats, Mallory's notebook entries recapping the previous adventures, world maps and other details can be found at:

www.avrilsabine.com/series/gotrt

The notebook entries will contain spoilers if you haven't read the book they refer to.

Chapter One

Mallory glanced down the hallway to the closed door before she checked her phone again. If they didn't leave in an hour, they'd be late getting to their father's place. It had taken a lot to convince their mum to let Ryan drive them up the coast. They'd told her he planned to take the so-called exchange student to the Sunshine Coast after school today and stay there for the weekend so he could show him around. There was no other way they could have explained Jorgen other than to say he was an exchange student.

Mallory glanced at the closed door again. Their appointment was meant to be fifteen minutes ago and she'd been told to set aside an hour when she'd rung the Guardian's headquarters to arrange the assessment appointment. Maybe they could use the excuse that traffic had held them up. As long as they weren't stuck here too long. What if their appointment went over time and they were held up by traffic? The last thing they needed was for her and Brodie to be grounded again.

She looked at each of those waiting with her, smiling when she saw Callum was showing Danae a clip to explain why they'd laughed when Brodie took an arrow to the knee. Ryan was grinning and Brodie was glaring at Callum. He'd been doing a lot of glaring at things this week. They'd been stuck at home all week, having been told they needed to have their appointment before they returned to Inadon and Friday afternoon had been the first time they could make an appointment since they technically weren't allowed to go anywhere after school. At least they were allowed out on the weekend.

Not being allowed to go anywhere after school hadn't stopped them from calling into the place Ryan had rented, for a few minutes, checking out the changes that had been made by those they'd brought back with them from Inadon. Each day there'd been something new done to the place and she couldn't help wishing they could have stayed home from school and been a part of sorting the place out.

Brodie kept threatening to quit school and focus on Inadon as much as possible. He'd pointed out that he earned enough from questing to support himself. The only thing that had stopped him was Callum reminding him he couldn't be a Guardian until he was eighteen and they might not let him become one if he ditched school.

Danae looked up from Callum's phone, frowning. "I still don't get it. Why is it so funny?"

"See, I told you it wasn't." Brodie glared at Mallory.

She ignored his comment. He'd been in a bad mood all week, his mood getting worse the closer it came to having to stay with their father. Having to pay fifty dollars to have a message sent to Ninette to let her know they wouldn't be back straight away also hadn't helped his mood. They'd all pitched in to pay the fee, so it hadn't been that bad.

"Do you think your dad will let you come to the beach tomorrow?" Ryan asked.

Mallory shrugged, not saying the words that filled her mind. Brodie would probably upset him within an hour of arriving and neither of them would be allowed to go anywhere.

"I doubt it," Brodie muttered. "Or doubt he'd let me go. I'll probably be grounded."

"Just don't say anything to him," Mallory suggested.

Brodie opened his mouth to argue, closing it to turn and face the door at the end of the corridor when it opened. A man stood in the doorway, saying something over his shoulder before he stepped out and closed the door. "Hey, that's the one we met at the bank vault." Brodie hurried down the corridor before anyone could comment.

Mallory stared after her brother. "Do you think we should go talk to him, too?"

Ryan chuckled. "Looks like Brodie has it sorted. And the man did seem more focused on talking to Brodie when we met him at the bank vault."

The man clapped Brodie on the shoulder, with a grin and a nod, before walking beside him back to where everyone waited. "Thanks for that." He glanced around the group. "A heads up is always appreciated." He took a step away, stopping and turning to face the end of the corridor when the door opened again. He grinned at the man who strode towards him, waiting until he was close enough before he spoke. "From your expression, I guess you were given permission to permanently move to Inadon."

The man nodded. "They'll unbind me from this timeline tomorrow."

The man they'd met at the bank vault clapped the other one on the back. "Good to hear. Bet your family will be glad to have you there, with them full time."

Brodie looked from one man to the other. "You can do that? Move permanently to Inadon and not have to come back here."

The second man nodded. "If you have a good reason. I have a family there now. They could move here, like Richelle did when she married Dorset, but they prefer Inadon to this world."

"Don't blame them," Brodie muttered, sending a pointed look towards Mallory.

The second man grinned. "Nor do I. Which is why I'm moving there instead of them moving here."

Mallory was tempted to protest that she liked both worlds, but doubted it would make a difference to her brother. He obviously didn't feel the same way.

"Richelle is from Inadon?" Callum asked.

The second man nodded. "Yeah. Half-elf." He glanced around the group. "I better get going. I've a lot to organise before I relocate tomorrow."

"I'll give you a hand." After a farewell, both men walked away, the two of them discussing what needed to be done as they disappeared around the corner.

Brodie stared wistfully after them. "We should do that. Move to Inadon. Then we'd never have to visit Dad again."

The door at the end of the corridor opened, saving Mallory from having to come up with a reply. When the man standing in the doorway beckoned them forward, she hurried towards him, wanting to get on the road before it was too late and they arrived well after they were meant to.

The man waited until they were all in the room before he closed the door. He looked between the five of them and the three seats on this side of the desk, placing his hand on the doorknob again. "Did you want to bring in a couple of chairs from the corridor?"

Ryan shook his head. "I'm right."

"I can stand too," Callum said at the same time as Brodie spoke.

"I don't need a chair."

Eventually, after some back and forth, Callum took the seat and Brodie stood near the door, looking like he might bolt through it at any moment. Ryan stood behind the chair Mallory sat in.

The man sat behind the desk, shuffling some pages before looking at each of them. "I'm afraid I have you at a disadvantage since I know who all of you are." He paused before continuing. "I'm Carl Brooks." He paused again, continuing when no one spoke. "I won't keep you any longer than necessary. I just have a few questions for each of you."

"You mean we won't be stuck in here for an hour?" Brodie asked.

Mallory barely managed not to groan at her brother's question.

Carl chuckled. "We always suggest an hour since we never know what might crop up to make us late. Like the previous appointment. It went over schedule."

"Can anyone move to Inadon?" Brodie asked. "Like the last guy. Move there forever and not need to come back here."

Carl looked from Brodie to Danae. "That is a choice you might be able to make later. When you're a good few years older by this world's standards."

Mallory didn't bother mentioning it was more likely the thought of going to their father's place than wanting to be with Danae forever that had her brother asking about moving. She resisted the urge to check her phone. "What questions did you want to ask us?"

"How are the four of you finding Inadon?" Carl looked at each of them other than Danae.

"Awesome!" Brodie exclaimed.

"It's an amazing place and I'm enjoying learning everything about it," Callum said.

"It's good to know your actions can make a difference," Ryan said.

Mallory had no idea what to say and when Carl looked at her, she blurted out, "It's good." Feeling like it wasn't a sufficient answer, she added, "At first I was focused on going home since we didn't know anything about the place, but now I love going there and completing quests and exploring the world." When he continued to look at her, she added, "Exploring Ruby Isle. We do plan to go to other places, too."

"Do I make you nervous?" Carl asked.

Chapter Two

Mallory had no idea how to answer Carl, but before she could come up with something to say, Brodie spoke.

"Are you going to stop us from going to Inadon?"

This time, she was grateful for his interruption. Carl did make her nervous, but she didn't want to tell him that.

Carl shook his head. "You can always go there. What I assess is if you're good Guardian material."

"How do you do that?" Brodie took a step away from the door. "I thought we couldn't join until we're eighteen."

Carl smiled. "You can't, but your actions will let us know if you're suited well before that time."

"Are we?" Brodie asked.

Carl made a noncommittal gesture. "Time will tell." He looked at each of them. "Are you having trouble sleeping?" When they all shook their heads, he asked, "What did you dream about last night?"

"Blueberry pancakes," Brodie said. When everyone laughed, except for Carl, who only smiled, he demanded, "What? What's wrong with that?"

Carl, still smiling, looked at the other three, again ignoring Danae. "What about the rest of you?"

"I dreamt of Smudge," Callum said. "My companion animal."

"I don't think I had a dream," Ryan said. "At least not one I can remember."

"And you?" Carl faced Mallory.

Not wanting to mention it had been a nightmare about Rass, Mallory shrugged. "I can't remember either."

"Do any of you find yourself reaching for a weapon when you're startled?" Carl asked.

Brodie grinned. "Only on Inadon. We don't have weapons here."

Callum leaned back in his chair, resting his hands on the arms of it. "I always feel safe in this world."

Mallory studied Callum, trying to figure out why he'd answered like that.

Ryan moved to stand by his brother. "So do I. Shouldn't we feel safe here? Have we gained too much rep on Inadon?"

Carl shook his head. "No, no. Not at all. It's just a question." He smiled. "How about friends here? How are you managing your relationships with others in this world?"

"My best friend goes to Inadon with me," Brodie said with a glance at Callum.

"Same," Callum said.

Carl looked between Ryan and Mallory. "And the two of you?"

Ryan rested a hand on the back of his brother's chair. "We're having no problems keeping up with both worlds. We keep notebooks so we don't lose track of anything and make sure to divide our time between the two worlds. Currently we aren't dividing it evenly since we're trying to establish ourselves on Inadon. But as we get sorted, the time spent in each place will probably change. Become more equal."

"We got our own place here," Brodie said. "And brought some of our group back to help set it up."

Carl glanced at the paper stacked in neat piles on his desk. "Yes. I was informed."

"Is there a problem with me coming here?" Danae asked. "I was told most people in this world don't know about Inadon and to keep it a secret. So I haven't told anyone about my world."

Carl smiled reassuringly at her. "No problem at all. You've all been very discrete. You're welcome to return as long as you continue to be discrete regarding your origins."

Mallory wasn't at all reassured by Carl's words. She was starting to feel like they'd done something wrong.

"Everyone helped us set up our place, so now we're completely organised in this world. We just need to do the same on Inadon."

Carl studied Mallory for a moment before speaking. "What do you think being organised on Inadon would look like?"

"Levelling up further and finding the right location for our base," Mallory said.

"And getting better gear," Brodie added.

"How about you two?" Carl looked at Callum and Ryan.

Ryan grinned. "I can answer for Callum. Getting all the crafting ability books."

Callum chuckled. "That would be good. It's always nice to have information about things."

"What about you?" Carl looked at Ryan.

"The same answer as Mallory. Skills and a base."

Carl studied Ryan a moment longer before he turned his attention to Brodie. "Is dreaming about food new?"

When everyone laughed, Brodie glared at them before muttering, "No."

"His first dream was probably about food," Ryan said.

"I bet it wasn't," Brodie muttered.

Mallory smiled. "I'm with Ryan on that one. I'm sure it was."

Smiling, Carl turned to Callum. "Are you worried about your companion animal?"

Callum shook his head. "No. I miss him, but I know Ninette will take good care of him." He chuckled and glanced at Brodie. "Unlike some, I rarely dream about food. Just about the other things in my life that I enjoy."

"So no nightmares then?" Carl asked.

Mallory finally realised what Carl was trying to find out and Callum's comment made sense. Now she was glad she hadn't mentioned dreaming about Rass. That certainly qualified as a nightmare. After Callum shook his head, she said, "I rarely dream. But I guess I don't have nightmares either since I sleep well. Nightmares would wake you, wouldn't they?"

"Or you'd remember them if they kept you from waking," Ryan said.

Carl rose to his feet. "Let me know if that changes." He smiled. "Sometimes the differences between the two worlds can be difficult to become accustomed to."

"Are you kidding?" Brodie asked. "What's not to love about Inadon? It's the best place ever."

"Not everyone feels that way." Carl made his way to the door, resting his hand on the doorknob. "Maybe having no idea what to expect has made things easier for you in some ways."

Mallory rose to her feet at the same time as Danae, Callum not standing up for another few seconds. "Does that mean we can go now?"

"Unless you had any questions." Carl held the door half open, having stopped when she'd spoken.

Mallory shook her head. She'd thought about asking if Rass could go after them in this world, but that seemed like a bad idea after the questions Carl had asked them. What would happen if he learned of her nightmares? Would he stop her from going? She wasn't about to risk it.

Carl held the door fully open. "Then enjoy your weekend and we'll be interested to see how you progress on Inadon."

"Does that mean we passed this test?" Brodie asked.

For once, Mallory didn't feel the urge to hush her brother. He'd asked the very question she hadn't been able to bring herself to ask.

"It wasn't a test," Carl said.

"Are you sure?" Brodie asked suspiciously. "It felt like one. Tests always have heaps of questions."

Carl chuckled. "If only life was that simple." He stepped back. "I'll see all of you again another day."

Mallory followed Callum from the room, wishing he'd walk faster, then realising that bolting from the room wouldn't have been a good plan. She waited until she was in the front passenger seat of the van, that Ryan had borrowed from his mate again since there were so many of them, before she spoke. "It was about PTSD, wasn't it?"

Ryan started the engine. "Yeah."

Callum nodded. "It had to be with the questions he was asking."

"What is that?" Danae asked.

"Why would we get that?" Brodie asked. "There's nothing traumatic about Inadon. It's here that's traumatic."

While Callum explained post-traumatic stress disorder to Danae, Mallory checked her phone. The appointment hadn't taken as long as she'd feared it would. "We shouldn't be late."

Ryan pulled out onto the road, heading towards their place where the rest of their group waited. "We can always blame traffic."

She smiled. That had been her thought, too. Her smile faded. Not that the excuse was guaranteed to work. "Getting there on time would be better. Then we won't have to make excuses." Mallory looked out the window, assessing how much traffic was about. It wasn't too bad. They might even get there early. Much better than having to start the weekend off with an excuse. Their father didn't like excuses. They were for the disorganised. Or the easily distracted. And he disliked both traits very much.

When they reached their place, they didn't get the chance to get out of the van before Emica, Jorgen and Esben were coming outside, bringing the luggage they were taking to the coast for the weekend. They piled into the van, Emica glaring at Brodie.

"Don't take up all the space, Goblin Boy."

"I wasn't," Brodie protested, moving closer to Danae. Glancing at Danae, he reddened. "I'm not taking up too much space, am I?"

Danae smiled, resting her hand on his arm. "Not at all. You can move closer if you need to."

Esben closed the door, the last to enter the vehicle. "I wish we had cars on Inadon. It'd make getting places a lot quicker."

"We don't have portals here," Callum said.

Mallory smiled, listening to the discussion between Esben and Callum over the differences and which place had the better options. Her smile faded as she thought of the coming weekend. She wasn't looking forward to it. At least it had been ages since they'd had to go to their father's place. And hopefully, it would be months before they needed to visit again.

"You okay?" Ryan asked.

She looked over at him. "Yeah."

"You sure? Callum said your name twice," Ryan persisted.

Mallory half turned in her seat. "Sorry. What did you want?" She allowed herself to be drawn into the debate going on in the back of the van about the two worlds, pushing aside her worries about the coming weekend.

Chapter Three

When they pulled up in front of her father's house, Mallory checked her phone. They were ten minutes early. Relief rushed through her as she opened the door. They wouldn't need to make any excuses. And being early would impress him, getting them off to a good start for the weekend. Now if only Brodie could manage not to answer back.

"I'll grab your bag for you." Ryan was out of the car before Mallory could protest.

She'd planned to tell him he didn't need to see her to the door, but she'd spent the drive talking about the two worlds and forgetting her plan to tell him to just drop them and go. Hurrying after him, she tried to take her bag. "It's okay. You can get everyone to the house you rented for the weekend. You still have to organise dinner and everything."

Ryan stopped halfway to the front door to face her. "Are you embarrassed to introduce me to your dad?"

"No." She tried to think of a way to explain, but everything made things sound worse than they were. "You have plans for this evening. Everyone does." Everyone that was except for her and her brother.

"Taking a few minutes to meet your dad won't slow those plans down." Ryan turned to Brodie, who'd stopped beside them, moving to the side before he spoke. "You can go ahead. We'll be there in a minute."

"As if I'm going first," Brodie muttered.

Before Mallory could again attempt to take her bag from Ryan, the front door opened and she barely contained a groan when she saw her father. "Come on." She hurried forward. It was too late to send Ryan to the van now. "Hi, Dad." She pasted on a bright smile.

Her father looked past her to Ryan. "You're the boy who lives next door. The one without a job."

Ryan held out his hand. "I'm Ryan. And I do have a job."

When her father said nothing, only looked Ryan up and down, Mallory said, "My dad, Gerald."

"Mr Owens," Gerald corrected. He again looked Ryan up and down. "You're too old for my daughter."

Ryan turned to Mallory with a grin. "Should I be worried my beard is going to turn grey and I'll need a walking stick?"

Normally, she'd laugh at his comment. All she could do was give her father a quick look.

When she didn't respond, the humour faded from Ryan's eyes. He linked his fingers through hers, her bag still in his other hand. "Are you okay?"

She disentangled her hand from his, glancing towards her father. His lips were pressed together in a tight line. "Yeah. You should go. We'll see you Sunday night."

Ryan looked between Mallory and Gerald. "If you're sure you're okay."

Mallory took her bag from Ryan. "Yeah. Go and get settled into the place you're staying at."

Ryan let her take the bag, studying her a moment longer before he nodded. He took a step towards her.

She stepped back, seeing the hurt in his eyes at her avoidance. But there was no way she could kiss him goodbye with her father standing in the doorway watching them. Not even a quick kiss. Or even one on her cheek.

Gerald stepped back out of the doorway when Ryan strode towards his van. "Inside. The two of you." When neither of them moved, he added, "Now."

Mallory moved first, entering the house, Brodie following close behind her. Before she could step out of the entrance room, her father spoke.

"You will use the train in future if your mother is unable to drive you." He closed the door behind him, moving to stand beside the neatly displayed footwear in the shoe rack. They were all lined up in ascending sizes. "I will not have you arriving in that vehicle again. It looks like it should be put off the road. I don't know what your mother was thinking, allowing you in a vehicle that looks like it should be sent to the scrapyard. Has she no concern at all for your safety?"

"It isn't that bad," Mallory protested. The vehicle might not look the best, but it was roadworthy.

Gerald continued like she hadn't spoken. "Nor will I have you dating a boy who has no prospects or connections. Neither he nor his brother will ever amount to anything. Would you have yourself dragged down to their level when you can achieve far more in life than either of them?"

Mallory pressed her lips together, knowing it was a waste of time arguing. He never listened to what she had to say. Unless it was something that agreed with what he'd said.

"There's nothing wrong with them," Brodie stated. "They're our friends. Our team mates."

"Team mates! Have you listened to nothing I've taught you over the years? You can't rely on people. You need to fend for yourself. Take care of yourself. How many times do I need to tell you? No one will stand up for you and no one will stand by you unless it's of benefit to them."

"You're wrong," Brodie said. "They do stand up for me. And by me. All the time. And not because it benefits them."

Mallory wanted to tell her brother to stop arguing, to keep his mouth shut so they could get through the weekend without any dramas. That he was wasting his breath. Their father would never see their point of view. Yet anything she said would only make things worse.

"They'll want something in return." Gerald pointed a warning finger at Brodie. "You wait and see. They'll ask you for something and remind you of what they did for you and how much effort it took. Never put yourself in the position of owing someone. You're begging to be walked over. Stop wasting your time with losers. How dense are you? I tell you this every time. And you continue to disappoint me. Every single time."

A woman entered the entrance area, a hand resting on her well-rounded stomach. "Dinner is ready. Surely this can wait until later."

Mallory stared at Corrine, her father's partner. "You're pregnant." She regretted the words the moment she blurted them out. She should have taken her own advice and kept quiet.

"We planned to tell you today," Corrine said.

Mallory somehow stopped herself from demanding why they hadn't told them sooner. Corrine had to be at least seven or eight months pregnant. She closed her eyes momentarily at Brodie's next words.

"If we didn't visit this weekend, does that mean you wouldn't have told us?"

"Do not take that tone with me," Gerald warned.

Corrine scurried out of the entrance room, murmuring, "I'll tell Landon and Vincent to wash their hands and sit at the table."

"I wasn't using any tone," Brodie protested.

Chapter Four

"Brodie." Mallory kept her voice low, hoping her brother would heed her warning and that speaking a single word wouldn't annoy her father. From the way the two of them glared at each other, Brodie was likely to end up grounded for the weekend. Like always. She tried again. "Should we go to the table now? I'm hungry."

"Once your brother apologises for his behaviour," Gerald stated.

"Apologise!" Brodie exclaimed. "I haven't done nothing wrong." He continued to glare at his father. "I don't know why I bother. I'll never be good enough for you. No matter what I do or how much I try to follow your stupid ideas on how people should act, you'll keep telling me you're disappointed in me."

"Apologise immediately," Gerald ordered.

"Why should I apologise for saying the truth?" Brodie demanded. "You had me believing the only way to be successful in life was to be like you. If that's true, then I'd rather fail."

Mallory drew in a sharp breath at her brother's words. She felt like she was watching a train wreck she couldn't prevent from happening.

"Apologise. Immediately."

Mallory wanted to beg Brodie to apologise. Wanted to tell him not to say anything else so he didn't end up spending the entire weekend going hungry and stuck in the bedroom. "Brodie." Again, she tried to put all her warnings in his name, keeping her voice low.

Gerald spun to face her, pointing a finger at her. "You stay out of it. How will he ever learn if you always interfere?"

Brodie stepped between his father and Mallory, reaching for a weapon that wasn't there, standing toe-to-toe with his father. "Leave her alone." There was an unmistakable warning in his voice, a threatening tone he'd never used on his father before.

The crack of Gerald's palm connecting with Brodie's face rang out in the room, bringing with it silence.

Mallory automatically reached for a weapon that wasn't at her side, moving so she stood beside her brother. Her action stunned her, holding her in place. She'd been about to attack her father? Then it dawned on her. She hadn't been about to attack him. She'd been trying to protect her brother. Something she'd been doing for weeks on Inadon.

Brodie took a step back from Gerald, grabbing Mallory's arm. "We're getting out of here."

Gerald reached the front door before them, blocking their exit. "You will not be going anywhere. You'll spend the weekend in your room thinking over your behaviour. If you apologise, I'll let you join us for dinner Sunday night."

"I'm not about to stay here after you hit me." Brodie grabbed his bag off the floor, handing Mallory her bag.

"With the way you behaved this evening, it was long overdue," Gerald said.

Mallory slung the strap of her bag over her shoulder, taking out her phone and opening the camera app. "Brodie." When her brother faced her, her voice having been loud and sharp, she took a photo of the red handprint on his cheek. She sent the image to Ryan, along with a message for him to collect them.

"What do you think you're doing?" Gerald reached for Mallory's phone, stepping away from the door when she retreated.

Brodie slipped past Gerald and swung the door open.

"Delete that photo immediately," Gerald ordered as he tried to grab the phone again. "I'll not have you blowing this all out of proportion."

"I can delete it if you want," Mallory said. "But it won't make a difference. I've already sent it."

"You sent it to your mother?" Gerald demanded.

Ryan appeared in the doorway. "No. She sent it to me. But don't worry, I'll make sure their mum has a copy." He looked from Brodie to Mallory. "Let's go." He stepped to the side so they could leave the house, blocking Gerald when he tried to follow. "I don't think so."

"You have no right to come in here and throw your weight around," Gerald said.

Ryan smiled, his hands clenched into fists, and his eyes narrowed. "I didn't enter your house." He kept his gaze on Gerald. "Get in the car, Mallory."

Mallory backed away, not wanting to leave Ryan to face her father alone.

Brodie grabbed her arm. "Come on. Let's get out of here."

"I will call the police," Gerald warned.

"Good," Ryan said. "We'll see what they think about physical assault." He took a step back from the doorway.

When her father took a step towards Ryan, Mallory wanted to run to his side. Instead, she dragged her arm from her brother's grip and stopped where she was. "Cause trouble and I'll start screaming until all the neighbours are out here wondering what's going on, and one of them calls the police."

Gerald froze, only several steps from the front door. He pointed a finger at Mallory. "I'm calling your mother and we'll see what she has to say about this. The two of you will be grounded for the entire weekend when she rings to order you to return here." He remained by the doorway as they left.

Mallory stared out the window at him, highlighted by the light from the doorway. His hands were on his hips and even though she couldn't see his expression, she knew what it would be. Annoyance and disappointment. Not the sort of disappointment when someone missed out on going somewhere they'd been looking forward to visiting. No, the sort of disappointed look that bordered on disgust with a touch of stunned horror, as if what had been witnessed couldn't have occurred. Like the piece of cake you'd been about to eat was rotting and full of maggots. She continued to watch him, not looking away until they turned the corner and she could no longer see him. He hadn't moved out of the doorway the entire time. She looked at Ryan when he briefly rested a hand on her thigh.

"You okay?" Ryan asked.

Mallory nodded, then spoke, since Ryan was concentrating on the road. "Yeah. You were quick. I thought it'd take you longer to collect us."

"We hadn't gone far," Callum said from the back of the van. "We pulled up a street away. Ryan was going to give you half an hour to get settled, then check you were okay. He said he didn't like your dad's attitude."

"He said you looked worried," Emica said. "Were you?"

"Did he hit you?" Ryan asked.

Again Mallory shook her head. "No. He never has. I wasn't worried about me, I was worried about Brodie. About him getting grounded again and having to go without food for the weekend."

Emica looked Brodie up and down. "He does that to you? Starves you?"

Chapter Five

Mallory started to protest. The word 'starve' sounded harsh compared to the 'send you to bed without dinner' punishment their father always threatened Brodie with. But she supposed they amounted to the same thing.

Brodie nodded, not meeting Emica's gaze.

"What kind of father does that?" Danae asked. "My father would never let me go hungry. No matter what I did. And I've certainly tried his patience more than a time or two."

"Neither would mine," Emica said. "And he's told me quite a few times that I cause more trouble than a dozen members of the dark forces." Emica grinned. "I always take that as a compliment."

"Our father believes in punishments suited to the individual. He takes away what you love most." Mallory smiled wryly. "And we all know how much Brodie loves his food."

"How does he punish you?" Ryan pulled up in front of a lowset house, glimpses of the beach visible on either side of it.

Mallory stared out the window. "He doesn't."

"He threatens to punish me," Brodie said.

Emica opened the van door. "Harsh." She clambered out, grabbing a bag as she went. "Very harsh. But he does know what punishment will bother each of you the most."

Mallory got out of the van too, wanting an end to the conversation. "Will there be enough space for all of us?"

Ryan joined Mallory on the footpath. "We'll find space for you."

"You can share the room Emica and I are using," Danae said. "Ryan showed us a floor plan of the place and we've chosen rooms already. There are three bedrooms."

Before Mallory could answer, her phone rang. She took it out of her pocket to stare at the screen. Her mum. She wasn't looking forward to this call. Especially since her father had obviously called her first.

"What are we going to tell her?" Brodie asked.

Ryan gave Mallory a quick kiss. "I'm sure you'll figure this out. While you sort out the call, we'll get set up. There's a verandah on the other side of the house with an outdoor setting that overlooks the beach. It looked good in the pictures we saw of the place."

Nodding, Mallory headed down the side of the house, answering the call, her brother keeping pace with her. "We were going to call you, Mum."

"I can't believe the two of you would do this. You know how important this weekend is to me. As well as to Alicia."

"Put it on speaker," Brodie said as they reached the outdoor cane chairs scattered across the verandah.

"I'm putting the phone on speaker. Brodie wants to talk to you too." Mallory sank down onto one of the chairs.

Brodie sat in the chair next to her. "Mum, it isn't like what you think. I bet Dad didn't tell you anything that really happened."

"Did you threaten your father?" Norine asked.

"No!" Brodie exclaimed.

Mallory wasn't sure if she could say no. Brodie had been threatening, it just wasn't the complete story.

"He said the two of you were argumentative the moment you stepped in the door and that Brodie was in his face in a threatening manner and the two of you were overreacting," Norine said.

"I was protecting Mal. He was the one being threatening," Brodie argued.

Mallory started to speak, stopping when she recalled all the questions they'd been asked at the assessment. Had they been overreacting? Was it their fault? She pulled up the picture on her phone while Brodie protested he was never going to their father's again.

"Mum! He hit me," Brodie protested.

"He said you'd tell me that. He also said the two of you were arguing with each other and Mallory slapped you," Norine said. "I thought better of the two of you than that."

Mallory stared at the picture, her brother again protesting. The vivid red mark covered her brother's cheek. The sinking feeling that had started to form vanished. She interrupted the argument between her mum and Brodie. "I'm sending you the pic, Mum. And if you want, I can slap Brodie's other cheek so you can have a size comparison."

Brodie rose from the chair. "You're not hitting me."

Mallory grinned up at her brother, pretty certain she wouldn't need to. "But what if Mum thinks my handprint really is that big? Surely you can cope with another slap today, all in the name of proof." Her grin faded at the look of uncertainty on her brother's face. Before she could reassure him, Norine spoke.

"I'm coming home."

"No, you're not," Mallory said. "We're fine. Don't let Dad ruin your weekend with Alicia. We can stay here."

"You're never going to your father's again," Norine stated. "Has he ever hit you before?"

"No," Mallory said at the same time as Brodie.

"Are you sure?" Norine asked.

"He's only ever sent Brodie to his room without dinner. It's the first time he's ever hit one of us," Mallory said.

"And it'll be the last time," Norine said firmly.

"So we can stay here?" Brodie asked.

"No," Norine said. "Give me the address and I'll pick you up."

"Come on, Mum," Brodie protested. "There's lots of space here. It's an entire house. Mal can share a room with Danni and Emica."

"Danni? The girl that wears the funny ears?" Norine asked.

"Yeah," Brodie said.

Mallory smiled briefly, her thoughts momentarily turning to the conversation she'd had with her mum, Norine shaking her head over how many people wanted to look like elves because of 'The Lord of the Rings' movies. It had been hard not to say that Danae was actually a half-elf and not someone who wished they could be one.

Norine didn't answer Brodie straight away. "I probably won't be there until after midnight."

"Then we can stay?" Brodie asked hopefully.

"I never agreed to that," Norine said.

"What do you think we're going to do?" Brodie demanded. "What if we promise no drinking and no parties?"

"That'd only be the start of the list," Norine said dryly.

"How about if we promise no having sex with anyone either?" Mallory said with a grin. Her grin faded when there was no reply. "Mum? You still there?"

"I'm here."

"How about you trust us to only do what we know you'd let us do?" Mallory asked. "We're not little kids. Making us go straight home after school and never having anyone over of an afternoon isn't necessary. We won't be living at home forever. Another couple of years and we'll be out of home and trying to figure out how to look after ourselves. Why not give us the chance to start figuring out how to do it now? While we have you to help us if we don't get it right."

This time, it was Brodie who spoke when Norine didn't answer. "You there, Mum?"

"Yes."

"What do you think of Mal's idea? It's not like we'd starve or anything. I can cook. I can even clean up after myself in the kitchen. And I'd listen to Mal. She usually knows what she's talking about. Please, Mum," Brodie begged.

"Are you sure there's nothing else going on?" Norine asked hesitantly.

"What do you mean?" Mallory asked.

"The two of you seem to have changed. Other than a little teasing, neither of you have hassled each other or had any major arguments," Norine said. "Which is why I was surprised when your father said you'd been arguing."

Mallory grinned when she thought of all they'd done on Inadon. "Maybe you're only just noticing. We've been working on growing up for years."

"No. Well, maybe you have, but Brodie hasn't. He's changed a lot in the past week. I always feared he'd turn out just like your father. Now I know he won't."

Mallory stared at the phone before looking at her brother, who looked as stunned as she felt. "You did?"

"I'm never going to be like him," Brodie stated. "Never."

Chapter Six

Mallory rose to her feet and reached up to drape an arm around her brother's shoulders. "Of course Brodie won't end up like Dad. He's nothing like him." When her mum didn't reply, she asked, "Can we stay here for the weekend? You don't want to be driving on the road so late. It'll be two or three in the morning by the time we get home. What if you're too tired to drive?" When her mum started to disagree, she interrupted. "We also like Alicia. We don't want to be the cause of ruining your weekend with her."

"You like her?" Norine asked.

"Yeah, she's cool," Brodie said.

"She's nice," Mallory said at the same time as her brother spoke, adding once he'd finished, "She treats us like people. Not little kids."

"Come on, Mum. What's the worse that can happen?" Brodie asked.

Mallory nearly groaned at her brother's question, speaking before their mum could list all the things that could go wrong. "Nothing will happen. We'll make sure of it. Not just me and Brodie, but our entire team."

"Team?" Norine asked.

"Yeah, our team," Brodie said. "They help us fight against the dark forces."

Norine sighed. "They all play computer games?"

Mallory laughed. "You make that sound like it's a bad habit. Isn't it better than drunken parties?"

"Is that what you plan to do all weekend? Play computer games?" Norine asked.

"We might for a bit," Mallory said. "But we also plan to show them around. They haven't been to Australia before, so we're not about to keep them in the one room gaming all weekend." Mallory tried not to smile, keeping the rest of her thoughts to herself. Or take them back to Inadon before they had the chance to check out the Sunshine Coast.

"You will give me regular updates," Norine said.

"We can stay?" Brodie asked.

"If the two of you can't prove to me you can manage a weekend away from home, then it's back to straight home after school and no friends over during the week or games until the weekend," Norine warned.

"We can stay?" Brodie asked again.

"And you better not let your schoolwork slip again this year," Norine added.

Taking pity on her brother, Mallory asked, "Does that mean we can stay here for the weekend?"

"Yes."

"Hell yeah." Brodie victory punched the air.

"If you behave," Norine warned.

"We will," Mallory said, Brodie echoing her.

After some last-minute instructions, Norine finally hung up.

Mallory turned to Brodie, slipping her phone into her pocket. "Are you okay?"

Brodie didn't answer immediately. "I realised the only people who attack us on Inadon are enemies."

"He's not our enemy," Mallory said.

"Then what is he?"

"He's-" Mallory broke off with a shrug, glancing out to sea. There was no answer there for her. "I guess he's our biological father. Other than that, I don't know." She looked her brother up and down, the handprint having faded to a faint redness. "Are you sure you're okay?"

"Yeah. I feel like I can stop guessing everything now. Like my first thoughts or actions aren't always wrong. Like no matter what I do, it'll never be right for him. But I think that's okay because I don't think he's right." Brodie grinned. "He'd never make a Guardian, but I bet he'd fit right in with the dark forces."

Mallory grinned too. "Yeah, he probably would."

Brodie's grin faded. "Does that make him evil?"

Mallory struggled to think of an answer, seeing her brother clearly needed something more than a yes or no. She shook her head as she tried to come up with a better reply. "He assesses what will give him the best results. I don't think he cares how he gets those results, as long as they're the best ones for him."

Brodie frowned. "So he's evil then?"

"No. Just doesn't think about how what he does will affect anyone else. Only how it affects him."

"So he's thoughtless?"

Mallory smiled wryly, laughing softly at her inability to explain clearly. "I don't think that's it either." She shrugged. "Or maybe it is. He doesn't do things thoughtlessly, just doesn't focus on anyone other than himself." She shrugged again. "In some ways, I guess he is. He's thoughtless of how things affect others, but not thoughtless to the consequences of things. At least when it comes to how they're related to him."

They both turned at the sound of the back door opening. Danae peered through the gap. "Are you all right?"

Brodie nodded.

"Everyone is talking about taking a walk along the beach. Did you want to go?" Danae looked past Brodie to Mallory. "Both of you?"

"Sounds good," Brodie said.

Mallory waited until Danae had closed the door, leaving them alone again, before she asked, "Are you okay?"

Brodie frowned, nodding after a moment. "I think so." He grinned. "Yeah, I am because we never have to go back there ever again. Mum said so."

Mallory laughed softly. "So it was worth the slap?"

Brodie rubbed his cheek. "It still stings a little."

Mallory stepped forward and rested her hand on her brother's cheek. "Let me try something." The last of the redness faded as she watched.

Brodie's jaw dropped. "That worked. That actually worked. I can't feel anything. You can heal in this world. But, how? It's not like you have a wand to cast any spells."

"I didn't use a spell. I used rapid mend and weak increased healing. I know that's not exactly how they're used and they need mana, but your cooking skill works a little differently here." Mallory shrugged. "I don't know which one worked, but I thought it worth testing since you can cook better in this world after levelling up your cooking on Inadon." She lowered her hand. "I wonder if those people who can heal with laying their hands on others are actually people who've been on Inadon."

Before they could continue the conversation, the back door opened and everyone came out, headed for the beach. Only Danae and Ryan remained on the verandah with them.

Ryan slipped an arm around Mallory's waist. "Want to walk with me?"

She smiled up at him with a nod. Unlike on Inadon, there was plenty of light cast across the beach from the houses dotting the waterfront.

Danae stood in front of Brodie. "Would you like to walk with me, Brodie?"

His cheeks reddened, but he nodded, taking the hand she held out to him. He didn't speak until they reached the beach, having kicked his shoes off before they'd left the verandah, just like everyone else had done. "We should do the bandit quest when we return to Ursen."

"You want to help Relmir and Sarnla take back their farm?" Danae asked.

"I thought you wanted to go after the drake eggs," Mallory said.

"I do, but…" Brodie's voice trailed off and he shrugged. "I was thinking about what we should do next and when I thought of that quest, I kept hearing Dad's voice ask how it'd benefit me. So we should do it."

Mallory frowned. "What has that got to do with it?"

"He wouldn't think it worth doing, so it must be," Brodie explained.

Mallory sighed, slowly shaking her head. "It doesn't work like that."

Brodie let go of Danae's hand and stepped in front of his sister, stopping so that she did too. The rest of their group was well ahead of them along the beach. "How does it work then? I'm not going to be like him. Mum thinks I will be."

41

Chapter Seven

Mallory tried to think how to explain it to Brodie. "Mum said she doesn't think you'll be like Dad anymore." She struggled to figure out what to say next. Nothing came to mind.

Ryan tugged Mallory back so that he could face Brodie. "Why do you think we should do the quest?"

"What do you mean?" Brodie asked.

"Forget about what anyone else thinks. Just tell me your first reaction to doing the quest. The reaction you had when you first learned about it," Ryan said.

Brodie glanced at Danae before he returned his attention to Ryan. "That no one else was helping them."

"Perfect answer," Ryan said.

Brodie looked startled. "It was?"

Ryan nodded. "What made you decide you shouldn't do the quest?"

Again Brodie glanced at Danae. "Ahh… well." He glanced at Danae again before he continued. "That there must be a reason why no one was helping them and maybe we shouldn't either."

"That's when you stopped thinking like you and started thinking like Dad," Mallory said.

"So my thoughts were right?" Brodie asked hesitantly.

Mallory wanted to give her brother a hug, but she knew that would embarrass him. Instead, she nodded and gave him a smile. "They were until you started thinking like Dad."

"But–" Brodie broke off to glance at Danae. He swallowed visibly before continuing. "Why does Dad always keep saying they're wrong?"

Danae moved closer to Brodie and slipped her hand in his. "Maybe because he's the one who's wrong. How can someone who's wrong know when something is right?"

Brodie stared at Danae, shock clearly on his face. The shock slowly became a smile that turned into a grin. "He is, isn't he?"

Danae nodded.

Brodie continued to grin. "Dad is the one who's wrong." He spoke the words as if they were the most amazing thing he'd ever discovered.

Ryan chuckled. "Does that mean we're going to do the bandit quest when we return?"

"Hell yeah," Brodie exclaimed. "Let's do all the quests."

Mallory laughed. "I wouldn't go quite that far. We do have to keep working on our things, too."

Emica came running over to them. "Is it safe to walk in the sea? Not far, just up to my ankles."

Ryan nodded. "It's safe to swim. We can pick up some swimmers tomorrow, if everyone wants."

Emica looked at each of them. "What were you talking about?"

"Doing the bandit quest," Brodie said.

"We're going back now?" Emica asked. "I wanted to see more of your world. Even if it's strange and you have no way of knowing when you level up."

Brodie brightened. "We could go back now if we wanted to. We're all in the same place."

Callum joined them in time to hear the comment, having been walking ahead of Jorgen and Esben, who were talking to each other. "I think we should go back Sunday night like we planned."

"Why?" Brodie asked.

"Because of all the questions we were asked during the appointment," Callum said. "They want us to have balance in our life and they're keeping an eye on us to make sure we don't get PTSD. We need to show them we've got things sorted. Rushing back won't do that."

Ryan nodded thoughtfully. "Even though they won't stop us from going to Inadon, I don't just want to keep going back. I want to be a Guardian. It's good knowing I'm making a difference in both worlds."

"I guess we can wait until Sunday," Brodie said. "But I bet Fang is missing me."

"Maybe we could bring her with us next time," Ryan suggested.

"I wish I could bring Smudge, but someone would call the RSPCA if they saw me wandering around with a river otter," Callum said.

"There are potions that could help with that," Danae said. "Ones that can change an animal's form. Turn him into a dog or cat so no one looks twice at him."

Brodie brightened. "We could make him a dog so he and Fang can play together. Fang might not like a cat when she's in this world. She might want to chase it or something."

Jorgen and Esben joined them, Jorgen gesturing in the direction they'd been walking. "There's a group of people further along the beach. Did we want to keep going in that direction or try the other one?"

Ryan looked ahead, grinning. "Looks like a group of kids. It'll be okay. This place isn't like Inadon." He turned to Mallory, slipping an arm around her waist. "Want to continue our walk? We could walk along the waterline."

They spent another hour on the beach before returning to the house where Brodie made dinner. Mallory regularly checked on her brother, wanting to make sure he was okay. There were moments when she was sure he was still grappling with everything, but the looks of uncertainty quickly passed and she remained silent rather than risk drawing everyone's attention to him. She was fairly certain he wouldn't appreciate her doing that.

They sprawled out in the lounge room watching a movie, spending more time talking about the weekend's plans than actually watching the action movie while they ate dinner. Not that their weekend went exactly to plan. They did go shopping the next morning, but Mallory wanted to cut it short when she glimpsed someone who she could have sworn was Rass. Ryan suggested she was seeing danger where it didn't exist and that they were safe here. Their reputation wasn't high enough the dark forces would be coming after them in their world.

Everyone from Inadon marvelled over the variety of stores and how easy it was to get some things and after lunch, they spent the afternoon on the beach. There were regular calls and messages from Norine and Brodie suggested once that they ignore them, getting annoyed at all the interruptions.

The evening was spent teaching those from Inadon how to play games on the two laptops Ryan and Callum had brought with them. They focused on RPGs and spent a lot of time laughing at their attempts at playing. Jorgen was the one who mastered the techniques first, pointing out it was all about dexterity and coordination, something a rogue frequently used.

Early Sunday morning, after packing up and putting everything in the van, Ryan took them for a drive around the area, including into the mountains of the hinterlands. They briefly visited some of the tourist attractions as well as stopping for a break at a waterfall before heading to Australia Zoo after lunch.

Jorgen pointed to a crocodile lazily sunning. "We have creatures like that back home."

"Ours are bigger and have larger teeth," Esben said.

"Do they have them on Ruby Isle?" Callum asked.

At the same time, Brodie asked, "What are they called?"

"Primordial crocodiles," Jorgen said. "They're in a few places on Ruby Isle, but the main location is at the head of the river that comes out into the sea between Surith and Mer Point. We heard some sailors at one of the taverns talking about there being a large nest of them there and that when there's too much rain, sometimes the younger ones get swept down to the sea."

Mallory was about to ask a question about the primordial crocodiles when she caught a glimpse of someone in the crowds. She turned, but before she could point out the man who'd reminded her of Rass, he'd disappeared amongst a group of people heading away from them. She remained silent, not wanting Ryan to remind her she wasn't in danger. Was he right? Was it only her imagination? Was she having nightmares while awake?

Callum moved close to Mallory, keeping his voice low when he spoke. "What's wrong?"

She shook her head, glancing at Ryan, who was talking to Jorgen about the crocodiles.

"Are you sure nothing's wrong?" Callum asked.

Mallory shrugged. "I thought I saw Rass, but I guess it was someone who reminded me of him."

Callum studied her for a moment. "Is that the only thing out of the ordinary? I know you have bad dreams sometimes." He smiled. "As we all do. Except for Brodie."

"Yeah. That's all," Mallory said.

Callum scanned the crowds. "Then maybe you really did see him. What was he wearing?"

Chapter Eight

Mallory stared at Callum for a moment, wondering if she had imagined seeing Rass. "He was wearing an expensive-looking business suit." She sighed. "I don't know. Maybe I'm just seeing danger where it doesn't exist. I mean, Rass in a business suit?"

"I can picture him in one. If he was here, he'd wear something that makes him look important," Callum said.

"How would we know for certain if it was him?" Mallory found herself scanning the crowds again. There were no familiar faces.

"I don't know." Before Callum could say anything else, Ryan slung an arm around each of them. "We haven't shown them the koalas yet." He grinned. "Bet they'll find them interesting."

Like Ryan had predicted, all the Inadonians thought they were looking at drop bears. Danae slowly shook her head. "Are you sure they're not? I mean, how can you tell while they're sleeping? It's not like you can see their fangs when their mouths are closed."

Ryan grinned. "Because they wouldn't be sleeping if they were. Not with all these people around."

Danae smiled. "I hadn't thought of that."

By the time they arrived back in Brisbane, it was nearly six o'clock and Norine had messaged them several times to find out what time they'd be home. She'd given them until seven to arrive when she learned they were at the zoo, warning them that if they were late, they'd be back to straight home after school and losing all privileges.

Mallory helped take the gear into Ryan's place, leaving hers and Brodie's in the van. She dropped the last bag on the floor in the kitchen by the table, looking around at the mess. "Are we going back to Inadon or cleaning all this up first?"

Danae looked wistfully at the bag she carried. "I wish I could take some of these clothes back with me."

"You'll be able to wear them next time you're here," Callum assured her.

Danae turned to Callum. "I can come back?"

Ryan was the one who answered, glancing around the group. "You're all welcome to come back with us."

Jorgen took a step away from the table, his bag slung over his shoulder. "Then we'd better put our gear away so we don't have to deal with that first thing when we return."

It didn't take them long to put everything away, shower and dress in their clothes for the journey back to Inadon with Brodie pointing out they should have rented a place with two bathrooms. Once she was dressed in her clothes from Inadon, Mallory cornered Callum before he could join everyone at the kitchen table. "Did you see Rass at all today?"

Callum shook his head.

"Should we say anything?"

Callum hesitated. "No. We don't know for certain. We'll keep an eye out next time we're back and see what happens. Besides, we were told Friday that the dark forces shouldn't target us yet."

"The dark forces mightn't, but what about Rass?" Mallory asked. "He seems like the sort that'd do his own thing and he would love to see us dead."

"I don't know," Callum said. "But there isn't really anyone we can ask. Not without having them think we're not handling things. Like Ryan, I really want to join the Guardians."

"I guess." She tried not to sigh. She didn't want to risk not being able to join the Guardians Of The Round Table either.

"Come on," Brodie called out. "If you take too long, we'll have to go home and won't get time to go back tonight. Then we'll have to wait until before school tomorrow to return. Fang will be missing me."

Mallory joined everyone at the table, having made some notes in her purple notebook during the drive back. She hadn't made any notes about thinking she might have seen Rass because she hadn't been certain she had seen him. And if she had been the only one to have seen him, then maybe she was imagining things. "Is there anything else we need to add?" She nodded to the notebook on the table.

"Did you write that we have to be home by seven?" Brodie asked.

Mallory nodded.

"Then we're all good. Let's go," Brodie urged, barely able to stand still.

Mallory slipped the disc into the laptop, smiling at the message on the screen. She always wanted to return to Inadon. She clicked on 'yes', the screen went black and a few seconds later the world around her went black too. Sound came back first, then the world, but it was no longer their kitchen. They were back on Inadon. Mallory grinned. She always loved returning to this world. And she doubted that would ever change.

Her grin faded as she noticed an elderly man sitting by their campfire on a wooden stool. The campfire was currently out, only charcoal within the circle of rocks, the sun nearly directly overhead. The man was carving a wolf out of a piece of timber, the carving looking suspiciously like Fang.

At their arrival, the old man looked up from his carving, setting it and the knife on the stool as he rose to his feet, a smile in greeting. "I'm Relmir and Sarnla's neighbour." He gestured off to his right. "Young Ninette asked me to watch your wagon." This time he gestured towards the wagon parked under the tree.

Ryan stepped forward, holding out his hand. "I'm Ryan." He nodded towards, or looked at, each of those with him as he introduced them. "Mallory, Callum, Danae, Brodie, Jorgen, Esben and Emica."

"Sten." The man shook Ryan's hand.

Brodie's attention was focused on the carving, his mask already on, it having been the first thing he'd done when he arrived. "Is that Fang?" At Sten's nod, he continued. "Where is she?" He glanced around.

"Where is Ninette?" Mallory scanned the camp. Everything looked in order. Including, the horses were still shrunk and contained by the enclosure made from a few pieces of firewood that had been placed under the tree. All that was missing were Ninette, Fang and Smudge.

Sten gestured towards the main part of Ursen. "I came over yesterday to let Relmir and Sarnla know a travelling bank had arrived in Ursen. It's set up on the western edge of Ursen. Between the town and the ocean. Young Ninette asked if one of us could watch the camp while she visited it yesterday."

Mallory wanted to get her gear out of the chest, but also wanted to find out what was happening. Seeing only her, Ryan and Callum didn't have their weapons, she remained where she was. If anything attacked, the rest could hold it off while the three of them gathered their gear. "Where is she now?"

Sten glanced skywards. "It's nearing midday, so she shouldn't be too far away. Been gone well over an hour, but then the lines for the travelling bank have been rather long. They don't get out here very much."

"What is a travelling bank?" Callum asked.

"A representative of the Inadon International Bank who travels around with a compact bank and a group of guards. They visit most towns and villages at least a couple of times a year here on Ruby Isle. Some merchants pay them extra to return at a certain time of the year," Sten said.

"Why does she need to use the bank?" Brodie asked. "We were at one not that long ago." Before Sten could say anything, Fang ran into camp, leaping up on Brodie, who greeted her equally as enthusiastically. "I missed you too, girl."

Chapter Nine

Mallory smiled as she watched her brother hug Fang tightly, his face buried against her fur as he knelt on the ground in front of her. Another sound caught her attention and she saw Ninette coming towards them, Smudge in the makeshift sling Callum normally wore. He peered over the edge, paws held out as he chattered at the sight of Callum, who strode towards him and Ninette.

Sten gathered up his carving, along with his knife and stool. "I guess I'll be off then." He nodded towards Ninette, who'd now reached the camp, Smudge having left the sling to be carried by Callum. "Let me know if you need me to watch your camp again. It makes no difference to me whether I sit at home doing my carvings or sit by your campfire."

"Thank you." Ninette said. "Are you sure you don't want anything else for watching the camp?"

Sten shook his head. "I'm grateful your party's companions were willing to pose for me. I don't get the chance to study critters from the wild very often." He patted Smudge's head as he walked past Callum, giving a nod in farewell to them.

"Why did you go to the travelling bank?" Brodie asked Ninette before Sten had fully left their camp.

Mallory held up a hand. "Give me a minute to finish getting ready and then you can tell all of us."

Ninette nodded, handing over the makeshift sling to Callum, who still held Smudge.

It didn't take Mallory long to grab her gear, removing the extras from their party as she did, leaving only her, Ryan, Brodie, Callum and Danae in it. She joined Ninette by the fire, grinning when she heard Brodie muttering about needing stools like the one Sten had been using, so they didn't have to sit on the ground. "We have more important things to focus on. And they'd take up too much space." She turned from Brodie to Ninette. "Is anything wrong?"

Ninette shook her head, holding out a potion vial. "After I washed all the clothes and visited the travelling bank yesterday, I went fishing with Smudge and Fang and was able to sell some of the fish and buy you a dye removal potion to use on your boots."

"Thank you for this. And you didn't need to wash all the clothes, but thanks for doing that too." Mallory took the dye. "How do I use it?"

"Just tip it over your boots. Half on each." Ninette grinned. "And it's not me you should thank for the potion. It's Smudge. He caught most of the fish and there were far too many for the three of us to eat. I also thought it'd be best not to have such noticeable boots in case Rass asks after you."

Mallory had been smiling at Smudge, who was playing with his multicoloured bracelet, sending little rainbows across the ground from where the jewels caught the sunlight. Ninette's last comment made her smile vanish. Rass was the last person she wanted to find her. She stepped away from the fire pit before using the potion, surprised at how quickly the purple dye vanished from her boots. "So what was with the trip to the travelling bank? Is everything okay?"

"I sent a message through to Goswin to see what he'd pay for Thief's Bane. I also asked if he'd be interested in the rare items since no one around here is interested in them. They can't afford what they're worth," Ninette said.

"Which are the rare items?" Brodie asked.

"The brood mother heart and carrion rat heart. As well as the brood mother teeth, even though they aren't that rare. Everything else we can sell to a trading ship as long as we get all of it to them before they sail this afternoon. They'll pay twelve gold and five silver pieces for the carrion rat tongues, tails, claws, teeth and pelts," Ninette explained. "I told them you'd let them know if you were happy with the price."

"What about the jewel? What can we get for it?" Brodie asked.

Mallory had been about to ask the same question as her brother, not at all surprised he beat her to ask it.

"After the cost of the message, portal for one person and his fee is taken out, he'll pay three thousand and seven hundred gold pieces. He has several clients looking to buy it, but only one paying in coins. The rest are offering houses in various out of the way locations that wouldn't be easy to sell and only useful to those wanting to live in the locations. Mostly in the lands far to the north of us," Ninette said before adding, "And he'll pay three hundred and thirty gold pieces for the brood mother heart and teeth and ten gold pieces for the carrion rat heart." She held out a folded piece of paper. "Here's the reply from him if you want to sell the items to him. If you decline, we need to pay the delivery fee for the letter."

Mallory took the letter from Ninette, glancing over the information.

"Four thousand and forty gold pieces from Goswin, plus twelve and a half gold for the rest of the items," Callum said. "I say we sell it all. With the amount of times that jewel has been stolen, I think we should get rid of it as soon as possible."

Mallory nodded, slipping the letter into her satchel. "I agree with Callum."

When the rest of the party agreed, Brodie asked, "Who gets to go to Goswin?"

"Not you," Ryan said.

Mallory barely managed not to grin at her brother's protests. "You can go with Ninette to sell the rest of the items to the trading ship."

Brodie's expression brightened. "I wonder where they're going."

"I wonder if they have any different news about The Nelly," Jorgen said.

"Or if they've heard of coffee," Callum added.

It didn't take everyone long to separate into groups, gathering the items they each needed to sell. Danae and Emica remained in the camp while Brodie, Callum, Ninette, Jorgen and Esben went to the trading ship along with Fang and Smudge. Brodie had spent a moment torn between staying with Danae or going to the ship. In the end, he'd hesitantly said he'd go to the ship. Mallory also did average rapid mend on Relmir before they left since it had been more than twelve hours since the last time she'd used the ability on him.

Mallory walked beside Ryan, surprised when a notification appeared when they hadn't gone far. Checking, she saw it was experience points for a new location. She guessed the cottage Relmir and Sarnla lived in was far enough out of Ursen to not be considered a part of it. Other than Sten, their closest neighbour was about two hundred metres away from them.

"That's strange," Ryan said.

"XP?" Mallory asked.

Ryan nodded. "I hadn't noticed we didn't get location XP when we took Relmir and Sarnla home. I guess I was too focused on everything we had to do before we headed home." He checked the time when they reached the people lined up waiting to use the bank. "I wonder if the travelling bank has a closing time or if they remain open for as long as people need to use it."

Mallory peered past the woman in front of them, trying to count how many were ahead of them. She gave up after thirty, no one standing still as they shifted restlessly in the line. It didn't help that children ran in and out amongst the line, a parent occasionally calling out for their child to not wander so far. "I really hope not. This looks like it could take a while. I'd hoped to join the Adventurers Guild when we got back, not stand around all afternoon waiting." She tried to get a better look at the travelling bank, but only caught glimpses of it through the crowd. From what she could see, it was a small timber building that was about four metres across the front and she had no idea how deep.

Ryan checked his pocket watch again. "Just after midday. So it's a bit after seven the night before for them."

Again Mallory glanced along the line. "I hope it doesn't take us too long. Otherwise, we won't get to join the guild." Luckily, the Adventurers Guild had no qualms about people under the age of eighteen joining, like the Guardians Of The Round Table did.

Ryan grinned. "Don't tell me you need to use a bathroom already."

She slowly shook her head at his teasing, a smile tugging at the corner of her lips. She managed to repress it. "That's not the only reason I want to join them." Although she had to admit it was certainly on the plus side.

He slipped an arm around her shoulders, drawing her close, his grin remaining in place. "I know."

Chapter Ten

Mallory and Ryan fell silent, slowly moving closer to the front of the line at the travelling bank. The only time they spoke was for Mallory to ask the time. As it grew later, her hope of joining the Adventurers Guild diminished until two hours later, when they were several people away from the front of the line, they decided it was too late to visit since it was after nine at night. She thought longingly of their bathroom, holding back a sigh as they shuffled forward a few steps.

They were one person from the front of the line when Brodie and Callum joined them, Fang and Smudge also with them.

Brodie held out bacon and pineapple fritters. They were on a wooden plate, covered in a small piece of canvas that was drawn back so that only a quarter of the plate's contents were visible. "I finally got to try out the recipe."

Callum grinned. "You're lucky he saved you any with how many he ate."

Mallory eyed her brother suspiciously. "You didn't spend all the money from the things you sold, on food, did you? We've got more than enough food. We didn't need to buy extra."

Brodie shook his head. "Of course I didn't. They gave us the ingredients in the deal. You should have seen me. I'm getting really good at haggling."

"What about the prices Ninette had organised?" Mallory asked.

Brodie shrugged. "Nothing was agreed on. She said she'd take the offer to us and see what we thought. When I saw they had all the ingredients for the fritters, I thought it worth a try. What do you think? Aren't they awesome?"

Mallory had a bite, having to agree he was right. She nodded rather than speaking with her mouth full.

"So, maybe I should go through the portal since I'm getting so good at haggling," Brodie suggested.

Finished her mouthful, Mallory asked. "What did you do with the money?"

"In the chest. Everyone said to put it in the chest for group expenses. That we can split the more valuable stuff like the topaz," Brodie said. "What do you say about letting me go to Goswin? I might get more money for the topaz."

"I think it takes more than being good at haggling to successfully sell things." Ryan helped himself to a second fritter.

"Mal?" Brodie persisted.

"I agree with Ryan."

"Aw, come on, Mal. I won't buy anything. Just sell everything," Brodie pleaded. "I'll bring all the money back."

"Why do you want to go there?" Mallory took another fritter, supposing she'd best have another before they were all gone. There weren't that many on the plate.

"There might be things in the book to find around here. Treasures. It's taking us forever to get anywhere," Brodie said.

"Do you really need any more quests in your journal?" Callum asked.

"No, but there might be something good around here," Brodie protested.

"Next," the bank clerk called out through the open door. He was a tall demon with gleaming, dark red skin and tattoos covering his arms that were visible beneath his short-sleeve shirt.

Mallory glanced around, realising that they were the ones being called forward. Swallowing the last of her fritter, she entered the small building, shushing Brodie as she did so. "I have items to sell to Goswin at the vault." She took the letter from her satchel, holding it out to the bank clerk who stood behind a counter that went half the length of the building, which was only three metres from the door to the back wall. There were windows on either side of the door, but the rest of the walls were solid. At each window, both inside and outside, stood guards. Four of them in total.

After a glance at the letter, the clerk handed it back to her. "Leave your weapons behind and step on the portal." He gestured towards the floor to the side of the counter, a circle surrounding a compass rose taking up one end of the building. Tiles of demonic runes curved around the outside of the circle.

Mallory left her weapons with Ryan before doing as she was ordered. Her hand pressed against the bulges in her satchel where the topaz was stored along with the brood mother heart and teeth and the carrion rat heart, her satchel awkwardly full. She would be glad to sell Thief's Bane. The topaz was too valuable to carry around the countryside.

Standing in the middle of a circle, she stared down at it. The compass rose was a lot smaller than the previous one she'd used. There certainly wouldn't have been space for all her party to fit on it.

Like the previous portal she'd used at a bank, once it was activated by the clerk, the world went black, all sound, smells and sensations vanishing only to return moments later. She arrived in a large room filled with people, quickly stepping off the portal so others could use it, remembering how she'd been admonished last time for taking too long to move.

A dark-skinned demon stepped forward. "Where to?"

"Goswin."

"This way."

She hurried after the demon, who led her down one of the many corridors leading away from the main room. The place was exactly the same as it had been last time. Walls made of stone blocks, worn marble tiles on the floor and glass orbs hung from chains attached to the ceiling to fully light the place.

The demon stopped at a door, rapping sharply on it.

The door swung open, a nephilim remaining in the doorway, his folded wings making it impossible for anyone to get past him and for little of the room to be visible. "How can I help you?"

Thinking it easiest to show the letter again, Mallory held it out.

After reading it over and handing it back, the nephilim glanced over his shoulder before turning back to Mallory. "Welcome." He stepped back out of the doorway, waving her in.

Mallory smiled at Goswin, who was again seated at his desk, making notes in a large, leather-bound book, a wall covered by bookcases behind him. She couldn't help wondering if he spent most of his time filling his books with notes about treasures.

Goswin looked up, returning her smile, his bald head making his pointed ears more noticeable. He wore numerous rings on his fingers and had several jewelled armbands on both the lower and upper parts of his arms. His tunic was sleeveless to show them off. Rising to his feet, he gestured her forward with a sweep of his arm. "Let's have a look at it, then. As well as my letter of offer."

Mallory turned her back on the rest of the vault, which was separated from the entrance area by bars and a locked door. Behind the bars, the area was filled with shelves and chests, every space looking like it was packed. She placed the topaz, teeth and hearts on the desk, along with the letter.

After a glance at the letter, Goswin ignored all the objects other than the topaz, which he held up to the light, turning it from side to side. "It has been a very long time since I last saw Thief's Bane." After admiring it a moment longer, he placed it on the desk and met Mallory's gaze. "Are you happy with the offer I made?"

Mallory nodded.

"Was there anything else you needed while you're here? Spells? Tools? Enchantments? I have a new set of rogue throwing knives that arrived today. They automatically return to their sheath if left out of it for too long. A dozen of them in total."

"No, I just want to sell the items." Mallory was glad her brother hadn't been the one to come here. Would he have been able to resist the temptation? He'd complained often enough about having to collect his throwing knives.

"Are you certain? I seem to recall one of you is a rogue."

"I'm certain."

Goswin sat at his desk with a nod. "I'll write a note to the bank for the amount of four thousand and forty gold pieces to be drawn from my funds and paid to you." He wrote as he spoke, finishing it with a flourishing signature and a seal dipped in red wax. He held the folded letter out to Mallory. "How are you going with finding the False Hope Goblet?"

"We're still on our way there." She slipped the letter into her satchel, glad she no longer had so many things in it. And especially glad to have sold the topaz before someone tried to steal it from them. "We're hoping to be in the area within the next couple of days."

Goswin gave a single nod. "Let me know when you find it. I still have interested parties."

"Okay." Hearing the door open, Mallory turned to see the nephilim had opened it and the demon waited for her in the corridor. "Thanks." When Goswin gave another single nod, she headed for the door, assuming it was a dismissal.

Chapter Eleven

It didn't take Mallory long to return to one of the bank vault portals, the demon having led her to a different one than what she'd entered from. He changed out the tiles before informing her she could step on it. Before Mallory could thank him, she was back at the travelling bank.

"Did you look in the treasure book?" Brodie asked before Mallory had a chance to step off the portal.

"Was there anything else I can help you with?" the clerk asked.

Mallory took her weapons from Ryan, surprised by how odd it had felt not to be wearing them. She held out the letter to the clerk. "I need to draw money from Goswin's account." She noticed her brother no longer held the plate of fritters, the edge of the plate sticking up out of his satchel. She thought wistfully of the fritters before returning her attention to the clerk behind the counter. Leaving them with Brodie hadn't been a good idea if she'd wanted more.

"What would you like done with the money?" the clerk asked. "Coins or put into another account?"

"Oh." Mallory realised that part hadn't been discussed in amongst all the rest of their planning.

"In their accounts," Callum said. "We were talking about it while Brodie was cooking. We realised we hadn't decided that before we all went off to our separate tasks." He stepped over to the counter. "Four hundred and forty-eight gold in each of their accounts and eighteen hundred into ours." He placed his hand on the black tile the clerk held out.

"But it doesn't divide up equally nine ways," Mallory said.

Brodie grinned. "They said we could have the extra eight gold since we're the ones who spend most of the money on the things we all need."

"And the names for the rest of the accounts?" the clerk asked.

Callum gave the names of Danae, Ninette, Emica, Jorgen and Esben.

As soon as the clerk was finished, he looked at Callum again. "Was there anything else you needed?"

Callum shook his head. "No, thanks." With a smile, he turned and followed the rest of them outside.

"Do you think we should spend more of our money on gear?" Brodie asked as they headed back towards Sarnla and Relmir's home. "We should have more than enough for moving to the mainland, shouldn't we?"

"We don't know the prices in that area," Callum said. "For all we know, it could be dearer than anywhere on Ruby Isle."

"It might also be cheaper," Brodie argued.

Mallory dropped back, trailing behind her brother and Callum, not wanting to get into the discussion. She shared a smile with Ryan, who walked beside her, softly telling him about Goswin's sales pitch.

Ryan chuckled, keeping his voice equally low. "Good thing it was you who went to visit Goswin." He glanced at Brodie. "Otherwise, we might have been down quite a bit. I can't think something like that would have been cheap. And I doubt your brother would have been able to resist."

Mallory nodded, glancing skywards. "Do you think we'll have enough time to get rid of the bandits at Relmir and Sarnla's farm?" If they wanted to go after the goblet within the next couple of days, they'd have to leave here as soon as possible.

Ryan took out the pocket watch. "It's not quite two. We should have plenty of time if there aren't too many of them. We don't want to take too long to deal with them. Brodie found out all the coming locations of the travelling bank for the next couple of weeks."

"I take it that's good?" Mallory asked, taking note of Ryan's smile and tone.

Ryan put his pocket watch away. "Yeah. They're visiting a few of the places up this way, then heading south. They'll be at Buckneth on the twenty-seventh day of this month. If we can get the goblet within five days, we'll be able to take it straight to the bank vault. Or if we need another couple of days, they'll be in Wayholt on the last two days of this month."

"So we have between five to seven days to get the goblet." Mallory nearly groaned. "Brodie is going to be pushing us to get it done in that amount of time."

Ryan chuckled. "You have to admit, it makes sense to try and get it done by then. Otherwise it's a long trip to the nearest bank, with most of the banks being over towards Shadhurst."

At the mention of the capital, Mallory was reminded of Emica's father. "Has Brodie heard from Hisoki?"

Ryan shook his head. "Emica's already asked him a couple of times. Or at least that was one of his complaints."

They'd barely made it back to where their wagon was parked when Brodie asked, "We going to take on the bandits now?" He hardly paused for breath before adding, "Or we going to Donris Island to join the guild?"

Ryan consulted his pocket watch again. "It's after nine at night there. We'll go tomorrow morning. We don't want to drag anyone out of bed if they're having an early night."

"What if they want to sleep in tomorrow morning?" Brodie asked.

"At seven in the morning for us, it'll be two in the afternoon for them," Callum said. "They'll have more than enough time to sleep in."

"Oh." Brodie was silent a moment. "So we can go after the bandits now?" He took the plate and piece of canvas out of his satchel and set them beside the campfire.

Mallory glanced around at everyone. "What do you think?"

"If we leave the wagon here, I can ask Sten to watch it so I can help you deal with the bandits," Ninette offered. "It's only a twenty-minute walk to the farm. Sarnla explained to me how to get there."

"There's plenty of daylight left," Esben said. "Might as well use it instead of sitting around waiting for morning."

"If we're planning to do the quest, then there's no point putting it off," Emica said.

Jorgen nodded. "I'm happy to start now."

"Me too," Danae added.

Ryan looked to his brother, who nodded, before turning to Mallory. "We're ready whenever you are."

Mallory nodded before turning to Ninette. "Ask Sten to watch the wagon. We'll deal with the bandits this arve." She also checked with Relmir and Sarnla, who declined joining them, wanting to remain behind since Relmir's leg wasn't fully mended.

It was a quarter to three by the time they were in a wooded area looking over Relmir and Sarnla's farmhouse. Callum used the spyglass to see if he could spot all the bandits so they would know their health and levels to make it easier to plan their attack.

Mallory scanned the surroundings. There was a large grassed area out the front of the farmhouse that was clear of trees, only weeds dotting the ankle high grass. Along the right and left hand sides of the house were strips as clear as the front. Behind the house she could see trees well past the house, but other than that, had no idea what was behind it.

The house itself was made of weathered timber with a thatched roof, the straw peeking out in various spots. The windows were small and impossible to see through with the coating of dust on them. It seemed like the place hadn't been taken care of in quite some time. Relmir and Sarnla would have a lot of work ahead of them once they had their farm back.

"What's taking so long?" Brodie demanded. "I bet I could have spotted them all by now."

"I've found sixteen so far," Callum said. "A mixture of classes and health. From twenty-four health on level three archers, mages and rogues all the way up to fifty-seven health on a level four warrior."

"Is that the highest level?" Ryan asked.

Callum shrugged, putting his spyglass away. "I can't see if there's anyone inside or behind the farmhouse. Or even further along the side." He took out his spyglass again. "Someone just came out of the front door." He checked before adding, "Another warrior. Fifty-seven health." He lowered the spyglass. "I only saw two of them at that amount of health. I don't know if we want to take out the two with the highest health while we have the element of surprise or go after the ones with ranged attacks." He put his spyglass away again.

Chapter Twelve

Mallory stared at the farmhouse. "Is it normal to have such a large group of bandits?"

Emica shrugged. "It can be. Depends on what they're up to."

"What's the plan?" Ryan asked.

"We should group up, two in a team, and focus on taking them out before they can get us," Brodie said. "Mal can cast Vanish I on us. She doesn't need to be in a group."

"I'm not about to only be support," Mallory stated.

"What if you make one of us invisible in each group?" Callum suggested. "We can break into groups of three."

"I'm with Danni," Brodie said.

Ryan grinned. "What if I wanted to be in her group, too?"

Mallory laughed at the momentarily stricken look on her brother's face.

The look cleared and Brodie appeared relieved. "We can fit a third person in our group."

Ryan's grin remained in place. "That's okay. I have a group." He slung an arm around Mallory's shoulders, his grin never wavering.

The groups were quickly sorted. Ninette joined Mallory and Ryan while Emica joined Brodie and Danae, leaving Jorgen, Esben and Callum to form the last group.

"How about we take out the four archers who seem to be on sentry duty?" Callum asked.

"Then what?" Brodie asked.

"If possible, we can leave the warriors until last," Ryan said. "They have to get up close to attack us."

"Unless any of them are also hunters," Emica pointed out.

"I didn't notice any of them carrying bows," Ryan said.

"We should all come from different directions," Callum suggested.

"We'll go that way." Brodie pointed towards the south.

"We can take the opposite direction to Brodie," Callum said.

"Who do you want me to turn invisible?" Mallory asked.

"Me," Brodie instantly said.

"Other than Brodie," Mallory added.

"Why not me?" Brodie demanded.

Mallory slowly shook her head. "We don't have all afternoon to point out the many reasons why."

"Emica, Jorgen and Esben are probably the best choices with their abilities," Callum said.

"Only two. I don't have enough mana to do three straight away and I don't want to wait around for it to regen. Standing here while everyone else is attacking seems like a bad idea. We need to all attack at the same time," Mallory said.

"It only lasts a minute. That's not going to give us much time to all get into place and still have it be effective," Callum said.

"Aw, come on," Brodie complained. "Can't we just get on with it? At this rate, it'll be dark before we attack."

Mallory drew in a deep breath. "Is everyone ready?" When they nodded, she continued. "If you all head in your group directions and stop two metres away from me, I can still reach you to cast Vanish I. That'll give you a little bit more time before the spell runs out."

Ryan's arm slid down to Mallory's waist as everyone but him and Ninette moved away. He drew her close against him, speaking softly. "You've got this. Stop worrying."

"Maybe I should have went with Brodie. What if he does something stupid while trying to impress Danni?"

Ryan chuckled. "I think Emica is more than capable of keeping him in line."

With a nod, Mallory cast Vanish I on Emica and Jorgen. The moment the two were invisible, their groups circled around. Mallory looked up at Ryan. "Ready?" She glanced at Ninette too as she spoke. When they both nodded, she faced the archer she could see through the trees. "I'll make you invisible, Ninette, and you can go after the mage off to the right of the archer." When Ninette nodded, Mallory cast the spell, her mana having regened enough, before stepping away from Ryan and attacking the archer.

Ryan, who'd readied his hunting bow the moment Mallory stepped away from him, attacked the archer a few seconds after her. A shout went up from the bandits, replies coming from the north and south that they were under attack too.

Mallory attacked the archer again, noticing Ryan had shot him a second time. The archer ran towards the house, the mage trying to do the same, but unable to with Ninette attacking him. The archer nearly made it to the house, dropping to the ground before the doorstep.

Ninette had made short work of the mage and was now attacking two warriors who had tried to save him.

Mallory moved closer and made Ninette invisible again the moment she could be seen. She'd saved enough mana to do so, having attacked the warriors only once each. Ryan continued to help Ninette fight them, remaining back and using his bow. Mallory looked around, trying to decide what to do. Keeping Ninette invisible was tipping the odds in their favour. She needed more mana so she could not only fight, but also help those in her party. She didn't want to just be the support member of the group.

She didn't mind helping, but that wasn't all she wanted to do.

Spotting two rogues heading towards the warriors attacking Ninette, Mallory threw a fireball at each of them.

"I'll head over there and help." Ryan reached for his sword.

Mallory placed a hand on his arm, preventing him. "I can't keep two of you invisible and if you go out there, you'll make yourself a target. Remain back here and attack. Hopefully, we can take them out before they reach us."

Ryan nodded, returning to using his hunting bow. "Maybe I should multi class with archer so I can have a better bow for times like this."

They'd barely taken out all those attacking Ninette when Brodie shouted, "One of them is escaping on a horse. I'm going after him."

Having been about to check a journal notification, Mallory groaned. "What is he thinking?"

Ryan grinned. "That he's as fast as a horse?"

Mallory slowly shook her head. "See if you can stop him. I'll check inside." She strode towards Ninette. "Want to check inside the farmhouse with me?"

Ninette nodded, keeping her sword drawn. "Thanks for keeping me invisible. It made things much easier. They rarely hit me."

Mallory placed a hand on Ninette's arm as they started forward, checking her health. By the time they reached the front door, she'd finished healing Ninette. A quick check of her journal showed that only Brodie and Callum had lost any health and the two of them had lost five points each. A grin formed when she realised her notification had been about gaining a CAS point.

"Let me go first." Ninette stepped in front of Mallory.

Before Mallory could protest, the door opened, slamming back against the inside wall, and a warrior burst out of the house. She stumbled as she backed away, eyeing the sword the warrior wielded.

Ninette blocked his attack at the last second, the clash of metal ringing out.

Mallory cast Vanish I on Ninette, backing away when the warrior turned towards her. She automatically cast Fireball at him before realising she should have cast Vanish I on herself. A kitsune raced out from amongst the trees and launched herself at the warrior before Mallory had the chance to cast another spell.

Two arrows also struck the warrior, who vanished as if he'd never been there.

Chapter Thirteen

Mallory stared at the spot where the warrior had been, ready for an attack that wasn't needed. The bandit was gone, obviously having had a revive.

Emica shifted into human form, only her ears remaining that of a fox as she turned to Mallory. "I tried to stop Goblin Boy, but he likes to learn things the hard way. Jorgen was going to go after him, but I said he'd soon figure out he's nowhere near as fast as a horse."

"I'll check there's no one else inside," Ninette offered.

"I'll go with you," Callum, who'd joined them, said.

Since Callum was now close enough, Mallory healed him, also checking that her brother's stats remained unchanged.

Jorgen and Esben, who'd been trotting beside Callum in crystalline wolf form, shifted. Jorgen stepped forward. "Want me to help you search the place for any other bandits?"

Callum nodded, following Ninette, who took the lead as they entered the farmhouse, Jorgen the last to enter.

Mallory looked in the direction she'd heard her brother call out from. "Maybe we all should have gone after Brodie. What if it was a trap?"

Before Emica, who'd opened her mouth, could speak, Callum came back outside.

"It's clear. Ninette and Jorgen went out the back door to start searching bodies. If we want to leave this afternoon, we need to focus on finishing up here."

"I'll help," Esben offered.

Callum knelt by one of the nearby bodies with a nod.

Mallory looked between Callum and the direction she'd last heard her brother in. "We need that Locate Party spell."

Emica laughed. "I'll help you find Goblin Boy. He shouldn't be too hard to track down." She changed into a fox again, the fur the same russet colour of her hair.

Mallory hurried after her, once again worried about what trouble her brother was in now. She checked his stats. They were fine. But that didn't mean anything. His health could start plummeting at any moment.

They hadn't gone far through the trees when Emica became human again. "Ryan is closer than Brodie. Did you want to go after him first?"

Mallory nodded. They didn't need him lost, too. "Yeah."

With a single nod, Emica again changed forms, angling off to the right. When Ryan came into view, she raced ahead of Mallory, catching Ryan's attention before returning.

Ryan ran after Emica, slowly shaking his head as he reached Mallory's side. "Your brother is quicker than I expected. Not as quick as a horse, though. I have no idea where he is, but I can almost guarantee he didn't catch up with the horse rider. Not unless something happened to them, like being thrown from their horse."

Mallory continued to follow Emica, Ryan falling into step with her, the trees this far from the farmhouse growing much closer together than the ones near it.. "That's okay. Emica is tracking him down. We really need that Locate Party spell. I think it'll get a lot of use."

Ryan chuckled. "I think it will too."

As they walked, Mallory checked on Ryan's stats, making sure he hadn't lost any health since the last time she'd checked. It was full, but at some time during the fight, he'd gained a CAS point and added it to longsword so it was now at level twenty-eight. Checking the stats of everyone else, she saw Callum had also gained a CAS point. He hadn't used his and now had thirty-eight CAS points saved up. She couldn't resist a smile at the thought of the complaints her brother would have about Callum continuing to hoard the points. The smile faded as quickly as it had come. Where was her brother? Again she checked his stats. His health was unchanged.

They came out into a clearing edging a small pond to find Brodie crouched by the water's edge, the branches of a broad tree spread out above him and creating deep shadows around him.

"What are you doing?" Mallory demanded as they continued towards him.

Her brother rose to his feet, clutching a slim book. "He got away." He met them part way, Fang at his side. "Another person chased after him. He had a horse."

When Brodie reached them, Mallory started heading back towards the farmhouse, healing him as she walked. "You have to stop rushing into danger all the time." She glanced around, making sure they weren't walking back towards danger. As far as she could see, they were the only ones in the forest.

"I didn't," Brodie protested.

Emica shifted into her human form. "Two warriors burst out the back door. Callum said they were level five warriors. If that's not danger, I don't know what is."

"Brodie!" Mallory exclaimed. "What were you thinking? You didn't even have full health."

"It was only one of them. I wasn't trying to take on both warriors. The other one stayed to fight."

"The one that stayed behind had a revive," Emica said. "I wouldn't be surprised if the one who ran had one too, which doesn't make sense as to why he'd run."

"Could have been running to someone," Ryan suggested.

Emica slowly shook her head. "That doesn't sound good."

"What if they come back here and retake the farm?" Mallory asked.

"We got rid of most of them," Emica said.

"They might be going after help," Ryan said.

His words brought silence, no one speaking until they reached the farmhouse and Mallory asked, "Do you think we should track him down?"

Callum joined them. "Track who down?"

When everyone else came over to them, Mallory explained what had happened.

Callum gestured towards the book Brodie carried. "Where did you get that?"

Brodie handed it over to Callum. "It was out under a tree, near a flask of mead."

"You stole the book?" Mallory demanded. She'd assumed he'd found it on one of the bandits.

"It was left there," Brodie said. "And I only took the book. Not like I took the mead and drank it. You're always complaining I eat and drink everything I come across."

"How did you know it was mead?" Callum asked.

"I looked," Brodie muttered.

Ryan grinned. "Bet that was hard, not drinking it."

Emica laughed. "Don't tell me Goblin Boy has learned his lesson."

Mallory stared at her brother. "You stole the book. With the price of books, no one would deliberately leave it behind."

Callum opened the book. "The Returners Guild Handbook. Now that sounds interesting."

"You should return it. I'm sure the rogue wouldn't have gone far," Danae said.

"How do you know they're a rogue?" Callum asked.

"Only rogues are allowed to join the Returners Guild," Danae said. "And you really don't want to steal things from them. Their entire guild is based on returning property to its rightful owners."

Callum flicked through the pages of the book. "Looks interesting. They even offer a reward for the return of lost guild handbooks."

Brodie's expression brightened. "Does that mean I'll get a reward?"

Ryan chuckled. "I don't think it counts when you're the one who steals it."

"I didn't steal it," Brodie protested. "It was just lying there."

Mallory glanced around the area. "Should we do something with the bodies?" She'd noticed they'd all been moved to the edge of the treeline while she'd been searching for Brodie.

Danae shook her head. "Sarnla and Relmir will know who to notify in town to take them away. We collected everything off them. Not that they had much."

Callum handed five arrows over to Ryan. "They had enough arrows to replace all the ones we lost and have seven extra." He held throwing knives out to Brodie. "I also found all your throwing knives."

Brodie took them, sliding them into place before turning to Mallory. "What do I do with the book?"

"We return it." Again Mallory glanced around the front of the farmhouse. "If we're finished here, we can do it on the way back to Relmir and Sarnla's cottage."

"I don't suppose I could read it first," Callum said.

"Only what you get read on the way back to the tree." Ryan grinned. "Lucky you've spent a lot of time honing the art of walking and reading at the same time."

Chapter Fourteen

As all of them walked to the pond, where Brodie had found the Returners Guild Handbook, Jorgen gave Mallory six silver and twelve copper pieces and handed a pair of leather boots over to Ryan to store in his backpack.

"Is that all they had?" Brodie asked. "Didn't they have any jerky or anything like that?"

"Guess Goblin Boy didn't learn his lesson after all," Emica said.

Brodie sent a glare her way before turning back to Jorgen. "Did they?"

Jorgen shook his head. "That was everything. We were expecting more too, but I guess they were travelling light."

When they reached the pond, Brodie stared at the flattened grass by the tree. "The flask of mead is gone. Someone's taken it." He did a slow turn, searching the area. "There's no one here. What do we do with the book now?"

Emica breathed in deeply. "Only one other person has been here. The rogue must have returned for the book and mead."

Mallory had no idea what to do and didn't suppose, once again, pointing out to her brother to stop rushing into danger would help.

"Did you want me to track the rogue?" Emica asked.

Mallory was torn. Stealing something from the Returners Guild sounded bad, but who knew how long it'd take to track the rogue down. "Which way did the rogue go?"

Emica shifted forms, sniffing around before she stopped several metres away from them, becoming human again. "That way."

"What's in that direction?" Brodie asked.

"Wildebay," Jorgen said.

Mallory drew in a deep breath, hoping she wasn't making a mistake. "We'll return to Relmir and Sarnla and let them know we've taken out the bandits. Then we'll pack up and get on the road. If the rogue is going in the same direction we're going in, it'll make sense to take all our gear with us so we don't need to backtrack before we continue onto Wildebay."

"Are you certain?" Danae asked, glancing worriedly in the direction the rogue had taken. "The rogue is a member of the Returners Guild."

"The rogue is on horseback," Emica said. "And alone. He'll move faster than us."

"We might need our horses to catch up to the rogue," Ryan said.

"Scorch can catch up with anyone," Brodie boasted. "He's the best horse ever."

"Back to the cottage, then?" Jorgen asked.

Mallory nodded. Hopefully, they'd pack up quickly enough that Brodie taking the guild handbook wouldn't be a problem.

Reaching the cottage, Relmir and Sarnla came out to greet them before they could go around to the back of the building, both looking worried. "How was it?" Relmir asked.

Callum looked up from the handbook he was reading, having been working his way through it on the way back to the cottage. "There were eighteen of them."

Mallory hurriedly added everyone to their party before stating, "We didn't get all of them. One escaped and two had a revive for somewhere else. At least two of them were level five warriors. We also don't know if they have reinforcements in the area since we don't know why one ran instead of staying and fighting."

"We can deal with three if they come back," Relmir said. "It was the amount that kept us from getting our farm back. And I'd be surprised if they had many reinforcements. Some bandits run rather than losing their revives. Or their life if they're out of revives."

"I can't wait to return to our farm," Sarnla said. "We were beginning to think no one would help us. I know there are a lot of people in Ursen who are in need of help. You should check the noticeboard at the tavern."

"Mal?" Brodie asked hesitantly.

"We've got our own things we need to do," Mallory reminded him, almost pointing out they had a book to return.

"Yes, but…" Brodie's voice trailed off.

Mallory realised what was bothering her brother. "It's okay to focus on our things, too. It doesn't make us him."

Brodie glanced away, looking uncomfortable.

Taking pity on her brother, Mallory turned to Sarnla. "Thanks for the idea, but we have to be in Buckneth within five days and we've got a lot to get done before then." She didn't glance at the book Callum held, but it was an effort not to.

"Thanks again for your help. Especially since you're pressed for time," Sarnla said.

"We greatly appreciate all you've done for us," Relmir added.

"Let me get the reward for you." Sarnla hurried away.

"We left the bodies by the treeline," Mallory warned Relmir.

He nodded. "We'll go into town and organise getting them dealt with before we head out to our farm. And if you need somewhere to stay next time you're in the area, come out to the farm. This cottage belongs to Sten. His family stays in it when they visit him."

Sarnla came outside, handing over fifty gold pieces. "We can't thank you enough for what you did."

A journal notification appeared, but before Mallory could check it was a notification for the quest, Brodie started to speak.

"We need–"

Mallory interrupted her brother, fairly certain he was about to say they needed more quests like this one. "What we need is to get packed up and on the road. We still have an hour or so left of daylight." Hopefully that'd be long enough to find the rogue.

"You're welcome to stay the night if you wish," Relmir offered. "There isn't that much daylight left in the day that you'll make it to another town or village. Especially if you're heading to Wildebay. That's a good eight or more hours away."

"We can travel through the night if we need to," Mallory said. "But we'd best get packed while we have the daylight to get that done."

"Sten is out the back, keeping watch over your things," Relmir said.

"We'll let him know we've returned." With a smile and a nod, Mallory headed around the side of the cottage to where their camp was set up.

Sten rose from his stool, gathering it as he stood. "Looks like you all made it back in one piece. I take it you sorted out the bandits?"

"One escaped and two had a revive," Mallory said. "Do we owe you anything for watching our gear?"

Sten shook his head. "Your companions paid me with their willingness to let me carve their likenesses."

Smudge made soft sounds from where he was in the makeshift sling Callum wore, peering over the edge.

Callum laughed. "I'm sure he's saying you're welcome."

"Well, I better get on home and out of your way," Sten said. "I guess you'll be off on your journey come morning."

"We're heading off as soon as we're packed," Mallory said.

"It was nice to meet all of you," Sten said. "I wish you luck. You'll need it travelling the roads of a night."

"Thank you," Mallory said.

Sten inclined his head before ambling towards his home.

Finally, having the chance to check her journal notification, Mallory saw it was about the quest completion, like she'd expected. As she read it over, she placed the fifty gold pieces in the chest.

Overrun By Bandits: You rid the farm of bandits. You were rewarded with fifty gold pieces for your party. You also earned fifteen experience points each.

Once she'd read it over, she removed all the extras from their party, focusing on helping pack up. Her first task was to use Shrink Reversal on their horses and donkey, none of the animals looking like it had bothered them to be shrunk in size.

With all of them helping, they were driving around to the front of the cottage within fifteen minutes. Relmir and Sarnla stood out the front to wave them off.

Chapter Fifteen

Mallory stared out the back of the wagon, lowering her hand as Relmir and Sarnla went out of sight. "We seem to leave people behind a lot."

"That's what happens when you're an adventurer," Ninette, who sat across from Mallory, said.

"It also means you meet a lot of new people all the time," Jorgen said from beside her.

"But it is sad to say goodbye. Especially since we might not get up this way again." Mallory thought of the handful of things they had left to do before they went to the mainland. Drake eggs, a goblet and an enchanted staff. Not many things left to do at all. Although the drake eggs would take them all the way to the capital if they wanted to sell them when they hatched.

"You have your family with you no matter who else you might say goodbye to," Jorgen said.

Mallory rested her hand on his arm for a few seconds. "You'll get your family back. You know where they were taken now."

Jorgen nodded, not saying anything.

Emica turned on the wagon seat so she could face them, sitting beside Danae, who was driving. "Did you want me to see if I can find where the rogue went?"

"Not on your own," Mallory said. "That doesn't seem safe."

"We can go with her," Jorgen offered, glancing at his cousin as he spoke.

"Did you want us to wait here?" Mallory asked.

Emica shook her head. "Keep on the road to Wildebay and we'll find you. No point sitting around here waiting when we don't know how far ahead the rogue is." She leapt off the seat of the wagon, becoming a fox as she touched the ground.

Jorgen and Esben joined her, two large crystalline wolves racing at her side.

Mallory stared after them. "You have to admit, that's a pretty amazing sight."

Ryan chuckled. "A lot of things are an amazing sight in this world."

"Yeah, I don't blame that Guardian moving here permanently." Brodie glanced at Danae. "I'm going to do that one day. It's way better in this world than it is in our world."

Callum looked up from the book he'd finished reading. "This is a really interesting guild. You should all read the handbook while you have the chance. I mean, even the motto is interesting. 'Retrieval with a hint of revenge.' They have some really cool curses. Whoever came up with them is extremely clever. Curse Of Speak Gibberish doesn't sound like that much of a problem, but can you imagine spending a week being forced to speak gibberish and having no one understand a single word you say? That would be extremely frustrating."

Ryan took the book from Callum. "We can't join every guild we come across."

"I know, but it's still interesting to learn about them," Callum said.

Mallory thought longingly of the bathroom at Drohgolrik Castle. Was that really the best way to choose a guild? "Did you want to join the Returners Guild instead of the Adventurers Guild?"

Callum shook his head. "I'm not interested in becoming a rogue. I just enjoy learning about different guilds. The Adventurers Guild is not only an interesting guild, but they're also in need of help. We can make more of a difference by joining them."

"You sure it wasn't their library that convinced you to join?" Ryan teased, looking up momentarily from the handbook he was now reading.

Callum laughed softly. "It may have helped a little." He glanced at Mallory. "But not as much as the bathroom did for some of us."

Mallory laughed at his pointed comment. "You have to agree, a bathroom is a big advantage. As well as a chest to store things in."

"When did everyone gain CAS points?" Brodie blurted out.

"Danni didn't," Mallory said.

"We should gather resources." Brodie moved to the back of the wagon.

"We need to stay close to the wagon," Mallory said. "We don't know how far away Emica, Jorgen and Esben are."

Brodie stopped at the back of the wagon, turning to speak to his sister. "We can still gather resources without going too far from the wagon. You can stay in the wagon if you're worried."

"I'll skip gathering for now," Ryan said. "I want to read the handbook before we need to return it. We probably should learn more about the different guilds in this world. You never know, one day we might need the Returners to take back something that is stolen from us. It'd be good to know how they work."

After some more discussion, it was decided that Brodie, Callum and Ninette would take turns gathering resources. Ryan kept reading and Mallory joined Danae on the wagon seat, scanning the area for Emica, Jorgen and Esben. As it grew dark, she needed to cast Tracking Magelight every five minutes, wishing each time that it lasted fifteen minutes like Magelight did. At least these days she didn't have to worry as much about her mana when she had to regularly recast a spell and they weren't in combat.

Emica, Jorgen and Esben returned about half an hour after they'd been travelling along the road. The two crystalline wolves trotted alongside the wagon while Emica changed forms to join Mallory and Danae on the wagon seat.

"The rogue headed for the road and joined it at about a quarter of a kilometre ahead of us. We might have to take the spare horse along with Scorch and Augusta." She glanced at the back of the wagon to where the three horses were tied, along with Bobbi, the donkey, the wagon being pulled by Bug and Sun Lily.

"You mean Dodger," Callum said, arriving back at the wagon with Brodie and Ninette, the three of them carrying hessian bags containing the resources they'd gathered.

"No one agreed to that," Brodie said.

"Ryan said he didn't mind," Callum pointed out.

"Ryan just didn't want to figure out a name." Brodie tossed his hessian bag in the back of the wagon.

Mallory spoke before the debate could continue. "Who would stay with the wagon?"

"I can stay with it if you want," Ninette offered.

Jorgen became human in mid-stride. "We can stay too."

Esben, remaining in his wolf form, snorted.

Mallory grinned, assuming Esben wasn't impressed with the offer. "Do I take it that was an agreement from Esben?"

Jorgen returned her grin. "What else would it be?"

Esben snorted again, still remaining in his wolf form.

"We'll go ahead and catch up with the rogue?" Emica asked. "I can track him down for you."

Callum faced Mallory. "I'll go with Brodie on Scorch. You and Ryan can ride Dodger, while Danni can ride Augusta."

It didn't take them long to get sorted, including lighting a couple of lanterns for Ninette. They followed Emica along the road at a faster pace than they could travel in the wagon.

"It'd be good if we could go this fast all the time," Brodie said. "It'd take us no time at all to get to all the places."

"We wouldn't be able to take the wagon with us if we went this fast," Mallory pointed out. "We'd have hardly any space for carrying things."

"I suppose," Brodie muttered, his expression falling. His expression brightened almost immediately. "We could take turns scouting out places to see if there's anywhere interesting that's off the roads."

"Then you wouldn't be able to gather resources while we travel between towns and villages," Callum said.

"Oh. Yeah. I guess." Again Brodie's expression fell.

Chapter Sixteen

Mallory barely managed not to smile at how disappointed her brother sounded. "I think the way we're doing things works for now. Maybe if we end up in an area with no resources, not even ones a little further from the road, we might do some exploring."

"Cool," Brodie exclaimed. "I can't wait to find out what's away from the roads. I bet there's all kinds of things. Look at where the treasure map took us. It wasn't really on a road. We should follow any tracks we find."

"They might be tracks made by deer," Danae said.

"Oh." Once again, Brodie's expression fell, immediately brightening. "We should get more treasure maps. Then we can find all the interesting places."

"They aren't easy to come by," Danae warned. "Usually they're expensive."

"How expensive?" Brodie asked.

"It's hard to say," Danae said. "It all depends on the value of the treasure and the difficulty in reaching it. But that's no guarantee someone else didn't reach the treasure first. You could spend a small fortune on a map and end up with nothing at the end of it."

Before Brodie could ask more questions, Emica slowed, all of them doing the same. She became human, jogging alongside them. "We aren't far. I can hear fighting off to the left."

"What are we waiting for?" Brodie asked.

"Stop rushing into danger, Goblin Boy," Emica said.

Brodie glared at her. "I'm not. But what if the rogue gets killed before we can return his book? He could have a revive that could send him to another country."

Mallory tried to figure out how far ahead of the wagon they were. Approximately a kilometre. They didn't want to risk Ninette coming unexpectedly into danger. "Let's get closer and see what's going on. It might not be the rogue. I'm sure there are other people travelling this way too."

With a nod, Emica became a fox, picking up her speed.

Mallory recast Magelight, not wanting to waste mana when they reached the fight. As much as she'd prefer not to have a light to give away their location, with the moon being just over half visible, it wasn't bright enough to light their way.

The trees grew close to the road along this section and a bend in the road hid the fight from them, that Mallory could now hear. Coming around the bend, they all slowed at the sight of a masked rogue taking on four warriors, fighting by the dim light of two lanterns placed on the ground. The closest warrior was less than five metres from her, so she cast Tracking Magelight on him, the ball of white light clearly showing those fighting. The rogue was struggling to avoid the attacks of the warriors, their greater numbers giving them an unfair advantage.

"That's the rogue who owns the book." Brodie pointed towards the masked rogue.

"How do you know?" Ryan asked.

"I recognise his mead flask." This time Brodie pointed to the object hanging from a hook on the rogue's small backpack.

Callum chuckled. "Brodie might recognise people by their drink flasks, but I recognise the face of one of the warriors. It's the one who escaped from the farmhouse."

"Do we attack?" Emica asked.

"Since one of the warriors is a bandit from the farmhouse, it makes sense they're probably the ones in the wrong here." Ryan slipped off the horse and readied his hunting bow.

Mallory joined him on the ground. "Want to be invisible, Emica?"

"Yes." Emica instantly changed into her fox form, racing forward the moment Mallory had cast her spell, the sounds of her paws barely heard on the loose pebbles at the side of the road, impossible to hear once she reached the grass.

Mallory threw a fireball at one of the warriors, wondering if she should take out her diplomat glasses to check which had the lowest health so they could focus on that one. In the end, she threw a fireball at each of the warriors, ignoring Brodie's pleas to make him invisible.

Arrows from Ryan, Callum and Danae punctured the warriors, Brodie having thrown a dagger at each of them. In less than a minute, the five of them were lowering their weapons, two of the warriors having had revives and the other two lying on the roadside. The one who had run from the farmhouse hadn't had a revive.

Emica retreated to Mallory's side, becoming human. "What now?"

Mallory stared at the rogue, who watched them warily. Slipping her wand back in the loop, she stored it in, she took a step forward, saying softly, "Wait here." When she was only a few metres from the rogue, she spoke. "I'm Mallory. We've been trying to catch up with you because we have something we think is yours."

"What might that be?" the rogue asked, his tone conversational.

Mallory half turned. "My brother found your book under a tree." She gestured Brodie forward.

Brodie took the book from Ryan, who currently had it, and made his way to Mallory's side. Holding the book out, he took another step forward so the rogue could reach it. "Cool mask." Brodie nodded towards the black, half mask the rogue wore that wasn't as moulded to his face as the one Brodie owned.

The rogue grinned as he took the book, opening it to the first page before nodding and closing it. "My mask isn't half as interesting as yours. Demonic I take it?"

Brodie nodded.

The rest of the group came forward, Callum in the lead. "I hope you don't mind. I read your book." He smiled, a self deprecating one. "I can never resist reading a book. Or collecting them." He held out his hand. "I'm Callum, by the way."

The rogue shook it. "Dannan." Letting go of Callum's hand, he smiled. "I can understand being unable to resist reading a book." He held the book out to Callum. "It's yours. Not many would track me down to return my property, but to help me out on top of that, it's the least I can offer in exchange."

"I didn't know the Returners Guild was on Ruby Isle," Danae said.

Dannan looked her up and down. "You're a local. Unlike most of your friends."

Danae nodded. "I have family in Simria and Wayholt."

"The Returners Guild doesn't typically have a presence here. There's not much call for it. Something changed recently and there have been reports of things happening over here. Knowledge is important and can help solve future ownership issues, so I volunteered to see what was going on," Dannan explained.

"What is happening?" Mallory couldn't resist asking.

Dannan shrugged. "No one knows yet. We're still gathering information. But we know a lot of items have been changing hands and not legally either. There are more members of the dark forces on Ruby Isle than are typically here. I dare say we'll have requests coming in soon to restore property to its rightful owners."

"Do you mind me asking what rank you are in your guild?" Callum asked. "I'll understand if you don't want to share the information, but I found your guild interesting from what I read in the handbook."

Dannan didn't answer straight away, studying Callum for a moment instead. "I'm a Guild Keeper."

"That's kind of like a librarian, isn't it," Callum said. "A rogue librarian that no one would want to mess with. But you're more than that. You're also second in charge of an area, with the Guild Custodian being the one in charge."

Dannan shrugged. "That's one way of putting it. Mainly I look after my local guild library, including guild records, keep track of quests for members of my local guild and help assess the information coming in to determine the rightful owner of items." He looked behind them. "Someone is coming this way."

Mallory turned, scanning the area and catching glimpses of light through the trees. She faced Dannan again. "Hopefully, it's the rest of our party. We rode ahead so we could catch up with you. We didn't want to miss giving you back your book."

"Sorry I took it," Brodie said. "It was just lying there, like no one wanted it and I know how much Callum likes books. I didn't take your drink. I left it alone."

Emica grinned. "Which is amazing considering Goblin Boy eats and drinks everything he comes across. But maybe he's learning a bit of caution." She continued to grin. "Although I wouldn't bet my sword on it."

"Goblin Boy?" Dannan asked.

"He drank goblin ale without getting goblin blight," Emica said.

This time, Dannan studied Brodie. "Interesting. Are your parents from here? Maybe one of the races that have a natural immunity."

"We only found out about Inadon recently," Mallory said.

"Could be an ancestor such as a grandparent or great grandparent. I doubt it'd be a great great grandparent. I don't think that would be a close enough ancestral link to pass on any of their natural immunity," Dannan said.

"Not as far as we know," Mallory said.

"That'd be cool if one of them was from here," Brodie said.

Chapter Seventeen

Mallory glanced over her shoulder when the wagon drew to a stop a few metres behind them, smiling reassuringly for Ninette, Jorgen and Esben. She faced Dannan again. "I don't know if it'll be of any use, but we were in Cutthroat Harbour recently and the dark forces are planning something. They've been gathering information about the routes for the Thornlight Shipping Company, they had several copies of 'Lost And Powerful Myths Of Misplaced Staves' and a silver piece from Eswen. As well as a lot of clothes warm enough to wear in a snowy location."

This time, Dannan studied Mallory, eventually inclining his head. "That information does help." He studied her a moment longer. "If you learn anything else, I'd appreciate hearing about it. You can send me messages through the demonic bank. Guild Keeper Dannan from Maregan. Send word if you need help yourselves. Those warriors have been tracking me down since I stepped foot on Ruby Isle and making a nuisance of themselves. At first it was only two, lately it has been more."

"We were glad to help," Mallory said.

"Yeah," Brodie said. "They'd taken over a farmhouse we had a quest to take back for the owners. Sarnla and Relmir."

"I'd heard about that and had sent word to my guild there were people in the area who might be in need of help and with limited resources to gain that help," Dannan said. "Did you complete the quest?"

Brodie nodded. "Yeah. This arve. But some of them had revives. And one of them ran. That's when I found your book. Trying to chase after him."

"I spotted him too and thought it was time to deal with him again. He was moving fast, so I didn't have time to gather all my items." Dannan glanced around at them. "Once again, thanks for your help." His gaze stopped on Brodie. "And thank you for returning my book." His gaze swept across all of them. "The Returners Guild is always looking for people with integrity."

"We're joining the Adventurers Guild," Brodie said. "They've got a castle that can grow."

Dannan laughed softly at Brodie's comment. "I'm not sure Drohgolrik would appreciate being referred to in that way." He took a step back. "I better get on my way. I've a few more things to look into. Just remember, if you need help, send a message. Tell the bank clerk there'll be no charge to you. I'll pay the fee for the message."

Mallory watched him slip through the trees, quickly vanishing from sight. Had he used a potion or was he a high enough level rogue to use a skill like shadow cloak or vanish? Maybe it was the lack of light and the density of the trees. Not knowing, she turned away from the direction Dannan had taken, facing the rest of her group. "We ready to get going?"

"Yeah, I want to level up some more," Brodie said. "I think I'm getting the hang of this RPG stuff. Dannan thanked me for bringing his book back. Not that he ended up keeping it."

"Only Brodie would come out of something like that looking like a hero," Callum said.

Emica grinned. "I think it was more that Dannan found him an interesting specimen when he discovered he could drink goblin ale."

"I wonder if we have an ancestor from here." Brodie turned to his sister. "You should try drinking goblin ale and see what happens."

Mallory took a step back, hands raised in protection. "No thanks. I don't have any interest in testing the theory that way. I still can't understand you drinking it with how terrible it smelled."

Callum, who'd been searching the bodies of the two warriors, looked up with a laugh. "I found something for Brodie." Rising to his feet, he held out a piece of paper.

"What is it?" Brodie asked as he took it. "Oh."

Mallory couldn't figure out if her brother was disappointed or surprised. "What is it?"

"A seagull pie recipe," Brodie said. "I'm not sure I really want to know what they taste like. Not now we have real food."

Mallory couldn't help laughing at her brother. She'd figured it out. He was both disappointed and surprised. She turned to Callum. "Was there anything else?"

Callum shook his head. "Even the lanterns ended up broken during the fight. I think Brodie used up all our luck by not having everything end up a complete disaster when he took the handbook."

"I did not," Brodie protested.

"We better get moving." Mallory stepped off the road and gestured Ninette forward, noticing she had put the lanterns out. Mallory glanced at her brother before returning her attention to the approaching wagon. "One day you'll take something you shouldn't and it won't turn out well." Gathering the reins of the spare horse, she tied him to the back of the wagon, keeping pace with the slowly moving vehicle. "We really need to come up with a good name for this horse."

"He already has a name," Callum said. "It's Dodger." He patted the neck of the horse. "He doesn't need another name." He looked at the horse. "Do you?" Turning back to Mallory, he asked, "How far do we plan to travel tonight? Wildebay is approximately forty kilometres from Ursen. Although if we don't go into Wildebay, we can save a bit over eight kilometres and head straight for Wayholt."

"What about Roast?" Brodie asked. "I thought we were going to visit Roast. It's been ages since we've seen him. I wonder what he's doing these days."

"We do need to go to Buckneth. Will that be quicker going through Wildebay or Wayholt?" Mallory asked.

"I'd have to work it out," Callum said.

"We have time. More than thirty kilometres to travel before we have to worry about it," Mallory said.

"So, who gets to gather resources while we travel?" Brodie asked.

Mallory nearly groaned. She supposed she should have expected that question. "I need to write in my journal. Whoever is interested can gather and someone should give Ninette a break from driving the wagon. We can't expect her to do all the driving."

"I can drive for a bit," Danae said before turning to Callum. "Are you going to join the Returners Guild?"

"Why ask me?" Callum asked. "I don't think his comment about his guild was directed to anyone in particular."

"Dannan let you keep the handbook. That's like giving you an invitation to join them. If he didn't think you'd make a good member, he would have kept the book, no matter what he said about it being payment for helping him."

Callum stared at Danae for a moment, stumbling on the rough track. "I didn't realise."

"You're not going to leave us and join them, are you?" Brodie asked.

Callum shook his head. "I have no interest in becoming a rogue. Or an archer rogue, since only rogues can join his guild."

"Maybe you'll change your mind in the future. I don't think there's an expiry date on the invitation. Not unless you did something that went against what they believe in," Danae said. "But I can't see you doing that." She headed towards the front of the wagon, clambering up on the seat.

Mallory grinned at Callum's stunned expression before getting in the back of the wagon. "You going to work out how long each direction takes?"

Callum nodded, joining Mallory in the back of the wagon. "I didn't realise it was an invitation. That's pretty cool. I wonder what made him offer."

Mallory shrugged. "I guess you'll have to ask him if we see him again."

"I think we will," Callum said. "We're sure to have more information for him in the future and I don't mind giving it to someone who'll use it to help people get their belongings back."

Danae glanced over her shoulder, already driving the wagon. "Even if it might be someone from the dark forces who they're helping?"

"That part is strange, but I suppose they have just as much right to justice as anyone else." Callum took out his map at the same time as Mallory's Magelight went out.

"Sorry," Mallory said. "I usually keep better track of it and recast it before it runs out." After recasting the spell, she took out her journal and made herself comfortable in the back of the wagon. They'd barely been back on Inadon and already she had plenty to write about.

Chapter Eighteen

Once Mallory was finished writing, she put her journal away, looking over to Callum, who was still calculating distances. "I thought you would have been finished by now."

Callum looked up from the map. "I am. Or at least the first calculation I did. Give me a minute while I finish the second lot." He went back to his task, looking up again a few minutes later. "Okay, Buckneth via Surith is less than five kilometres longer. At the most, an extra hour."

Brodie returned to the wagon with some herbs in time to hear Callum's comment. "Does that mean we get to visit Roast?"

Mallory nodded. "We can if everyone wants." She turned back to Callum. "What was the other calculation you were doing?"

"The quickest way to Shadhurst once we have the drake eggs. If we visit Wayholt so Danni can say goodbye to her mum–"

Brodie interrupted Callum. "And pick up NFB."

"Even going from there," Callum continued, "it would still be about an extra twenty-two kilometres going south than if we went north. Give or take a few kilometres since it's hard to measure using string. Especially in a moving wagon on a bumpy road."

"So we go north again after the drake eggs and the goblet," Mallory said.

"What about the staff?" Brodie asked.

"I don't know," Mallory said. "I'd like to go after it, but it might be beyond what we're capable of for now. It won't take us long to get the eggs and goblet and then what? Do we wait around for weeks while we level up more?"

"I bet we could do it," Brodie stated. "Look at all we've done. And we've got plenty of help these days."

Mallory held back a shudder as she thought of the undine. How could they avoid being snared by that creature's song? "We'll get everything else done and then see what levels all of us are at."

"You better help gather, then," Brodie said. "That staff could get us a house." He dumped the hessian bag, he'd been carrying, into the wagon before striding off, picking a nearby herb when he was only a couple of metres away.

Mallory sighed. She was sick of gathering resources. But it did help get them levels and they needed all the levels possible with the plans they had. A house in the area they wanted to travel to would save them a lot of money. It'd also be good to have a home base in this world. Somewhere they could store all the things they wanted to keep and work on the crafting abilities they were interested in.

They all alternated between gathering herbs and vegetables and sleeping, with Ninette, Danae, Emica and Jorgen doing most of the driving. Ryan and Danae even managed to shoot a couple of rabbits each so they'd have fresh meat next time Brodie cooked.

They arrived on the outskirts of Wildebay around three in the morning, the wagon overflowing with hessian bags of herbs, berries and vegetables, so there was no room for anyone in the wagon other than those on the driver's seat. For the last hour of the trip, everyone else had been forced to either walk or ride. They set up camp on the beach, not wanting to wake Roast to ask him if they could camp behind his house. They were also too tired to travel to the Adventurers Guild and decided it'd be best to have at least a few more hours of sleep first.

During the journey to Wildebay, they'd all gained plenty of experience points and CAS points. Brodie had been excited Fang had levelled up and now had an extra twenty-five percent attack damage and was at level five. She only had another fifteen levels until she was maxed out, as he'd exclaimed excitedly. Mallory had been tempted to point out Fang still had a long way to go before max level, but she let her brother keep his excitement. Brodie had also gained CAS points and was struggling to decide which crafting ability to put them in, torn between putting them in bartering and cooking or finally starting to add some to brewer.

Smudge had reached level five, too. Barely. He was only nine points into the level. Like Fang, he'd gained an extra twenty-five percent attack damage. Callum had gained more CAS points and now had forty-two of them saved up, much to Brodie's disgust.

Ryan had gained enough CAS points to max longsword out to level thirty and still have two CAS points left. Ninette had gained enough CAS points that she now had six of the ten needed to reach level five. She'd put her CAS points in smithing, but mentioned she was a long way from being able to do anything decent with her crafting ability.

Emica had gained a level and was now level four, putting her class point in warrior, so it was level four as well. She hadn't said if she'd done anything with her CAS points and Mallory hadn't thought it polite to ask. She also had no idea how much experience or CAS points Jorgen or Esben had gained, as they hadn't mentioned either of those details.

Danae now had twenty-four CAS points saved up and suggested she head to Merrow sooner rather than later, so she could add them to her alchemy crafting ability after she received recipes from the academy for her first nine levels.

Mallory could barely contain her smile when she heard her brother speak, pausing in setting up a tent.

"But don't you want to travel with us?"

"I do, but I also want to study at the academy," Danae said. "If I go there ahead of everyone, I can level up my alchemy and learn to make something more useful than health tea."

Too tired to decide if she should use some of the ten CAS points she now had saved, Mallory stifled a yawn. She was also too tired to listen to her brother trying to convince Danae to stay with them a little longer. "Brodie, keep setting up that tent. We need some sleep before we head to the Adventurers Guild. Standing around talking isn't getting either task done."

Muttering under his breath, Brodie did as ordered.

Mallory didn't bother trying to figure out what he was saying. All she wanted to do was sleep. It had been far too long a trip and they'd gathered too many resources. She thought longingly of the bath at Danae's mum's place. She yawned, crawling in the tent that was now set up, falling asleep before she'd barely laid down.

Early morning light woke Mallory far too soon and she realised neither she nor Ryan had drawn the tent flaps closed when they'd stumbled into the tent earlier that morning. Rolling over, she saw Ryan stir.

He grinned when he opened his eyes. "Keen to get to the Adventurers Guild and try out their bathroom?"

She laughed softly. "That's not why I'm awake." She glanced towards the opening of the tent. "Too much daylight."

Ryan sat up, stretching awkwardly in the limited space. "We should probably get going. We've still got a lot of kilometres to travel today."

Mallory groaned. "I'd rather not think about that. Wagons are too slow sometimes." As well as bone jarring along the more rutted roads.

"Go back to sleep," Callum called out from the tent next to theirs. "It's too early to wake."

Ryan left the tent with a grin. "No time for sleeping. We've got a guild to join. Who's coming with us?"

Everyone was soon out of the tents, Callum sending his brother daggered looks and mentioning coffee several times. Jorgen, Esben, Ninette and Emica volunteered to stay behind and watch the gear, since none of them planned to join the guild.

Ryan rose to his feet. "Let's go then."

"What about breakfast?" Brodie protested.

"What about coffee?" Callum asked.

"After we've been to the guild." Ryan took out his pocket watch. "It's already a quarter past two in the afternoon there. If we leave it too long, who knows what might interrupt our plans. At this rate, we'll never get to join."

"It shouldn't take too long to join the guild," Danae said. "We've already read the handbook and they've assessed our suitability. It'll just be a matter of telling them we wish to join, collecting our personal portals so we can travel to and from the guild, be given access to the party's storage chest and gain our four recipes."

"What about the hundred mana we each need to give the castle before we're allowed to leave?" Callum asked. "Ryan only has twenty mana and he only regains four a minute. It'll take him twenty minutes to repay Drohgolrik."

"Mallory can offer to repay some of ours since hers regens so fast," Danae said. "She'll just need to let Drohgolrik know."

"That's good. She'll have hers repaid in about half a minute," Callum frowned. "Didn't Jofren say he only gave us a single use portal to return there? Does that mean only one of us can use it?"

Danae shook her head. "It means the person who took it from him needs to go through last. After they enter it to go to the guild, no one else will be able to see it. And when they use it to return here from the guild, then it'll vanish permanently."

Chapter Nineteen

Mallory took the portal from Ryan since she'd been the one to take it off Jofren, Callum having been too focused on the guild handbook at the time. "Maybe I should also place it down. Just in case." She put it on the sand. It looked like a piece of black fabric while also seeming to have an appearance of depth. "Are we all ready?"

Ryan grinned. "You just want to use their bathroom."

Mallory returned his grin. "Then everyone better hurry up or I'm going without them." She waited until Brodie, Danae, Ryan, Callum, Fang and Smudge had stepped through the portal, sending a smile towards those who were staying behind before she stepped into it too.

Sight, sound and smell vanished momentarily before she was stepping out of the portal and into the entrance hall of the Adventurers Guild. In front of her was a solid timber door she knew from her last visit was Jofren's office. Or maybe it'd be called a study in this world.

Stepping past everyone, she knocked on the door, which opened almost immediately.

A man stood there who appeared to be in his thirties. She knew he was more than a hundred years old from Darwil's comment when he'd shown them around the guild. "We've made our decision."

Jofren smiled. "I assume you're planning to join."

Mallory nodded, those with her either doing the same or murmuring in agreement.

"This way then." Jofren led the way to the font they'd been taken to last time. "Place your hands in the font."

Before she did, Mallory turned to Jofren. "Can I use my mana to replace that of the rest of my party, since mine regens the fastest?"

Jofren nodded. "Tell Drohgolrik each time you arrive if you want him to do that. He'll know for this time since he always listens to what we have to say so he can help us."

"Can I just have him automatically do that until I say otherwise?" Mallory asked.

Jofren nodded. "He can do it that way if you prefer."

"It'll take us just over four minutes to repay the mana for the five of us if you help," Callum said.

Mallory smiled. That was far better than waiting the twenty minutes it would take for Ryan to repay his mana. "I want him to take it from my mana, every time we come here, until all of us have repaid the cost of our portal." Mallory placed her hand in the deep stone dish of the font.

The pedestal part was intricately carved stone. There was a mixture of woodland creatures peering out from amongst vines and she couldn't resist looking at a few of them, amazed by how lifelike they were. The warm stone beneath her hand pulsed in and out regularly, like it breathed, and she found it just as disconcerting as last time. Around her, the rest of her party also placed their hand in the font. When nothing happened, she asked, "What do we do now?"

"Tell Drohgolrik you willingly join the Adventurers Guild," Jofren said.

The five of them repeated the words. A glow emanated from the font once they'd all finished speaking, pulsing brighter until it dimmed and went out.

Mallory checked the journal notification that appeared and discovered she had a new tab. One called Guilds and Factions.

Jofren smiled. "You can take your hands from the font. You're now members of the Adventurers Guild. Follow me and I'll show you where the relevant things are." He led them back to the entrance hall and into another room where a set of stairs led downwards. There were rows of large timber chests and he stopped in front of one. "Everyone place a hand on the lid. All of you at once."

They did so. After a moment, the timber warmed beneath their hand and Mallory had to force herself not to move back in surprise.

"You can take your hand off it now," Jofren said. "This is your chest to store items in. You'll also find your personal portals inside it."

They each took out the portals that looked the same as the one they'd used to reach here. Puddles of black fabric.

"There are recipes in here too," Brodie exclaimed. "And a spell." He handed the spell over to Mallory after closing the chest.

Jofren inclined his head. "Darwil left a Locate Party spell here for you. He said he offered it to you as a welcoming gift. Any letters or notifications for your group will be added to your chest, so you should check it regularly."

"Like a mailbox?" Brodie asked.

"I guess you could say that," Jofren said.

"Who puts the letters and notifications in there?" Callum stared at the chest.

Mallory had been about to ask the same question, worried about the security of the chest.

"Drohgolrik," Jofren said. "Don't ask me how he manages. I put them in the font and tell him who they're for and he puts them in the correct chest. Now the chest is yours no one else has access to it."

Mallory was relieved by his answer.

Brodie opened the chest again, peering inside it before closing the lid. "That's cool. Our own mailbox."

Jofren took a step back, gesturing the way they'd come. "I'll show you to where you can find quests and our various services as well as the dormitories."

It didn't take long for Jofren to show them around and he returned to the entrance hall with them when he was done. "Do you have any other questions?" When they all shook their heads, he took out a folded piece of paper and handed it to Callum. "This message was sent here for you. Normally I'd have Drohgolrik put it in the chest, but since I hadn't yet explained about letters being added to it, I thought I should give it to you in person."

"Me?" Callum stared at the paper with his name written neatly across the front.

Jofren inclined his head. "Don't hesitate to ask me or the other guild members if you have any further questions about anything." He retreated to his study before they could speak.

Callum continued to stare at the paper.

"Aren't you going to open it?" Brodie asked.

Mallory had been about to ask something similar. "Is it from Deneg?" She couldn't imagine who else would send Callum a message.

Callum shook his head. "I don't recognise the handwriting."

"Then open it," Brodie said.

"I don't know," Ryan said. "I think it's more fun watching Brodie trying to figure out who sent it."

Callum laughed softly. "Maybe I should put him out of his misery." He opened the letter, then frowned. "It's from Dannan."

"What does it say?" Brodie tried to peer over Callum's shoulder.

"Dannan?" Mallory asked. "As in the rogue from the Returners Guild?"

Callum nodded before reading out the letter. "I heard of a quest during my travels that I thought you might find of interest. If I hadn't a quest that needed to be done in a timely fashion, I would have looked into it myself. It's intriguing. There's an inn west of Estwater and Eastvale called the White Horse Inn. It's regularly being attacked by a unicorn, which is quite out of character for such a creature as they usually only attack when threatened. A few have tried to solve the mystery, but none have as yet been successful. If you discover what is happening and why, I'd be interested in learning what is causing the problem." Callum looked up from the letter. "He's also drawn a basic map of how to find the location."

"We've been given a quest for it?" Brodie asked. "But we're nowhere near it."

Chapter Twenty

Mallory had opened her journal when the notification icon appeared, only seconds before Brodie had spoken. She read the quest over, as surprised as Brodie to have been given one.

Aggressive Unicorn: Discover why a unicorn keeps attacking the White Horse Inn.

"Maybe he doesn't like having an inn named after him," Ryan suggested.

"How are we going to do the quest when we're nowhere near the inn?" Brodie asked.

"We'll get there eventually and if the quest is still available, we can do it then," Ryan said.

"How are we meant to figure out why the unicorn is trashing the inn? Are we meant to negotiate with it or something?" Callum asked.

"They aren't a sentient race," Danae explained.

"What if we bribe it with apples to go away?" Brodie asked.

"If we can't negotiate with them, then how are we meant to bribe it?" Ryan asked.

Brodie shrugged. "I don't know. Send a virgin to lead it away? Isn't that what they do in all the old stories?"

"They're obviously not stories from Inadon," Emica said. "I've never heard of that being a thing."

Brodie's expression brightened. "Hey, isn't there someone who wants a unicorn for his collection? What if we catch it and sell it to him?"

"I know you said they're not a sentient race, but well…" Mallory's voice trailed off. "Should we be capturing and selling unicorns?"

"It's no different than catching and selling a horse," Danae said. "They're just a magical horse. The only reason they're so expensive is they tend to avoid areas with people. I'm surprised the owners of the inn haven't asked hunters to come in and shoot it since it's being so dangerous. Although, even if they have, they might not have been able to find it. Unicorns might not be one of the sentient races, but they are smart."

"So we can catch it and sell it?" Brodie asked. "We don't have to figure out why it's trashing the place?"

Callum shrugged. "We can sell it, but the quest says to find out. We might have to discover why it's being aggressive before the quest is completed. But there's no reason we can't do both. Find out why and sell it."

"It still feels weird talking about catching and selling a unicorn," Mallory said.

Danae studied Mallory. "You'll buy a horse, which means someone has sold it, but aren't willing to do the same when it comes to a unicorn."

"It's probably all the myths we've grown up with regarding them," Callum said.

"So we're going after the unicorn?" Brodie asked.

"If it's still there when we're over that side of Ruby Isle," Callum said.

"Let's get going then." Brodie took a step towards the portal.

Ryan grinned, glancing at Mallory before his gaze swept across the group. "Anyone need to use the bathroom before we return to Ruby Isle?"

Mallory made a face at him, but headed to the bathroom, anyway. It was going to be good to have a portal here. Her own personal portal that she could use at any time of the day or night. And a locked chest they could store things in that they didn't want to carry with them.

Before leaving the bathroom, Mallory looked through a window set high in the wall at the dusty red ground outside. The outer wall was as close to the castle as it had been last time, leaving very little space between the castle and the wall. Today there didn't seem to be any creatures on this side of the wall. Would the outer wall move away from the castle as they did quests to help provide more mana to Drohgolrik? She didn't know, but was looking forward to finding out. And would the castle grounds improve, becoming less dry and parched, and no longer like something that could be found in the middle of a desert? Something else she couldn't wait to discover.

Returning to the entrance hall, Mallory waited until everyone else was through the portal before she stepped through. The single use portal vanished once she'd exited, not even dust left behind. A grin formed when she saw Roast sat across from Ninette, who'd lit a campfire. Water was bubbling away, but no food was cooking. She supposed Ninette wasn't interested in hearing Brodie's complaints about her lack of cooking ability.

Roast looked up at their arrival, grinning back at them. "I was told there were adventurers camping out on the beach. Why didn't you come and see me? You're always welcome to camp behind my house if you'd rather stay with your wagon instead of sleeping in my home."

"Didn't Ninette tell you we arrived around three this morning? We didn't want to wake you," Mallory said.

"How've you been, Roast?" Brodie asked as he made coffee and began breakfast preparations. "Anything interesting happening?"

"I haven't long arrived at your camp," Roast said. "Ninette told me of a few of the places where you've been, but we've barely covered anything. I'm sure your tales will be more interesting than mine."

Mallory glanced around the camp. "Where are the other three?"

"When Roast arrived, they said they'd go fishing while I had someone here with me," Ninette said. "We've got so many vegetables, but only the four rabbits to go with them."

"We need to sell most of what we gathered," Mallory said. "Otherwise, the wagon is going to be very crowded on the way to Wayholt. Not to mention we won't have space to store any new resources we gather."

Brodie used some of the blueberries they'd collected to make blueberry pancakes. "We're going to need more flour, sugar, oil, milk and eggs. I used the last of the oil and we're getting low on the other ingredients."

By the time Brodie was serving, the other three had returned with seven fish between them, Emica having caught three. They were halfway through breakfast, listening to Roast talk about finding more charms so he could learn how to use all types of magic, when Brodie burst out, "We need salt and pepper. We have spices, but no salt and pepper."

Roast stared at Brodie for a moment. "Why would you want salt and pepper on blueberry pancakes? Maple syrup would taste much better."

Brodie shook his head. "For the fried fish cakes."

Chapter Twenty-One

Mallory frowned, trying to make sense of what her brother was saying. Then she noticed the paper on his lap. "Fried Fish Cakes are one of our new recipes?"

"Why have we never bought salt and pepper?" Brodie asked. "They're basic condiments. We have spices and they aren't anywhere near as basic as salt and pepper."

"We can get some today before we leave Wildebay," Mallory suggested.

"You're moving on so soon?" Roast asked.

At the same time, Callum asked, "What other recipes did we get?"

Brodie turned to Roast. "Everyone wants to rush back to Buckneth." He turned to Callum the moment he'd finished speaking, not giving Roast a chance to say anything in reply. "They all look good. As well as the Fried Fish Cakes, we also have Adventurer's Stew, Long Lasting Biscuits, and Date And Oat Bars. The bars seem to be like a muesli bar. They've got oats, flour, eggs, honey, dates and water in them. I'm not so sure about the Adventurer's Stew. There's no meat in it. You put four different types of vegetables in it, choosing from two different veggies each time. And two herbs. But there's no meat."

"Adventurers aren't always hunters," Emica pointed out.

"I suppose." Brodie shrugged. "I guess we'll have food if we don't find anything to hunt. We've always got plenty of veggies."

Ryan checked the time. "We should head into Wildebay as soon as we've eaten and try to sell some things. We've only got four days until the travelling bank is at Buckneth."

"There's a travelling bank on Ruby Isle?" Roast asked.

Danae nodded. "It should be in Wildebay some time today and then be at Surith tomorrow and the next day."

"That's wonderful news," Roast exclaimed. "I need to get money out of the bank to pay for a charm. I was worried I'd have to travel to one since I had no idea when a bank would be due here again." He rose to his feet. "You'll come and see me before you leave, won't you? Merry would love to see all of you again. I need to hurry into Wildebay and let other people know about the travelling bank. Also to let the charm seller know I'll have the money for it today rather than in a couple of weeks' time like I previously thought. They weren't certain if they wanted to hold it for me that long." He backed away as he spoke, glancing several times over his shoulder towards Wildebay. "You will come and say goodbye before you leave, won't you?" he asked again.

Mallory smiled reassuringly. "Of course we will. We were hoping to see Welby while we're here, too."

"Welby and his brother are out hunting," Roast said. "They left two days ago and won't be back for at least a week."

"Oh." Mallory pushed away her disappointment. At least they'd been able to see Roast. "We're not sure when we're next likely to be out this way, but if you ever need to get in touch with us, you can send word to us through the Adventurers Guild at Drohgolrik Castle on Donris Island."

"He's a sentient castle," Brodie said. "And we have a mailbox there."

Roast's eyes widened. "I've heard of sentient castles. You'll have to tell me all about him before you leave. You all end up in such interesting places." With a wave, and another glance over his shoulder, he hurried back to Wildebay.

"What level are the recipes?" Callum asked once Roast had left. "The handbook said there'd be none over level three."

"There isn't," Brodie said. "The stew is level one, the biscuits are as well and the fish cakes are level two while the bars are level three. They can all be cooked on a campfire using one of those camp oven pots. There are also instructions for the oven and stove top as well. Which is good because if you don't follow the instructions exactly, recipes don't work out properly here. Not like at home, where as long as something is cooked in a pan, it doesn't matter whether it's on top of a stove or over a campfire."

"If you can receive messages at the Adventurers Guild, can you let my father know?" Emica asked. "In case he needs a different method of getting in touch with me."

Brodie nodded, taking out the duplication paper. "There's no new message from him."

Emica slowly shook her head when she saw what Brodie had written. "What sort of message is that? You can send messages to us at the Adventurers Guild. We have a mailbox there. Or at least a chest that mail goes in."

Ryan grinned. "It's a Brodie sort of message. You did leave the wording of it up to him."

"You're right," Emica said. "I should have known better."

"There's nothing wrong with what I sent." Brodie returned the duplication paper to his satchel, muttering that Emica couldn't have done any better.

The moment they'd finished eating, they packed up and travelled the last few hundred metres into Wildebay.

Other than Ninette, who drove the wagon, the rest of them walked.

Brodie tugged on Mallory's arm, drawing her back from the rest of the group, the two of them falling a little behind. "Should we check out the quests in each town? Or village. We're only going so quickly because it's something we want. Doesn't that make us as selfish as him?"

Mallory smiled reassuringly at Ryan when he looked over his shoulder at them, shaking her head slightly when he slowed. Seeing Ryan had picked up his pace again, falling back in beside Callum, she turned to Brodie. "Wanting to do things for ourselves doesn't make us selfish. It's when the things we want are bad for other people. We don't need to do every quest we come across or help every single person. Some quests will be unimportant and we aren't the only people going around completing quests and helping others."

"How do we know the difference? Sometimes quests seem unimportant, but lead to important ones."

"We won't always get it right." Mallory hurriedly spoke again when it looked like her brother was about to ask another question. "It's okay to get things wrong sometimes. Everyone does. It's when you go ahead and do something knowing it'd be bad for someone else just because it's something you want."

"Are you sure he's not evil like the dark forces?" Brodie asked.

Mallory laughed. "Being selfish doesn't make you evil." Or at least she didn't think it did.

"So we should still go to Wayholt?" Brodie continued to sound uncertain.

Mallory rested a hand on her brother's arm for a moment before she spoke. "Danae will get to see her mum, and that's a good thing that isn't focused on you. Sometimes what we want fits in with what someone else wants, or needs."

Brodie was silent a moment before he spoke again. "I never thought he'd hit us."

"I didn't think he would either." Mallory thought back over the years and the times they'd spent with their father. He'd never even threatened to hit them when they'd misbehaved.

"I keep seeing the look in his eyes when he hit me. It's taken me this long to figure out what it was. Shock followed by satisfaction. Or maybe triumph. Did I do something to make him hit me? I mean, something wrong."

"He hit you, not the other way around. It doesn't matter what you said, he shouldn't have done that. And you weren't being that obnoxious. I think it was the tone of your voice when you were defending me that set him off."

"I shouldn't have said anything. Like you kept warning me," Brodie said. "I mean, I hate going there, but…" His voice trailed off. "He's our dad."

"Just because he's our dad, doesn't mean we have to see him." Mallory studied her brother, their slow pace having caused them to fall well behind the rest of their group. She wasn't sure what to say.

"Does Mum blame herself? What she was saying when we talked to her. Does it mean she blames herself? I don't want her thinking it's her fault. If I'd just shut up, she wouldn't be thinking it was her fault," Brodie said in a rush.

Mallory was tempted to wrap an arm around her brother's shoulder, but she knew he wouldn't appreciate that. "Everything that happens to us, Mum always thinks it's her fault. That she could have stopped it somehow. Could have protected us better." She smiled slightly. "Why do you think she always says you're going to make her a nervous wreck one day with how you rush into danger all the time?"

"I do not," Brodie automatically protested.

"Yep, you do." Mallory sobered. "You can't change Mum either. She's always going to worry about us. Especially about you. I'm not saying she loves you better, just that you worry her more."

Ahead of them, the wagon pulled up on the side of the road. Brodie glanced ahead, his steps slowing further. "It'd be so much easier if we could just stay here."

"What about Mum?"

"She wouldn't know we were gone. We could take timeless potions and return years from now."

"It'd be strange growing up yet not growing up. We'd be adults in children's bodies. I've been thinking about it a lot. We should keep travelling back and forth like we're doing. Grow up first before we think about extending the life we have. Otherwise, we'll be going back to our world as children and that's how people will treat us." She glanced ahead to where everyone waited for them. "You going to see what you can get for the resources we gathered?"

Brodie answered with a nod, not walking any faster, but also not saying anything else.

Chapter Twenty-Two

Mallory felt extremely inadequate. Callum would have been the better one to talk to Brodie. He knew so much more than she did. Had she made it worse? Would Brodie keep dwelling on their problems with their dad? She had no idea and only hoped that when they returned home and Brodie saw their mum wasn't too upset by it all, that he'd start putting it behind him. She'd thought he had, but obviously she'd been wrong.

They stepped into the general store, taking hessian bags with them. The rest of their group, other than Ninette, did the same. Ninette stayed with the wagon, watching over it since Wildebay was busy along the waterfront where the shops were situated.

While Brodie haggled with the shopkeeper, Mallory realised she hadn't learned her new spell. Worried she'd need to learn it before she misplaced any members of her party, such as her brother, she stepped outside. It would have felt odd learning the spell in the general store while they were trying to sell their resources. Mallory didn't even have the chance to take the spell from her satchel before Ryan joined her.

"Are you okay?"

"Yeah. I came out to learn the new spell."

Ryan grinned. "Before your brother gets lost again."

Mallory laughed softly. "Something like that."

Ryan's grin faded. "Is he okay? Callum was worried when the two of you dropped back like that and wanted to see if he could help. I told him to let the pair of you talk."

Mallory was again lost as to what to say. "I think it's going to take a bit for Brodie to figure things out." Her brother had spent a lot of years trying to gain their father's approval. Of trying to be the person he wanted him to be. "He'll be okay, though." She'd make sure of it. She just wasn't sure how.

Ryan nodded. "You might not want to stay out here too long. I think we're going to end up with a lot of groceries by the time Brodie is done. We might need help carrying everything."

Mallory laughed again. That certainly sounded like her brother. "I guess we do go through a lot of food with how many of us there are to feed these days."

With a grin, Ryan headed back inside the shop.

Mallory took the spell out of her satchel, reading it over. The paper crumbled away to nothing once it was read. She opened her journal to check the details of the spell.

It cost fifteen mana to cast and had a cooldown of five minutes. Which wasn't a problem, since the spell lasted for five minutes. It only worked on five party members, but didn't say if that included a party member's companion animals or if they were counted separately. It also only worked on members within five kilometres.

Mallory sighed. She really needed to know what levelling the spell up would do. It was a pity spells didn't tell you that information. In an effort to figure out how many would show up on her journal map, Mallory cast the spell. She grinned. Companion animals weren't counted separately. Luckily. Otherwise, she wouldn't have been able to see everyone on her map. When everyone else was in the party, she'd have to figure out how to cast it only on the ones she needed to find. Or discover if increasing the levels would increase the amount of people she could see. But she'd worry about that later.

Each of the members of her party was represented by a dot on her journal map and had a name next to them. Even she had a dot on the map to represent herself. Which would make it easier to discover where everyone was in comparison to her.

Finished with the spell, Mallory took a step towards the shop, stopping when everyone came outside, laden down with full hessian bags. They put them in the wagon, taking some of the bags of resources before returning inside. She grabbed hold of Ryan's arm when he would have followed everyone back inside the shop. "What's going on?"

"Brodie couldn't get them to buy everything, but there are a few other places we can try after this. We were told the bakery will buy berries and some vegetables for their tarts, pies and pasties."

"Need me to grab any hessian bags?" Mallory gestured towards the ones still filling the wagon.

"Another two and that'll be all the shopkeeper can take. Approximately a quarter of them."

Mallory collected two hessian bags and hurried inside with Ryan.

By the time they'd left the shop, having sold a quarter of the resources they'd collected, they'd earned twenty-five gold and three silver pieces along with the food.

"I got salt and pepper and dates and honey," Brodie said.

"A kilo of dates," Emica pointed out. "What are we going to do with a kilo of dates?"

"Make Date and Oat Bars," Brodie said, his tone implying she should have known.

"I hope you're not expecting us to eat them all the time," Emica said.

Ryan grinned. "With how much Brodie eats, they won't last that long."

Mallory peered into one of the hessian bags. "What else did you get?"

Brodie rattled off his shopping list. "A kilo each of salt and pepper, five kilos of flour, two kilos of sugar, four litres of cooking oil, a litre of milk, two dozen eggs, a kilo of dates, a kilo of honey and four kilos of rolled oats." Brodie pointed to one of the hessian bags. "That one is for Danae's mum, in case she wants to make us some beef and vegetable pasties. It's all the ingredients she'll need other than the ones we'll take out of the resources we gathered."

"What if she doesn't want to make pasties for all of us?"

"I got twice the amount of ingredients so she can make some to sell too."

Mallory slowly shook her head, not knowing how to reply. Would it be considered bribery? And should Brodie be trying to convince Danae's mum to cook for them? She had no idea what the etiquette of the matter was.

By the time they'd visited every other shop possible, they still had a quarter of the resources left and had earned fifty-one gold pieces from the other shops in total, as well as two dozen medium-sized beef and mushroom pies from the bakery. Mallory dropped all the coins in the chest, wondering if it was time to add more to their bank account rather than carry so much money around with them. Or leave some in their chest at Drohgolrik castle.

They pulled up in front of Roast's house just before midday, relieved to find him at home. It had taken far longer to sell the resources than any of them had expected.

Brodie clambered down off the wagon. "I wonder if Roast is having lunch."

Mallory joined her brother on the ground. "Don't you dare ask him for any of his food. We've got pies from the bakery for our lunch."

"I thought he might want a couple if he hasn't had lunch. They smell awesome." Brodie was off before Mallory had a chance to say anything.

She slowly shook her head as she watched her brother grab the two baskets the pies had been placed in. She owed him an apology. When she tried to catch him before he reached the front door, and attempted to apologise, he interrupted her.

"Is this going to take long? I'm starving." He stepped around her and knocked on the door.

Roast swung the door open, Merry at his side, waving them all inside. "I'm afraid I don't have enough chairs for everyone. I put the stools at the table, but even that isn't enough."

Brodie held out a basket to Roast once they were all crowded into the house that seemed rather small with all of them in it. "Want a pie? They're from the bakery. Beef and mushroom. We don't need to sit to eat them."

"Well, if you're sure." Roast looked uncertainly at the timber table and four matching chairs, two stools looking out of place amongst them.

Brodie sat the baskets on the table. "There's enough pies for two each." He took one out for himself. "They're still hot."

Mallory laughed. "Brodie isn't about to let a little thing like lack of chairs distract him from food."

Roast laughed, taking one of the pies. "I guess not."

Chapter Twenty-Three

Mallory drew one of the chairs back from the table, sitting while she ate her pie and listened to Brodie tell Roast and Merry about some of the places they'd been and things they'd done, peppering Roast and Merry with questions in amongst his tales.

While she ate, Mallory glanced around the room. It looked exactly the same as the last time they'd been here. Floor made of timber planks, several windows that allowed plenty of light in and a stone fireplace across from the table. Left of the fireplace were shelves covered in crockery and food, with a workbench to the right of the fireplace. On either side of the entrance door were two wooden chests and a tall cane basket was beside the chest on the right of the door.

After everyone had eaten their two pies, and Smudge and Fang had eaten one each, Ryan collected the baskets off the table. "We should get on the road. It's just after one and we plan to reach Wayholt today."

"That's a long way to travel in a single afternoon," Roast said.

Merry nodded in agreement. "You're welcome to stay here the night and get an early start tomorrow. I'm sure it'd be much safer than the risk of arriving in the dark."

"It's only about four hours if we don't run into any trouble," Callum said. "So we should reach Wayholt well before dark. We rarely get attacked with how many of us are travelling together these days."

"Great," Brodie muttered. "Now we're sure to be attacked."

"At least it'll be more XP for you, Goblin Boy," Emica pointed out.

Brodie brightened instantly. "We need more of that if we're going to get the staff."

Roast walked outside with them, Merry at his side. "You will visit again if you come to Wildebay in the future, won't you? Next time you're here, Welby and his brother might be home. They'll be disappointed they missed you."

"Tell them we said hello," Callum said.

Mallory nodded. "Let them know we're sorry we missed them."

It took a few minutes for goodbyes to be said after which they turned the horses towards Wayholt. Mallory stared out the back of the wagon, waving to Roast and Merry, who stood arm in arm. It was getting to be a habit, leaving people behind. "Do you think we'll visit Ruby Isle after we head to the mainland?"

Ryan, who sat beside her, said, "I'm sure Danae will want to visit her parents sometimes."

"I'm going to miss this place." Mallory continued to stare out the back of the wagon, even though she could no longer see Roast and Merry.

"You'll enjoy Merrow," Jorgen assured her.

"I hope so." Mallory turned away from the receding view. "Who wants to gather resources?"

"Me," Brodie said instantly.

Mallory grinned. She should have known he'd be the first to answer.

After some discussion, it was decided they'd focus on Brodie, Ryan, Callum, Danae, Ninette and Emica since they were all still character level four. Emica protested she had experience points at home in Shadhurst, but Callum pointed out that was a lot of kilometres away.

The first half hour there were barely any resources to be found, much to Brodie's disappointment, since he was the one gathering first. Danae went next, followed by Ninette, Ryan, then Emica. Callum was about to start his half hour turn, with the half hour after him to be split between Mallory, Jorgen and Esben, when Smudge made his warning cry.

"I can't see anyone." Brodie drew his dagger, his mask activating and covering his body in armour.

"It might be a creature," Danae suggested.

"How will we know when it's safe to gather resources again?" Brodie continued to hold his dagger.

"When Smudge stops warning us," Callum said.

Mallory scanned the trees set back from the road, trying to see if there was anyone or anything hidden amongst them. "I was beginning to think we'd make it all the way to Wayholt without any problems."

"We might still manage that," Danae said. "No one has come out to attack us. They might be staying hidden because we're too large a party for them to defeat us."

"Or we're not in the right position for them to attack." Callum had no sooner finished speaking, than a dozen arrows came out of the trees to rain down upon them.

Mallory dived behind the wagon, that Ninette was currently driving, having pulled up at the rain of arrows. "Should I shrink the horses so they can be protected more easily?"

Ninette joined Mallory at the side of the wagon. "They aren't aiming at them. Whoever it is, they want the horses too."

The rest of their group joined them beside the wagon, pressed up close against it. Jorgen peered around the edge of the wagon. "We can't stay here all day."

"I can make you invisible," Mallory offered.

"Why do you always say that to everyone but me?" Brodie demanded.

Mallory ignored her brother, casting Vanish I on Jorgen when he nodded. Another volley of arrows landed around them, one grazing Ryan, who hissed at the pain. She healed him. "We definitely can't stay here."

"Turn each of us invisible so we can make for the trees," Emica suggested. "We'll have more cover over there and can attack rather than hide."

Mallory nodded. "You ready then?" she asked the kitsune.

Emica grinned. "Always." She shifted into her fox form a moment before Mallory made her invisible.

Hoping she wouldn't regret the decision, Mallory turned to her brother. "You ready to become invisible?"

Brodie victory punched the air. "Hell yeah!"

Mallory cast the spell on Brodie and Fang, waiting until her mana was fully back before casting it on Callum and Smudge. She sent Esben over next, followed by Danae, all the time checking Brodie's health to make sure he wasn't doing anything stupid. Like trying to attack as many as possible while he was invisible, so that everyone wanted to target him when he could be seen.

Before Mallory could turn anyone else invisible, Jorgen dashed out from amongst the trees to return to the side of the wagon. "There are others on the other side of the road. They're trying to make us leave the wagon unprotected so they can take it."

"How do you know?" Ryan asked.

"I don't for certain, but I caught sight of two archers hiding on the opposite side of the road amongst the trees over there." Jorgen gestured in the direction. "And neither of them have attacked, so I can only assume they're waiting for something."

"What if they're not with the ones attacking us?" Mallory asked.

"It seems unlikely," Jorgen said.

"You go with Jorgen while Ninette and I guard the wagon," Ryan said.

"Okay." Mallory cast Vanish I on the two of them, grateful when Jorgen spoke softly.

"Straight ahead from us, about three trees back from the road. Quiet now," Jorgen warned.

Mallory automatically nodded, then spoke softly. "Okay." She continued moving forward, trying hard not to make any noises. It was impossible. There was leaf litter, twigs and loose rocks. All causing her to make sounds. Jorgen, though, was silent. An arrow flew towards her, the archer ducking back behind the tree that hid him. It flew wide, but she couldn't count on that happening each time one of them released an arrow.

Seeing the time was nearly out for the spell, she cast it again, scanning the area for Jorgen as she continued moving towards the archer. She spotted him near an archer, dagger in hand. The archer spun to face him and she cast the spell, causing Jorgen to vanish. The archer threw himself to the side, but it didn't help.

Another arrow came towards Mallory, reminding her there was a second archer. She cast Fireball at him, stepping to the side when he tried to attack her again. This time, the arrow struck. She drew in a sharp breath at the pain, attacking the archer with Fireball again, relieved when Jorgen joined the attack on the archer and helped make short work of him so she could focus on healing herself.

Jorgen appeared in front of Mallory. "If you want to search the bodies, I'll scout this side of the road to make sure no others are hidden here."

"We can search them later." Mallory was more focused on helping the rest of her party.

"You might not find them later," Jorgen pointed out. "You can barely see them in the undergrowth. It'll be quicker to search them now."

Chapter Twenty-Four

Rather than waste time arguing with Jorgen, Mallory searched the bodies, gaining four silver pieces, two arrows and a brown, long sleeve shirt. She cast Vanish I on herself before returning to the wagon, where Ryan and Ninette waited for her. "Jorgen is searching the area to make sure we didn't miss any on that side of the road."

"Want us to remain here while you help the others?" Ryan asked.

Mallory was about to say no when she saw Callum's health plummet. "Okay." She ran towards the trees, casting Locate Party as she ran. Spotting where Callum was on her journal map, she hurried to his side. He was being attacked by five archers, no one else helping him. Healing him, she waited the few seconds needed to cast Vanish I on him and Smudge before turning her attention to attacking those who attacked Callum. Rather than use her magic, she drew her dagger, wanting to recast Vanish I since hers was nearly out of time. She alternated between attacking and healing, relieved when Emica and Brodie joined them to finish off the last three. Mallory continued to heal Callum, keeping out of reach of the fight so she could focus on his health.

When the bandits fell to the ground, Smudge fell silent.

"We get them all, Smudge?" Brodie asked.

Smudge made soft chattering sounds.

"I think that was a yes." Callum rubbed Smudge's head, smiling down at him. "Thank you for warning us."

"If all of you want to search bodies, I'll run back to the wagon and see if Ninette and Ryan are okay," Mallory said, finally finished getting Callum's health back to full. When they nodded, she hurried to the wagon where Jorgen was with Ninette and Ryan.

"There was another one hidden amongst the trees, trying to make a run for it." Jorgen held out two copper pieces. "This was all he had."

"The rest of them have been dealt with." Mallory rested her hand on Jorgen momentarily, checking his health.

Jorgen grinned when she healed him. "Thank you. It wasn't necessary. I hadn't lost much."

"We're not in Wayholt yet. Who knows what else we might encounter." Mallory healed him twice more, bringing his health up to full.

By the time they'd finished searching the bodies, finding nine silver pieces, two hundred grams of deer venison that Brodie started eating, fourteen arrows and a short bow, and got back on the road, it was nearing five. Seated beside Ninette, who was driving, Mallory checked where the sun was. If they encountered nothing else, they'd make it before dark.

Callum took a turn gathering resources next, with the last half an hour into Wayholt split between Mallory, Jorgen and Esben. Once again, they entered a village with hessian bags filled and the wagon near to overflowing with the resources they'd gathered. At least this time there was just enough room for everyone, four of them needing to sit together on the wagon seat.

As they pulled up in front of a timber cottage, the door opened and Sarisa stepped out, hurrying over to Danae who leapt off the wagon seat. Sarisa enveloped her daughter in a tight hug. "You've made good time. Your father said you left Simria on the twenty-first of this month. You must have come straight here."

Danae drew away with a grin. "We stopped to do a quest along the way and join the Adventurers Guild, but other than that, we travelled straight through."

Sarisa opened her mouth, closing it with a shake of her head before turning to Ninette, who had been driving the wagon. "You can set up camp behind the house. I'm sure you're all needing a break after your journey." She glanced at Danae. "There'll be time to hear everything you've done once you're settled."

Brodie scrambled out of the wagon, bringing with him the hessian bag of ingredients for Sarisa. "We thought you might like these. It's all the ingredients you need for your beef and vegetable pasties."

Sarisa chuckled, peering into the bag. "Am I to understand you need dinner?"

"There's more than what we'd eat for dinner," Brodie protested.

Sarisa raised a brow. "Are you going to help?"

Brodie looked between the wagon disappearing around the side of the house, Mallory, Ryan and Callum having first hopped off it, to Sarisa's front door. "I've probably got to help set up camp."

Hearing the disappointed tone in her brother's voice, Mallory said, "If you're helping prepare dinner for us, we won't mind if you don't set up camp."

Brodie's expression brightened. "I can help." Barely pausing for breath, he added, "Where's NFB?"

Sarisa gestured towards the front door. "He's inside. He has his own pen."

"I'll help set up camp and be in once we're done." Danae took a step away, coming forward again as she took a piece of paper from her satchel. "Duplication paper so you can keep in touch with me, too."

Sarisa took the paper from Danae. "Your father said he sent some with you." She smiled. "It'll be nice to know where you are and what you're doing." She started towards the front door, glancing back to say, "I'll see you when you've finished setting up camp."

Brodie followed Sarisa inside, Fang at his heel, chatting away to Sarisa about some of the recipes he'd gained since he'd last seen her.

Mallory laughed softly. "Brodie is in his element. Talking food and about to prepare some."

Ryan chuckled, draping an arm around her shoulders and one around Callum's. "We'd best get out the back. It's as good as dark now and I bet everyone is wondering where the magelight is. No point in wasting money on lamp oil if we don't need to." He grinned. "We'd never hear the end of it from Brodie."

It took them longer to set up than usual. They'd needed to shuffle resources so they could take out the tents and other gear they planned to use. Once the tents were set up and a campfire was burning, Mallory stared at all the resources in the wagon. "I hope we can sell the majority of these tomorrow."

"I'd be surprised if you can." Danae took out the compact alchemist's station, setting it up close to the house. "There's a lot of them. Maybe you can exchange some as well." Stepping back, she activated the compact alchemist's station, so it became full size. "I'll take out some of the herbs and store them so I can use them to make herbal teas when we need them. I really am going to have to travel to Merrow soon, so I can level up my alchemy. I could make herbal infusions and tinctures with all my current CAS points. They'd be a lot more helpful than tea."

"What about using a portal to take you there once we complete all our current quests? Including the unicorn one. That will take us over to Eastvale, where there's a bank," Mallory suggested.

"It would be expensive." Danae sorted through one of the hessian bags of herbs, glancing up. "Very expensive."

Callum joined them. "What do you consider to be expensive?"

"More than four thousand gold pieces." Danae placed herbs in the cupboards of the alchemist's station.

"Okay." Mallory drew the word out as she thought of what they had in the bank. Less than twelve thousand. Taking four out of it would be too much. "Obviously not a good plan."

Danae smiled, stepping back from the station so she could close the cupboards. "It's all right. I can catch a ship from Estwater, Eastvale or Shadhurst. They have a lot more ships coming and going than many of the other places on Ruby Isle. It's not urgent for me to travel to Merrow yet. I just want to contribute more."

Ryan, who'd been sitting by the fire, came over. "Enjoy not being able to make herbal infusions and tinctures. Brodie will keep you making them once you know how so he can sell them at all the shops we find." He grinned at Danae.

She laughed at his comment before glancing towards the house. "I should see how the cooking is going. And prepare myself for the many questions from my mother. After I return this to the wagon." She glanced at the half empty hessian bag she held.

Ninette, who'd finished hanging out the brown, long sleeve shirt she'd washed, asked, "Do you think your mother will need any help cooking?"

Danae shrugged. "I don't know. It depends on how much other cooking she has to do other than for us. I'll let you know if she needs a hand."

"I'll put this away for you." Ninette took the bag, putting it in the wagon before she joined Emica, Jorgen and Esben at the campfire, where they talked about their favourite weapons.

Chapter Twenty-Five

Mallory, Ryan and Callum walked around the side of Sarisa's house with Danae, only Smudge chattering away from his sling that Callum carried him in. Danae let them in the front door, closing it behind them.

Mallory slowly shook her head as she watched her brother pop what looked like a sweet pastry in his mouth, him and Sarisa seated at the table with an array of pastry style foods between them. "How can you eat anything else after having all that jerky not that long ago?"

Brodie looked up at the comment. "That was ages ago. You should try some of these pastries." His attention returned to the contents of the table. "Especially these ones. They're called Custard Clouds. They're so light and melt in your mouth. It's like they're made of clouds." His expression fell. "They're a level nineteen recipe, though."

"You could put more points in cooking," Mallory said.

"But what if I need them for bartering?" Brodie asked. "Or maybe I should add some to brewer."

Callum laughed. "Now you see why I'm keeping mine?"

"No." Brodie shook his head. "There's keeping some for spares and then there's not using any at all when you could be putting them into something useful."

Not wanting to get into the same old discussion, Mallory asked, "Where's NFB?"

Brodie's expression brightened. "You should see his pen. It's a garden." He dusted his hands off on a cloth that sat on the table in front of him. "Come and look." He led her to where two chairs sat by a fireplace, stopping between them and a window on the opposite side of the room. A small table was set up at the window. On the table was an open timber box which had a miniature garden that contained a closed box with an arched opening in the side. To the side of the closed box was a miniature trough with shavings of fruit and vegetables. A set of tiny stairs led up to the garden so NFB could come and go as he pleased.

Mallory shot Sarisa a grin. "Someone has been spoiling NFB."

Sarisa grinned sheepishly. "He's such a sweet little thing. He likes to go with me when I deliver my orders." She gestured towards the brick oven. "The food won't be ready for a bit. Brodie said I might want to have a look at some of the resources you collected along the way."

They went outside with Sarisa, who had to stop and admire the compact alchemist's station before she went through some of the resources. She filled a couple of baskets with fresh vegetables and berries, along with a handful of cooking herbs, but the amount she took didn't make much of a difference.

"How much would you like for them?" Sarisa asked, glancing towards what she'd taken.

Brodie shook his head. "You're making us beef and vegetable pasties."

"You bought me twice what I needed to make them," Sarisa pointed out.

Brodie shrugged. "Danae helped gather the resources, too."

Sarisa inclined her head. "Fair enough." She paused a moment. "Are you certain you wish to take NFB with you?"

"I've missed him," Brodie said.

"I doubt you've missed him anywhere near what I've missed my daughter," Sarisa said.

"Are you going to stop Danae from coming with us?" Brodie hurriedly asked.

"No, it's her choice if she wishes to travel with you. I've seen how you treat her and know you look out for each other. But having NFB helps with the loneliness," Sarisa said. "Although he does tend to get into mischief as much as Danae often did."

Danae's cheeks reddened. "I wasn't that bad."

Sarisa laughed before turning back to Brodie. "What if I was to give you some recipes in exchange for him? How about Cinnamon scrolls? And Toffee Snaps."

"Aww," Brodie groaned. "That's not fair." He drew in a deep breath. "I can't leave him behind. I don't know when I'd see him again."

Mallory held back a smile at the struggle her brother was having, choosing between food and NFB.

"What about a Chocolate Pudding Pie recipe? It's only level eight and not that complicated to make," Sarisa offered.

"Chocolate Pudding Pie." Brodie closed his eyes, opening them and shaking his head. "I saved his life." He sounded uncertain.

"Almond Syrup Slice?"

Mallory was amazed her brother was able to shake his head, although he did look rather pained.

"Nutty Oat Bar. It's a recipe you can make while travelling and lasts very well," Sarisa said.

"I don't know. I've missed him heaps," Brodie said.

"Custard Clouds. Not many people have that recipe. I hunted around for a copy for months."

Brodie groaned. "You'll look after him? Make sure he's always got something to eat?"

"Of course I will," Sarisa said.

"Okay," Brodie said. "He's yours."

Emica burst out laughing. "I'm amazed Goblin Boy held out that long. After all, we're talking food here."

Mallory somehow managed not to laugh with Emica. Especially when her brother sent Emica a daggered look. "Did you want me to make NFB normal size again?"

Sarisa shook her head. "I think he's happier being little. He enjoys being carried around. I certainly couldn't do that if he was full size." She turned to Brodie. "I'll copy out those recipes for you." Before she left, she glanced around the group. "The water carrier visited today if you wanted to use the bathroom. I'm sure it's been a while since you've had the chance to soak in a tub. I had him drop off an extra couple of barrels in case any of you wished to use it."

Brodie took two dice out of his belt pouch. "Highest number goes first."

Mallory ended up being the fourth person to have a bath, which meant dinner was ready before she had one and there was plenty of time to write in her journal. By the time she crawled into her tent later, that she shared with Ryan, she was already half asleep.

"Long days travelling aren't as much fun as actually doing things," Mallory said as she snuggled in close.

Ryan draped an arm across her waist. "We'll do something soon. Tomorrow we'll learn where the drake nests are. Collecting them should be interesting."

Mallory thought of the caged drake she'd seen at South Peak Mine what felt like months ago with how much they'd done in this world. "Hopefully not too dangerous, though."

Ryan chuckled. "I have a feeling what you think is dangerous might be a little bit different to what your brother thinks is dangerous."

Mallory groaned. "Don't remind me." She felt silent, drifting off to sleep to the sound of Ryan's heartbeat and soft breathing.

Mallory woke not long after sunrise, the sound of someone putting water on to boil disturbing her. Stumbling out of the tent, she wasn't surprised to see it was Ninette getting things ready for the day. Half tempted to tell her she could sometimes sleep in, she instead made use of the bathroom, coming back out to find everyone else rising.

Standing by the campfire, Mallory scanned the area. Being in the shadow of the mountain, it felt like the day was overcast. But from previous times she'd been in Wayholt, she knew the day would brighten as it went on.

The sound of the front door opening proceeded Sarisa, who brought out two baskets of pastries for breakfast.

After all the sweet pastries had been eaten, Emica, Jorgen and Esben had decided to have a wander around the village while Ninette offered to help Sarisa with her orders for the day. Brodie slowly shook his head, pointing out that Sarisa would have very unsatisfied customers if she let Ninette do the cooking, but she'd be good at cleaning up and running errands.

"I don't have any levels in cooking. I've been keeping them to put in longsword," Ninette said apologetically. "And smithing."

"She makes a good guard," Brodie said. "So she'd deliver anything you need delivering without someone taking it from her."

"If that's you trying to be complimentary, you might need to practice a bit more," Callum said to Brodie.

"We've got things we need to sell." Brodie stalked outside, muttering under his breath, Fang on his heel with her tail wagging.

Ninette smiled. "It's okay. I can't cook, but I can fetch and carry as well as help clean up and deliver. He wasn't saying anything that wasn't true."

"Including you're good at protecting things," Mallory reminded her before glancing around. "Everyone else coming?"

"I might stay behind too," Danae said with a glance at her mother, who smiled happily at the comment.

They headed out to the wagon, Callum offering to drive.

Chapter Twenty-Six

Since it was open first, they made their way to the apothecary. It was a timber building with a wood shingle roof and a sign hung above the open front door with the word 'Apothecary' in fancy script. Inside, several windows let in what little light there was in the day, the shutters wide open. The shelves along the far wall were filled with herbs, bottles, containers and cloth bags.

The apothecary smiled as they entered. "It's been a while since I've seen all of you. I don't suppose you brought any canines with you this time."

Mallory shook her head. "We only have herbs today." She put the two hessian bags she carried on the table, Ryan, Callum and Brodie doing the same with the bags they'd brought in. "I don't know if you need any, but you can sort through them for any that are useful."

The apothecary checked inside three of the bags before facing Mallory. "It might take me a while to sort through them. Did you want to wait or come back in an hour?"

Mallory glanced around her group before turning back to the apothecary. "We'll come back."

They went to the tavern next, going to the back door since the main part was closed. The tavern keeper bought three gold pieces worth of vegetables, lightening their load a little. Mallory couldn't help thinking about the tavern noticeboard where there had once been a house for sale for a thousand gold pieces. At the time, it had seemed like an impossible amount of money.

Back at the wagon, Callum surveyed what was left. "I don't think we're going to sell all our resources today. Unless they want some in Buckneth when we get there later today."

"We've still got the Trading Post to visit," Ryan pointed out.

"I wonder if the secondhand shop wants any," Brodie said.

"I doubt it." Ryan climbed up onto the wagon seat. "But we do have a few other items they might want."

They were able to sell the leather boots and short bow at the secondhand shop, if they were interested in at least five gold pieces of the value being in items from the shop. Callum spotted a secondhand crafting ability book for eight gold pieces, leaving them with six gold pieces from the trade.

Brodie slowly shook his head as they returned to the wagon, having been unable to talk the shopkeeper down in price for the book. "I can't see how artist will be any use. Why do you need the books for crafting abilities you wouldn't choose? Besides, we've already unlocked artist so it's not like we even need it to unlock the ability."

"Unlocking it and knowing what can be done with it are two different things." Callum sat on the wagon seat and gathered the reins.

"You should be happy he has it," Ryan said.

Brodie eyed him suspiciously. "Why?"

Ryan grinned. "Because that's one less book he needs to find before he can start putting points in an ability."

Ignoring her brother's mutterings, Mallory joined Ryan in the back of the wagon. "What's the time? Has it been an hour yet?"

Ryan drew out the pocket watch. "As good as. We can return to the apothecary now."

They went straight to the apothecary, learning she wanted less than three quarters of what they'd brought into her shop. She offered ten gold pieces.

Mallory took the unwanted bags of herbs and handed them to Ryan and Callum, taking the money offered before her brother could try haggling. They were lucky to have sold as many as they had. "Thank you."

The apothecary smiled, closing her belt pouch. "Thank you for letting me choose the ones I needed."

Back in the wagon, Brodie stared at what they still had to sell as Callum drove towards the trading post. "We've only got one shop left. They're not going to take the rest of what we've got."

Mallory shrugged. "Maybe not, but we'll be in Buckneth later today. We can see what can be sold there."

Brodie brightened. "Then we can go after the drake eggs." His expression fell. "Or should we get the goblet first?"

"Eggs," Mallory and Ryan said together, grinning at each other.

When the wagon pulled up in front of the trading post, Brodie jumped down from the wagon with two hessian bags. "Bring more of them in," he threw over his shoulder before he stepped inside.

While Brodie haggled with the shopkeeper, the rest of them wandered around the shop to see if there was anything they were interested in. Callum found three crafting ability books and took them to the counter.

"Are you interested in more of the herbs and veggies if we buy these?" Callum asked.

"Aww, come on," Brodie protested. "You can't seriously be interested in cobbler, farming or scribe."

"It might be handy to make our own boots," Callum said.

With a sound of annoyance for Callum, Brodie turned back to the shopkeeper. "Where were we?"

While Brodie continued to haggle, Mallory wandered around the shop a bit more. Discovering a book listing available spells, including what each level of the spell gained, she flicked through it, stopping when she found Locate Party. It might actually be a spell worth levelling up. It cost less mana as it was levelled, the duration increased and the cooldown decreased. For the first five levels, the range went up at a kilometre at a time and then doubled every five levels after that until it was three hundred and twenty kilometres at level thirty. It also showed the location of an extra party member each level until, at level thirty, it could show the location of thirty-five members. She doubted she'd ever have a party that large, but the distance would make it worth completely levelling up. Unless there was a better version of the spell. She'd have to ask Danae later. Maybe she'd know, since her father was a trader and may have had such spells in his shop.

Returning to the front counter, Mallory grinned as she listened to her brother, surprised when the price went from them owing ten gold pieces to the shopkeeper owing them three silver pieces and him taking half their resources.

They returned to Sarisa's house, where they discovered everyone was still out. Brodie grilled the fish so they'd have food for the journey to Buckneth, while the rest of them packed up the tents. By the time everything was done, the rest of their group had returned.

Sarisa hugged Danae tightly. "Regularly let me know where you are and what you're doing."

"We still have a few things to do in this area before we travel to Shadhurst," Ryan said.

"We can call in here before we leave for the capital," Mallory offered.

"I would appreciate that," Sarisa said. "If you wait a moment, I'll grab the sweet pastries I cooked this morning for you to take with you." She hurried off before anyone had a chance to reply.

Ryan grinned. "I wonder if it's a bribe to make sure we come back here. So that Brodie is demanding we visit before we head to Shadhurst."

Emica laughed. "I bet it works. Goblin Boy is easily bribed with food."

"I don't know," Callum said. "Look how long he held out when it came to NFB."

They were all still laughing when Sarisa returned, transferring the contents of her basket to one of theirs. She stood out the front of her house, watching them go, the basket handle clutched in both hands, NFB's head poking out from her belt pouch.

Chapter Twenty-Seven

Mallory studied Danae, who watched her mother get further away. "Are you sure you still want to travel with us to get the drake eggs? You could stay and visit with your mum until we come back this way."

Danae turned to Mallory, her mother no longer in sight. "I'll miss her, but I'd miss the adventures more." She smiled. "As well as all of you."

Brodie peered in the basket Sarisa had filled. "Is anyone else hungry?"

"It's only been a few hours since you had breakfast," Mallory protested.

"Exactly," Brodie said. "It was hours ago."

They shared out the pastries so Brodie would know how many he could have and the rest could leave theirs until later. He was disappointed to learn there were only four each.

Callum opened up the crafting ability book for cobbler, reading the start of it and passing it along so everyone else could unlock the ability. He did the same with the one for farming before settling in to read the books in full for the abilities they'd unlocked.

After she'd unlocked cobbler and farming, Mallory got comfortable. She might as well get some sleep while she could. There was a good chance they'd be going after the drake eggs today. And she had no idea how far they were from Buckneth.

She had no memory of actually falling asleep, but was woken by Ryan gently shaking her shoulder. She looked up to see him grinning. "What happened?" She glanced around as she sat up, seeing they were nearly at Buckneth, the area sparsely treed.

"You missed Brodie's complaints about no resources to gather in the area and Callum pointing out it's probably because we've gathered all of them previously," Ryan said.

Mallory laughed softly. That sounded like her brother. They pulled up near one of the larger groups of trees that were well off the road and Mallory frowned. "What are we doing? Aren't we going into Buckneth?"

"Sending Ninette in to see if there's anyone waiting for us," Ryan said.

"Oh. Of course." Mallory stifled a yawn, wondering if she should have spent the last few hours sleeping. Maybe something to eat would help her wake properly. And she was hungry now, since it had to be around midday. "Do we still have pastries left or did Brodie lose the battle between his self control and food?"

Ryan chuckled. "He ate his fish and complained he was still hungry, but there were pastries and fish left for everyone else. He had a couple of carrots while saying he'd make more food next time. Your pastries and fish are still in the basket, but everyone else has had theirs."

Mallory helped herself to the pastries, raising her voice so her brother could hear over his discussion with Ninette about how to look for dark forces members. "I'm sure she knows what she's doing, Brodie. And you can have my fish if you want. I won't fit it and the pastries in." She grinned when Ninette hurried off the moment Brodie was distracted by the food.

Ryan leaned in close to Mallory. "I bet Ninette is wishing you said that the moment we pulled up and she tried to head into the village."

Mallory took a bite from one of the pastries, closing her eyes as she savoured the flavours. "I can't wait until Brodie can cook this well."

Hearing his sister, Brodie said, "I put five points in cooking earlier. I had recipes I couldn't make. And five in bartering. I didn't want it to get behind. Now I've only got three left and I still don't know if I should put any in brewer."

"I bet that was a tough decision," Callum teased.

"It takes so long to get CAS points," Brodie complained. "But I can make basic quality food and have a twenty percent chance of receiving a discount when purchasing multiple items."

"If you added one level into brewer, you'd be able to use casks and make inferior quality ale," Callum said. "See how useful the crafting ability books are?"

"It's taking forever to collect them all," Brodie muttered. "At this rate, we'll be level ten before you start using any of the CAS points you're hoarding."

Finished her pastries, Mallory joined Danae on the wagon seat. "Is there a higher level spell for the Locate Party spell? Or is the one I have one that'd be worth levelling up?"

"There is a higher level spell, but I think you have to be level fifteen mage. It gives greater range and allows you to locate larger parties," Danae said.

"That's ages away." Mallory checked how many CAS points she had. Eleven. Did she really want to use nearly half of them to level the spell up to level five so she could find ten party members for a distance of up to ten kilometres? A sigh escaped. Brodie was right. It took forever to earn CAS points. Surely there had to be a way to earn them faster. Even with power levelling on resource gathering, it was still taking too long. Especially when they went through areas they'd already harvested.

Mallory turned to Danae again. "What is the higher level Locate Party spell called?"

"Locate Legion."

Mallory stared at Danae. "Legion? As in something to do with battles and armies?"

Danae smiled. "It can be, but it's often used by organisations that want to keep track of everyone during a large undertaking. A legion can also refer to a group of parties who've joined up to work on something together. Either permanently or temporarily. But the spell works just as well on individual parties too, showing a much greater distance."

Before Mallory could ask any other questions, a sound caught her attention.

Ninette came running through the trees, grinning. She came to a stop by the wagon seat, her gaze scanning the group of them. "We can go into Buckneth. Darwil's group took out the dark forces members that were waiting in the village for us. When I went to the tavern, Ahron said they'd been making a nuisance of themselves and the villagers were glad to see Darwil and his party arrive. They were also glad to hear we were all doing well."

"Are we driving into Buckneth, then?" Brodie asked.

Mallory nodded. "We'll go to the tavern and see if Ahron wants to buy any of the resources we have left."

"The hunter is at the tavern too, having his midday meal," Ninette said. "He plans to wait there for you. I let him know you're ready to go after the drake eggs."

They parked the wagon out behind the tavern, taking some of the hessian bags of resources in with them. Ahron smiled at the sight of them. "I put something aside for Callum. I don't know if you have it yet, but when someone offered it to me, I thought of you." The last was said to Callum as he took a book out from under the counter. "I can sell it to you for seven gold pieces if you're interested."

Callum picked up the book, a smile spreading across his face. "Cooking." He turned to Brodie. "Now you have to admit this one is useful. You'll learn what you can unlock at each level."

Mallory laughed at her brother's expression. He looked torn between arguing and wanting to grab the book. Instead of saying anything to Brodie, she turned to Ahron. "Would you be interested in exchanging some of the resources we gathered along the way for the book?"

"Let me see what you have." Ahron reached for one of the bags.

"There's more in the wagon," Brodie added.

In the end, Ahron ended up paying them two silver pieces for the amount of resources he bought, including the four rabbits Brodie had been reluctant to sell until Callum pointed out he had the new recipe to try that didn't contain meat. They still had approximately two thousand resources left and Mallory feared they'd be stuck with them. Especially since they had a few things to do in the area before they went anywhere else.

Chapter Twenty-Eight

Once the bartering was concluded, they all joined the Buckneth hunter at the table where he was nursing his drink, having already finished his meal. They were the only ones still in the tavern, the couple of patrons that had been in there when they'd arrived having left once they'd finished their meals.

Brodie leaned forward, resting his arms on the table. "So where's the nest?"

"At the start of the river, that leads to between Surith and Mer Point. It's only a bit over a kilometre from here. Not that far away at all. You won't be able to take your wagon all the way, but more than half the way there's a track you can follow. When you reach a clearing where you can see the remains of an old campfire, you'll have to turn the wagon around. There's nowhere else to turn it around down near the river. You certainly don't want to get stuck down there."

Brodie's gaze narrowed. "Isn't that the place with the crocodiles?"

Callum corrected him, "Primordial crocodiles."

"I hope that wasn't meant to make it sound better," Ryan said.

Callum shook his head. "No, just stating the facts."

Mallory turned to the hunter. "Can we take on primordial crocodiles?"

The hunter shrugged. "I'd planned to avoid them. Skirt around them and raid the nest before racing to safety."

"It depends on how many are there," Jorgen said. "It also might be advisable to take out the primordial crocodiles, so we don't risk having both them and angry drakes after us. Providing there's only one or two of them."

Callum took out the map, placing it on the table. He marked the location with a finger, another finger touching Buckneth. "It doesn't look too far. Maybe we should leave the wagon behind and take the horses. It'd be quicker to escape on horseback."

"Nothing can catch Scorch," Brodie added.

The hunter rose to his feet, still using crutches. "I'll leave you to your planning, then."

"Wait." Mallory rose from the table too. "I'll heal you again before you go. I can do average rapid mend."

The hunter nodded, sitting down again. As soon as Mallory had finished, he again rose from the table. "Thanks for that."

Mallory smiled. "That's okay." She sat at the table, glancing around at everyone. "So what do we do? Leave the wagon and go on horseback? Try to avoid the crocodiles or take them on?"

"Horseback and scout the area before we decide what else to do," Emica suggested. "It's always best to have as much information as possible before finalising a plan."

Everyone else either nodded or verbally agreed to Emica's suggestion.

Mallory drew in a deep breath. "All right then. I'll ask Ahron if we can leave the wagon here for him to keep an eye on so we can all go after the eggs."

"I can ask one of my brothers to watch it," Ninette offered. "I'm sure they'd be happy to watch it for a copper piece. Especially with how little Pa pays them."

"What if your father sees you?" Callum asked. "We don't want you getting into trouble with him."

"Farlie and Martie will be somewhere hiding from Pa by now, trying to avoid being given more chores for the day after having completed their morning ones." Ninette smiled. "I know all their hiding places."

"Your younger brothers?" Mallory guessed.

Ninette nodded. "Yes. They're twins." She paused a moment. "It's nearly their fifteenth birthday. It'd be nice if we could be in Buckneth for it, but I'd understand if we can't stay around here that long."

"When's their birthday?" Mallory asked.

"In six days' time on the last day of the month," Ninette said.

Before Mallory could answer, the door was flung open and Osbert Junior entered, clearly out of breath. He grinned when he spotted his sister.

Closing the door behind him, he hurried over to her. "I heard there were adventurers in the village. I was hoping it might be you. It wasn't the last time adventurers came to Buckneth."

Ninette laughed. "What good timing. I was about to look for our brothers to see if they can watch the wagon while we go after some drake eggs. We're only going to the start of the river north of here, so we'd be back well before dark."

Osbert shook his head. "Pa has them cleaning out the barn. He hasn't let any of us out of his sight for more than a few minutes at a time."

"How did you get away?" Callum asked.

"I've been delivering wool to one of the weavers, so I can't stay long," Osbert said. "If you didn't turn up within the next six days, I was going to leave a message here with Ahron for you. We're leaving when Farlie and Martie turn fifteen. Pa has become a lot worse since you left. He never smiles anymore and we can't even say your name without him yelling at us."

Turning to Ninette, Brodie blurted out, "But you're fifteen." He stressed the word 'you're'.

Callum chuckled. "It only takes nine months to have a baby, Brodie. Although twins are often born early."

"They were only born a couple of weeks early," Ninette said. "But I'll be sixteen next month. On the eighteenth day of the third month. Osbert turns seventeen on the twenty-sixth day of the third month."

"You should have said it'll be your birthday in twenty-three days," Brodie said. "I need time to find a birthday cake recipe. Do you think they'll have one that can be cooked over a campfire? Or maybe we'll have our oven by then. We need to reach rank six at the Adventurers Guild."

"It takes a total of seventy points to reach rank six," Callum pointed out.

Brodie frowned. "That's four, no, three, no–" He stopped in mid-sentence with a shake of his head.

"Three points a day with one day of four points," Callum said.

Brodie groaned. "If we only get a point for every four quests completed, that's going to take forever."

"Bounties would give us points quicker. We'd get a point for each bounty completed," Callum said. "But we don't have time to worry about that right now. Who's going to watch the wagon?"

Emica grinned. "Goblin Boy always gets distracted by food."

"Where are you going to go?" Ninette asked Osbert. "It's not safe on the roads out there and if you remain too close to Pa's farm, he'll come after you."

Osbert shrugged. "I don't know."

"I have money," Ninette said. "But it's in the bank."

"The travelling bank will be here on the twenty-seventh and in Wayholt on the twenty-eighth and twenty-ninth," Callum reminded her.

Osbert turned to Callum. "Are you certain?"

Callum nodded. "We spoke to the bank clerk. He gave us a list of places he'll be this month and early next month."

Osbert turned to Ninette. "If you could give us some money, we could pay for a ride to Surith next week. We just need to sneak all our gear out so Pa doesn't stop us from taking it with us."

"What do you plan to do in Surith?" Danae asked.

"I want to unlock crafter and focus on husbandry and farming. More than just sheep. Cows, pigs, horses, chickens and a few other animals too. I'd like to grow some of the feed for them as well. I'm not interested in being a fighter or adventurer like Ninette." He turned to his sister. "Our brothers want to be rogues."

Ninette shuddered. "I don't know if that's a good idea. They get into enough trouble without learning skills like shadow cloak or vanish."

"That's why I was hoping you'd come with us," Osbert said. "I can't look after them on my own. They get into too much trouble if no one is watching them and they don't listen to me anywhere near as well as they listened to you."

Brodie brightened. "What about our house?"

Mallory had no idea what her brother meant. "We don't have a house."

"Not yet. But we will when we get the staff," Brodie said. "We're going to want someone to look after it while we're out doing quests."

"We don't know if we'll be high enough a level to go after the staff by the time we're ready to leave here," Mallory reminded him.

"That's actually a good idea, Brodie." Ryan turned to Ninette. "Would you be interested in that? Guarding our home and keeping it safe. Osbert could have his animals and your younger brothers could scout the area and help you protect it."

Ninette laughed. "You obviously don't know our younger brothers. If anything, they're the ones the place would need to be protected from."

"You could travel on the ship with me to Merrow," Danae suggested. "It'd be nice to have company."

Chapter Twenty-Nine

"We don't have the staff," Mallory reminded everyone.

Ryan grinned. "Not yet." He slung an arm around Mallory's shoulders. "We've got this. Between us all, we can figure it out."

"What about Emica, Jorgen and Esben?" Mallory asked. "We can't expect them to trail along on a dangerous quest with no reward in it for themselves. They have plans for their future, too."

"I wouldn't be surprised if there was other treasure with the staff," Emica said.

"Smudge found a pearl in the area where we think it is," Callum said. "So it's logical the rest of the pearls might be out there."

Mallory sighed. This wasn't getting anything done. "First, we go after the eggs. Then we return here and find the goblet in Bard's Hollow before the travelling bank arrives. Then we work out what to do next." She glanced around the group. "But who is going to watch the wagon today?"

"Do you think you can be back in two hours?" Osbert asked. "If you park the wagon out of the village a bit, I can hide out there and watch it and tell Pa I heard a rumour about the travelling bank and wanted to find out if it was true for him."

"That won't get you in trouble with your father, will it?" Mallory asked.

"Does he hit you?" Danae asked.

Before Osbert could reply, Brodie said, "There are worse things than being hit."

Osbert shook his head. "Not really. He's threatened a couple of times and lately he's gone to hit one of us, but we step out of the way and he doesn't try again for a bit."

"Should you go back there?" Callum asked.

"Our brothers can't leave home until they're fifteen," Osbert said. "I can't leave them alone with him. Not with how much they get into trouble. It's only five more days. And they were born early in the morning, so we can leave before daybreak. He won't even be up then."

"He might be," Ryan warned. "If he suspects you're waiting for your brothers to turn fifteen so you can leave."

"I'll come and get the three of you if you don't get out of there by daybreak," Ninette stated.

"You'll be here then?" Osbert asked.

Ninette nodded. "I'll make sure of it."

"So we're going after the eggs now?" Brodie asked.

Mallory looked at each person, relieved when they either nodded or spoke in agreement. She turned to Osbert. "How about you show us the best place to leave the wagon?" She waved to Ahron as they left, the tavern owner giving her a nod since he had his hands full of tankards he was putting away behind the bar.

They unhitched the horses once they reached the location Osbert suggested. It was within view of the village, but there were enough trees that unless someone came this way, they wouldn't notice the wagon.

Mallory and Ryan rode Bug, Danae rode Augusta, Ninette rode Sun Lily, Brodie was on Scorch with Fang in front of him and Callum was on the horse he insisted was called Dodger while Smudge remained in the sling he wore. Emica, Jorgen and Esben shapeshifted and ran alongside them.

The ride was quick and uneventful, taking barely ten minutes at the pace they set. Mallory began to hope that meant they were in for an easy task. Pulling up in sight of the river, she drew in a sharp breath when she spotted six primordial crocodiles. "I really hope we don't need to take them on. They're almost as tall as the horses and far too long. Look at the sharp spikes along their back and tails."

"Scutes," Callum said.

"I prefer the word spike. It describes them perfectly." Mallory couldn't drag her gaze away from the spikes. They looked like they'd do a lot of damage.

Emica shifted into her human form, her ears remaining that of a fox. "What's the plan?"

"We need to find the nest," Ryan said.

"Would it help if I cast Vanish on you?" Mallory asked Emica.

"The primordial crocodiles use all their senses to hunt. Smell, vibration, hearing and sight. Take away one of them and they're still left with the rest," Emica explained. "Being invisible wouldn't help."

"We can't take on one of them, let alone six," Mallory stated. "Look at their size." Jorgen had obviously overestimated their capabilities if he thought they could take on two primordial crocodiles.

"The hunter planned to skirt around them to reach the nest," Callum said. "That means the nest must be far enough away that the primordial crocodiles wouldn't notice us."

"They can hear a heartbeat in the water nearly a kilometre away, but on land, the distance is a lot shorter," Emica said. "Two or three hundred metres. If you keep to a slow pace, making as little noise as possible, you should remain unnoticed."

"How are we going to find the nest?" Brodie asked.

"We should have asked if it was to the left or the right of the river," Callum said.

"I could go back and ask," Ninette offered. "It's not that far."

"Not on your own," Mallory said.

Jorgen shifted into his human form. "Esben and I can go with her."

Esben snorted.

Mallory smiled. "Okay. We'll see what's to the left while you're gone. See if you can get a better idea of the location other than you get to it by skirting the crocs."

With a nod, Jorgen shifted into his crystalline wolf form again and the three of them headed back the way they'd come.

"Should we retreat a bit before we head to the left?" Callum asked.

Mallory continued to watch the primordial crocodiles. One of them opened its mouth in a wide yawn, sharp teeth gleaming in the sunlight. They ranged in size from that of throwing knives to daggers. They looked like they'd cause more damage than the spikes. "Sounds like a good idea to me." She didn't want to be anywhere near those creatures.

They retreated until the river was barely visible through the trees, which were much thicker along with the underbrush being more dense this far away from the village.

"What does a nest look like?" Callum asked.

Emica grinned, pointing ahead of them. "That."

Mallory leaned around Ryan to see what Emica pointed at. The nest was about forty centimetres in diameter and made from water reeds, grasses and leaves that had long since dried. Within the nest could be seen feathers amongst the eggs, creating a soft lining for them.

Brodie, still mounted on Scorch, said, "I can see another two past the first one. We're going to have tonnes of eggs."

"Leave one egg in each nest," Danae said. "Sometimes they'll remain to protect the last egg if you leave one behind."

"I don't think there's-" Brodie broke off as a drake flew in and landed in one of the nests. The red scaly creature was less than half a metre long from the tip of its nose to the end of its tail. It was draconic looking with leathery wings and a body like a frilled necked lizard, but without the frill. The eggs in the nest were about one and a half times the size of a chicken egg and she curled her body around them. "I guess we only have to worry about one drake."

"One is more than enough," Emica said. "Especially when it comes to fire drakes. She could set this entire area alight."

"I have a spell to take care of that." Mallory opened her journal, going through her spells until she reached the one she wanted. "Water manipulation." She checked the amount of water she could shift at a time since it had been a while since she'd last used it. Five litres. Would that be enough to put out any fires the drake started?

"If we're going to raid the nests while the other drakes aren't here, we better start now," Emica warned.

"Nightfall," Callum suggested. "Blind it, then cast Slow Target and lead it into a lightning trap. Brodie can lead it away on Scorch before coming back this way. That'll give the rest of us time to raid the nests."

"Take all the eggs from the nest with the drake in it," Danae said. "If we plan to attack it, we don't want to leave the egg to die if we end up taking out the drake."

"Why do I have to be bait?" Brodie demanded.

Ryan grinned. "You've got the fastest horse."

"We all ready?" Mallory asked.

Everyone nodded.

Chapter Thirty

Mallory drew in a deep breath, not sure she was ready to go after the drake eggs. But they were here now and there was no reason to put it off. She pushed thoughts of the primordial crocodiles from her mind. "Okay. I'll put the lightning trap north west of the nest and cast Vanish on you and Fang, Brodie. Then I'll follow so I can cast the rest of the spells on the drake once I'm close enough and you've distracted it."

"Make sure you have your armour activated, Goblin Boy," Emica warned. "Just in case the drake manages to get an attack in."

Brodie drew out a dagger, holding it along with the reins, the armour sliding over his body.

Ryan slid off Bug. "I'll hop on Callum's horse in case you need to make a run for it if the drake focuses on you instead of Brodie."

As soon as Ryan was mounted, Mallory asked her brother, "Are you ready?" When he nodded, she cast the spells, grinning when what appeared to be a riderless horse headed for the drake. Should she have cast the spell on Scorch too? She didn't know, but it was too late now. They were out of range. Not that she knew if her level of Vanish would have worked on him being he wasn't a typical horse. Or a companion animal.

The drake swooped Scorch and Brodie led it towards the lightning trap. Mallory rode after them, the rest of her party stopping at the nest when she continued onwards. As soon as she was close enough, she cast Slow Target and Nightfall. The drake breathed fire towards Brodie, who was well out of range.

The drake circled around, screeching angrily, focused on Mallory, able to see again.

Mallory headed off to the left, not wanting to lead the creature to where the nests were being raided. Nor in the direction her brother had taken. As soon as she could, she cast Nightfall on it again. This time, when it circled, trying to get its bearings, she cast Beacon in the centre of where it flew then veered off towards the village, not wanting to become lost.

Leaving the drake behind, hoping the bright light of Beacon distracted it, Mallory bent forward over Bug to avoid any low-hanging branches as they raced through the trees. The last thing she needed to do was get knocked off the horse. She didn't even know if Bug would stop for her if that happened.

Hoping she was within a five kilometre range of the rest of her party, Mallory cast Locate Party, finding they were scattered around the area. She turned towards Brodie first as he was the one furthest from everyone else. She circled well around where she'd left the drake, taking longer to reach her brother than if she'd gone directly to him. It didn't take her long to realise why he was still heading away from everyone. A primordial crocodile chased him, a lot quicker than she'd expected one to be.

Mallory raced towards them, urging Bug to go faster, wondering why Brodie didn't have Scorch going as fast as possible. Coming alongside him, she glanced across at him, not wanting to take her attention too long off the ground she raced across. Brodie was trying to keep Fang from falling off the horse.

Brodie glanced at Mallory. "Do you think we can fight it?"

Mallory cast Lightning Trap and Slow Target. The first spell seemed to make no difference and the second barely slowed the creature. Using Nightfall on it made no difference. It continued to come straight for them. "I doubt we'd survive." She checked her map, estimating where the drake had been and looking at where Ryan, Callum and Danae were. "Follow me." She abruptly changed direction, Brodie following.

The primordial crocodile didn't slow as it did the same, the distance between them not changing.

"Why do I get the feeling that creature could keep the same pace all day without tiring?" Mallory asked.

"I can't die," Brodie said. "If I do, it might get Scorch and Fang. And I don't know if Scorch would revive. His stats don't say anything about having one."

"How about we avoid dying and focus on getting to the rest of our group so they can help us take the croc out?" Mallory again checked her journal. Everyone was moving rapidly towards where they'd left the wagon. Why were they going that fast? Was something wrong? When they had circled out far enough to avoid the drake she'd left behind, Mallory headed directly towards the wagon. "Keep riding this way and you'll get to the wagon. I'll ride ahead and make sure everyone is ready to take on the croc when you arrive."

"What if something else comes after me?" Brodie asked.

"Don't slow and don't stop. I can keep check of you on my map." She urged Bug to go faster again, not waiting for a reply from Brodie. There wouldn't be much time to get ready to fight the primordial crocodile, considering how little distance was between them and the wagon.

Mallory kept checking on her journal, refreshing the spell as she approached the wagon, angry voices coming from the other side of it. She nearly groaned when she spotted Osbert Senior. That was all they needed. Slowing Bug, she called out, "Primordial crocodile coming this way."

Osbert Senior grabbed his son by the shoulder. "We'll finish discussing this at home. I want no part of this." He strode away with a protesting Osbert Junior.

"How far away?" Ryan asked.

"We need to meet up with it away from the wagon." Callum turned to Ninette, who, along with Jorgen, was at the wagon. "You take care of the eggs."

"This way." Mallory dismounted, tying Bug to the wagon before running towards where her brother's icon was on her map. She didn't need a horse to worry about when going after the primordial crocodile.

"Are you sure we should be on foot?" Ryan strode by her side, his hunting bow in hand. "They're massive."

"Keep moving," Jorgen advised. "The moment you remain still, you're dead."

"There they are." Emica pointed ahead before shifting into her fox form and running towards Brodie and the primordial crocodile.

Mallory didn't bother using Vanish I on anyone. The crocodile had clearly shown that lack of vision didn't impede it in the slightest. As she came close, she cast Slow Target, dashing out of the way when it swung towards her. Getting close enough to cast that spell might not have been the best plan. Slowing the creature by ten percent wasn't a big enough drop in speed.

Avoiding a lunge from the crocodile, and nearly stumbling, Mallory glanced through her spells, not sure what to use. She cast Poison Dart and followed it up with Fireball. The creature didn't even flinch, let alone slow in its attacks.

Wondering what health it had, she took out her diplomat glasses and slipped them on while the creature was busy trying to snap at Emica, who had darted in while still in fox form. Mallory took a step back when she saw the health of the level six primordial crocodile. None of their attacks seem to be doing much. "We're hardly doing any damage. It has one thousand one hundred and seventy-five health. Ryan, your hunting bow is doing nothing. Neither are your throwing knives, Brodie." Her brother had dismounted, leaving Scorch well back from the fight and Fang sitting on the horse.

Ryan drew his longsword, darting in to attack before jumping out of the way of a tail slash.

"Use your ice spell." Danae used her longbow, keeping well back. "What level is the primordial crocodile?"

"Six." Mallory cast Ice Shard. It took a single point of health from the creature.

"For every sixty points of health damage you do, you'll slow it by ten percent, capping at ninety percent," Danae explained.

Mallory cast Ice Shard repetitively, glad the cooldown was only two seconds. "That's going to take a bit, considering I'm only doing one damage at a time."

Danae dropped an arrow as the primordial crocodile did a spin attack, trying to avoid being struck. "At least it doesn't have a healing ability. Then it would be a problem with that little amount of damage."

Callum wasn't able to move as quick as Danae and was knocked back, falling to the ground. Scrambling to his feet and retreating as the primordial crocodile focused on him, being prevented from reaching him by the two crystalline wolves.

Shock rushed through Mallory at how much health Callum had lost. She cast Health I as she ran to his side, calling out to everyone else. "Don't get hit. That spin attack did twenty-four damage."

"What's its health now?" Ryan called out.

At the same time, Brodie demanded, "What am I meant to attack with if my throwing knives do no damage?"

"One thousand one hundred and forty-three." Mallory took the health potion from her satchel, using weak increased healing on it to double the amount of health Callum would gain from the potion.

"Thanks." Callum downed the potion, handing the vial back before readying his bow.

Chapter Thirty-One

Mallory cast Ice Shard another couple of times, nearly groaning when she saw how little health the primordial crocodile had lost. "If we kill this croc before dark, I'll be surprised."

"See if this does anything," Brodie called out before drawing his stiletto and running forward to leap on the creature's back. He stabbed with the stiletto before vaulting off and running out of the way.

"Brodie!" Mallory exclaimed, continuing to cast Ice Shard. "That only did one damage. Don't do it again. It wasn't worth the risk."

"What do you expect me to do? Watch?" Brodie demanded.

"You can help Ninette," Danae suggested. "We collected a lot of eggs. They need to be kept warm. If they're away from heat too long, we'll lose them."

Brodie's expression brightened. "How many?"

Danae stumbled backwards as the crocodile tried to bite her, following it up with a swipe from its claws. She barely avoided both attacks, unable to attack back while she was retreating. Out of reach, and the crocodile now focused on Jorgen, she readied her bow. "I don't know. You'll have to count them. We raided three nests."

"Cool." Brodie started retreating towards where he'd left Scorch. "Are you sure you don't need me? How much health is left?"

"One thousand and ninety-six." Mallory continued to use Ice Shard on the crocodile, having lost count of how much damage she'd caused. She must be getting close to sixty damage. "We're making progress. Go help Ninette. Those eggs need to be kept warm. Or did you want to lose some of them?"

"Of course I don't." Brodie mounted Scorch, giving the battle a wide berth, Fang remaining in front of him.

He'd barely left when Ryan was raked by the crocodile's claws, causing twenty-six damage. She didn't have a healing potion to offer him and very little mana with how she was constantly attacking the crocodile. "Have you got a healing potion, Ryan? I can use weak increased healing on it if you do." She moved towards him as she spoke, wanting to be next to him if he did.

Ryan, who'd retreated, took a potion vial from his satchel, holding it out to Mallory. The two of them dived in different directions as the primordial crocodile lunged towards them.

Mallory clung to the potion vial, using weak increased healing on it as she scrambled to her feet, heart racing at the close call. Ryan only had nineteen health. An attack would have killed him. When the crocodile spun to attack Emica, Mallory hurried to Ryan, giving him the potion to drink.

He downed the contents, handing the vial back before heading towards the crocodile, sword in hand.

Mallory healed him again before turning her attention to Emica, Jorgen and Esben, checking their health with the help of the diplomat glasses. They were fine. None had lost any health. She went back to using Ice Shard on the crocodile, nearly shouting in excitement when she noticed the attacks had slowed ever so slightly. "One thousand and thirty-two health and I think I've finally done at least sixty ice damage."

"It's a little slower, so I'd have to agree," Callum said.

"How about you work on slowing it down some more?" Ryan suggested.

Mallory, who hadn't stopped attacking, said, "What do you think I've been doing?" She breathed in sharply when Jorgen was sent flying with a swipe of claws. Like Ryan, he lost twenty-six health. She focused on healing him. They really needed more healing potions. And better healing spells.

Emica got in the way of the crocodile when it tried to go after Jorgen, who was only now getting to his feet, shaking himself after being knocked over.

Mallory was torn between continuing to heal Jorgen and attacking the crocodile. The more she could slow it down, the less likely it was that anyone would be attacked. She alternated between healing and attacking, hoping she was making the right choice. When the crocodile did another spin attack, this time Danae being hit, and Jorgen still wasn't at full health, Mallory felt a moment of fear. She pushed it aside, healing Jorgen twice more before healing Danae once. The half-elf had retreated, the crocodile now focused on Ryan who continued to attack with his longsword.

"What is the health?" Danae asked as Mallory moved closer to her.

"One thousand and five."

"I only have one health potion. If I use it this early in the fight, I'll have nothing for later," Danae said.

Mallory cast Health I on Danae again. "Are you sure?" Instead of alternating between attacking and healing, she focused on healing. Obviously, it hadn't been a good decision to do that earlier.

Danae smiled fleetingly, readying her bow. "Not at all, but no back-up plan in case things get worse isn't good either."

As soon as Danae was fully healed, Mallory returned to attacking the crocodile, having had to dash out of the way a couple of times. She really didn't want to get bitten by that snapping mouth full of dagger sharp teeth. It was sure to hurt. She was relieved when she could finally call out, "Twenty percent slower and only seven hundred and eighty-eight health."

"I'm going to run out of arrows at this rate," Callum said. "I'll be starting on my spares soon." He released an arrow before glancing at Danae. "Do you want half the spares?"

"I'm down to my last three," Danae said.

"I have forty-three spares I can split with you," Callum offered.

"I'll take twenty. That's all I can fit in my quiver." Danae released her last arrow before retreating to a point behind Callum, waiting for him to join her.

Mallory had no idea what they'd do if Callum and Danae ran out of arrows. The two of them were doing the most damage. The rest of them only did one or two damage with Ryan doing five every time he got close enough. Most of his attempts ended with him dodging out of the way instead of finishing the attack.

Ryan tried to get out of the way of the snapping jaws again, too slow to avoid them this time.

Mallory used what little mana she had left to heal some of Ryan's health. "That was twenty-eight damage. Avoid the teeth at all costs. Bite is obviously its strongest attack."

This time, Danae was forced to dash out of the way of the jaws, dropping her arrow as she did so. "If it was only facing a single attacker, tail spin would be its strongest attack. The damage might not be as high, but being knocked to the ground puts you at a great disadvantage."

Mallory continued to heal Ryan, who headed towards the crocodile. "What are you doing? Your health isn't full."

Ryan attacked with his longsword, barely avoiding being clawed. "Full enough I can survive one of its attacks. I can't stand back and leave all the work to everyone else. Not with how much health it has."

"Should one of us collect Brodie and tell him to leave Fang with Ninette and use Scorch to lead the croc away?" Mallory asked.

"It wouldn't help," Danae said. "It'd return here looking for him after Brodie lost it. Then it'd notice either us or the village."

"We're not about to let it go wandering into the village," Ryan stated.

"I'm halfway through my arrows," Danae said. "What is the health?"

Chapter Thirty-Two

Mallory cast Ice Shard, now Ryan's health was full again, almost cheering when the creature slowed another ten percent. "Five hundred and sixty-seven health and thirty percent slower."

"I'm halfway through my arrows too," Callum said. "We might need to lure it away from this area far enough that Danae and I can return and gather the handful of arrows the croc has knocked to the ground."

"That sounds like a terrible plan." Mallory had no idea what they'd do if the crocodile went towards their camp rather than follow them. "We're barely avoiding the attacks as it is. Even slowed, it'd still outrun us."

"Then slow it some more," Callum said. "Because I'm down to five arrows."

"Why don't the two of you keep your arrows and retreat?" Ryan asked. "Then you can attack it from a distance and we can head towards you when it goes after you."

"And if it doesn't take the bait?" Mallory asked.

"We need to try something," Callum said. "I have three arrows left."

"You two retreat," Ryan ordered. "It's better than leaving it to only five of us to take this creature down."

Ninette came running towards them, her longsword drawn. "We have the eggs settled and Brodie is watching them. He said you need my help."

"This croc still has four hundred and fifty-one health," Mallory said. "We need all the help we can get." She quickly explained what they were doing.

"Ready for us to attack?" Callum called out once he and Danae were far enough from the crocodile.

"Everyone drop back," Ryan ordered. "You two attack one at a time. Conserve your arrows in case it needs a bit of extra encouragement." Ryan retreated warily as he watched the crocodile, leaping out of the way when it lunged at him.

Emica, Jorgen and Esben were the first to reach Callum and Danae. Mallory wished she had their speed. She tried to get past the crocodile, but the creature had other ideas, ignoring the arrows to lunge for her. Instead of getting closer to where everyone else now stood, she ended up further away. Again, the crocodile went for her. This time it nearly got her, a rush of air from the passing claws letting her know how close it had been.

Not knowing what else to do, and the arrows not drawing its attention, she returned to casting Ice Shard at it. She wished she'd been able to keep count of how much damage she'd done since last time, but counting was the last thing on her mind. All she could focus on was avoiding the attacks and keeping everyone's health full.

"Do we return to attacking?" Emica, who'd shifted to her human form, asked.

"Not yet." Mallory cast Ice Shard four more times, grinning when the crocodile slowed. "Let me see if I can get past it now. Surely forty percent slower has to make a difference." Drawing in a deep breath, she added, "Warn me if it gets close." Spinning, she ran, circling around to head to the group waiting for her. Desperately wanting to look over her shoulder, she kept her gaze on Ryan, noticing his knuckles were white from how tightly he gripped his sword. Then she was running past him and slowing to look behind.

Emica was again in her fox form, attacking the crocodile along with everyone other than Callum and Danae, who were circling back to the place where they'd been before.

Mallory returned to attacking, trying to ignore her racing heart and catch her breath. She was obviously becoming as crazy as her brother, trying to outrun a primordial crocodile like that. A smile slowly formed. Although it had worked. "Four hundred health left."

"We must be about a third of the way." Callum rejoined the fight. "Going by what you said the health was when you first checked and how slowly we're taking it down, the initial health would have been around twelve hundred."

Ninette stumbled back, avoiding a tail spin by centimetres. "I'm glad it's been slowed, otherwise that would have hit me."

Mallory continued to use Ice Shard. "As long as no one gets hurt, I'll have it slowed some more in about another thirty or forty hits." She doubted there was any chance at all that she'd be able to keep a proper count of the damage she was doing. "I need more powerful spells."

"We all need more powerful weapons." Ryan tried to get out of the way of the claws, but the crocodile managed to attack him. "Sorry." He retreated, needing to run out of the way when the crocodile chased him. "Just get my health up enough I can survive the strongest attack."

"What if you get hit twice?" Mallory focused on healing Ryan, moving closer to him as she did.

"At least until you slow it down another ten percent. That should keep us all a bit safer," Ryan said. "Besides, even with full health, I wouldn't survive two attacks."

Mallory did as he suggested, making sure he had five extra health than the strongest attack, hoping there weren't any stronger ones than what they'd encountered. "Does it get a buff to its attack when its health is low?"

Danae released her last arrow. "Not that I know of." She scanned the area. "If you want to make it move to another spot, there are eight arrows we can collect here."

Callum also released his last arrow. "What health is it now?"

"Three hundred and seventy-three." Mallory sighed. "And I have no idea how many more times I need to attack to slow it down again."

"Eighteen or twenty-eight," Callum said. "We should wait until then if we're going to lure it away again. Although this time it'll have to be Mallory who does the luring since we're out of arrows."

"Are eight worth luring it away for?" Mallory asked.

"That's sixty-four damage," Callum pointed out.

"If we manage to hit it each time," Danae added.

Before Mallory could comment, claws raked across her side as she tried to get out of the way. Pain rushed through her and she healed herself, the pain immediately fading. She was forced to dodge another attack, retreating as she healed herself. The attack had been more painful than she'd feared. "We should have brought the health tea with us."

"We didn't have much time to get organised," Ryan pointed out.

As soon as Mallory's health was high enough to survive another hit, she returned to attacking the crocodile. Surely it couldn't be too much longer until it was slowed again.

Then she'd finish healing Ryan and herself. "It's three hundred and forty-nine health. This is taking so much longer without the arrows."

"Should we lure it away?" Callum asked.

Mallory didn't answer, continuing to cast Ice Shard. She grinned. "Finally! Fifty percent slower. And three hundred and thirty-one health. This fight is becoming ridiculously slow. We need the arrows."

"Retreat to where we were attacking it before," Ryan ordered. "Mallory goes first, along with Danae and Callum since they can't attack." He continued to attack the crocodile, barely avoiding the sharp teeth.

Mallory ran back to where they'd been, turning to face the crocodile and casting Ice Shard at it. This time, it ignored her. "Ninette and Ryan come over next since Emica, Jorgen and Esben move the fastest." She kept throwing Ice Shard at the crocodile, wondering if she should heal herself instead. But the longer the fight continued, the more chances there were someone might lose all their health. None of them had that many revives they could afford to waste them.

As soon as the crocodile took the bait and came after Mallory, Danae and Callum ran back to where their arrows were. They were still collecting them when the crocodile spun in their direction and headed their way.

"Look out," Mallory called. "It's coming back."

Danae looked up, firing one of her collected arrows at the crocodile, veering to the side as the crocodile went for her.

"I've collected them all," Callum finally said, joining Danae in attacking the crocodile. "We ended up getting nine in total so well and truly worth coming back for."

Mallory continued to cast Ice Shard at the crocodile, trying not to get too excited by the dropping health. The arrows wouldn't last long. By the time the last arrow had struck the crocodile, it had two hundred and twelve health. Mallory called out the number.

"We're going to need to buy arrows," Callum said. "We have twenty back at the wagon, but that won't fill three quivers."

Ryan grinned. "Don't tell Brodie or he'll tell you to learn fletcher so you can make your own."

"Speaking of Brodie, how many eggs did we end up getting?" Callum asked Ninette.

The young warrior dodged an attack, getting in one of her own, before she spoke. "There were seven in the nest we emptied. We took four from the next one and five from the last one."

"Sixteen eggs!" Callum exclaimed. "I bet Brodie was happy when he found out."

Ninette laughed. "Very happy. He's busy coming up with all the things the money can be spent on."

Ryan grinned. "So he's busy counting his drakes before they're hatched."

Mallory groaned, distracted enough by the comment that the crocodile nearly got her. "That was a terrible joke."

"I'm an idiot." Ryan exclaimed.

"I hope you're not expecting me to disagree," Callum said with a grin.

"I've got sixteen arrows left. Retreat and I can give them to both of you." Ryan retreated as he spoke, handing the arrows over to Callum and Danae when they joined him.

Chapter Thirty-Three

At the same time as Ryan, Callum and Danae retreated, Mallory called out, "Sixty percent slower and one hundred and eighty-eight health left. Maybe we will get this fight done before dark."

Danae and Callum rejoined the fight, the health dropping at a faster rate until their arrows were gone.

"Twelve health left." Mallory could barely contain her excitement, relieved the crocodile was so much slower when her focus on how little health it had left, nearly had her losing most of her own.

Then it was dropping to the ground, several arrows still sticking out of it. Mallory stared at the creature. "I can't believe we did it." But they had. The diplomat glasses showed there was no health left.

Emica shifted forms. "That would have been a lot quicker if I could have used my lightning attack." She glanced at Jorgen and Esben, not saying aloud that they suppressed her kitsune ability. There was also none of the annoyance or anger that used to be in her tone when she made that statement.

Callum gathered the handful of arrows left, giving Danae four and keeping three for himself. "Who's skinning it?"

Ryan eyed it up and down. "It looks big enough we can all have a go at the same time."

Ninette gathered Brodie's handful of throwing knives. "I'll return to camp and make sure the eggs are safe."

Emica laughed. "I don't blame you for wanting to check on Goblin Boy."

Ninette smiled as she left, not saying whether or not Emica was correct in her assumption.

Mallory handed over the two empty potion vials to Danae, finished healing herself and started on Ryan. "Let's hope we get something from the croc. It's going to cost us a fortune to replace all the arrows. We can't exactly take on Bard's Hollow with no arrows." She glanced at her stats. "And we only ended up with eight XP each from killing it."

Danae slipped the vials in her satchel, glancing in the direction Ninette had taken. "I can't wait to return to camp. That fight took forever."

Ryan checked his pocket watch before taking out his skinning knife. "It took just over two hours. Way too long a fight. I could do with a rest too."

Callum joined him, taking out his hunting knife. "I wonder what Brodie has cooked while we've been here."

Ryan grinned. "I have no idea. But I bet he's cooked something. And eaten some of it too."

Jorgen and Esben joined them, both using their stilettos to gain resources.

Danae and Emica kept watch while Mallory checked everyone's health and finished healing Ryan before she put her diplomat glasses away. About to ask if they needed any help, Ryan rose to his feet with a large hide draped over his hands, both ends dragging on the ground.

"I wonder what this is worth."

"Maybe the hunter will be interested in it," Mallory suggested.

"It'll probably be worth more than what he can afford," Danae said. "We could travel to Wayholt tomorrow and sell it and anything else we gain as well as restock on arrows." She came forward with the two empty vials Mallory had given her.

"What are you doing?" Callum asked.

"Their blood is used in some potions." Danae turned to Jorgen and Esben. "Do you think you can help turn it over so we can try to get the heart? It'll also be the easiest area to take the blood from."

Mallory, Emica, Callum and Ryan joined Jorgen and Esben and between the six of them, they pushed the crocodile onto its back. By the time they finished, as well as the hide, they also had twenty-five teeth, six claws, eight kilograms of meat, a gold ring, seven silver pieces, two potion vials of blood, eighteen stomach scales and the heart.

Esben studied the ring. "I wonder if it has an enchantment on it." He slipped it on. "Nothing shows up. Either it doesn't have an enchantment or the circumstances aren't right to trigger it." He removed the ring, giving it to Ryan, who carried most of the resources they'd gained in his backpack.

"We should return to camp and make sure everything is still okay." Mallory didn't like the idea of leaving her brother in charge of everything for too long. Not with his tendency to rush into danger so often.

Emica laughed. "You worried about what Goblin Boy will get up to?"

Mallory didn't bother answering. It wasn't like she could deny the comment. Using the Locate Party spell, she checked her journal map. Brodie was still at camp. And his health was fine. She smiled when she noticed his stats. It looked like he'd earned experience points from when they'd taken out the primordial crocodile. He was sure to be happy about that.

It didn't take them long to return to the camp and Mallory had been correct. Brodie was excited about the experience points he'd gained for a kill he hadn't been there for at the end. "I wonder how far away you can be and still get XP." Before anyone could answer, he continued. "I made a pot of Adventurer's Stew. It's not bad. Does everyone want some? Is that the hide from the croc?" He started serving up stew before anyone had even answered his question about wanting some.

Ryan placed the hide on the back of the wagon. "We got a few resources from the croc, but we ended up with next to no arrows after taking it out."

"Ninette found all my throwing knives." Brodie handed a bowl of stew to Ryan when he returned to the campfire.

Callum collected the twenty arrows from the wagon, sharing them out between himself, Danae and Ryan so that, including the ones Callum and Danae already had, they each had nine.

Brodie gave a bowl of stew to Emica, having already given one to Esben, before turning to Mallory. "We need another basket. I don't think the eggs are going to stay warm enough with how many are crowded into each basket. They aren't all against the warmed rock that's in the middle of them."

Mallory sighed heavily. "I really wanted to go to the Adventurers Guild and get cleaned up after that fight, then have something to eat. I don't even know where we'd get another basket from."

Ninette took a bowl of stew from Brodie. "The weaver two doors along from the tavern sometimes has baskets for sale." She sat by the fire.

"How much?" Brodie looked around the group, another bowl of stew in his hands. He gave it to Danae.

Ninette shrugged. "Around four or five copper pieces. I'm not sure exactly."

"I can see if they have any," Brodie offered. "I've already eaten."

"We were going to see if anyone wanted to buy some of the resources we gained from the croc," Mallory said.

"I can go with him," Callum said. "We can load it all up on Bobbi and I can eat when we're back."

Mallory hesitated. She really didn't want to go anywhere. She wanted to collapse in front of the fire and take a break. After she'd washed.

Callum smiled. "There isn't much mischief to get into in Buckneth."

Mallory was tempted to sigh again. It didn't take much for her brother to find mischief. "Okay. Fine. Don't buy anything other than a basket and arrows."

"Hell yeah!" Brodie victory punched the air. "I'll get more XP from bartering."

Mallory slowly shook her head, not bothering to point out he was likely to gain one and a half experience points at the most. She glanced around the group instead. "Does anyone want to join me for a trip to the Adventurers Guild to wash up?"

While Brodie and Callum went into Buckneth, having first taken forty silver pieces from the chest, Mallory took

Emica and Ninette with her once they'd finished eating. When they returned, Ryan and Jorgen went to the guild, followed by Danae and Esben.

Mallory sat at the fire, eating her stew, watching Ninette, who'd been quieter than usual. She was changing the heated rock placed in the middle of each basket, wrapping it in a cloth before she put it amongst the eggs. She tried to think of a way to ask Ninette what was wrong without making the warrior feel like she had to explain herself. "You're quiet."

Ninette looked over to Mallory, not speaking straight away. "I didn't expect to have to look after my brothers so soon." She sat down beside Mallory, staring at the campfire that had burned low. "I wanted to see a few more places before I found somewhere to stay with them."

"You will see more places. We have the unicorn quest still to do, which is on the other side of the island. And then you're going to Merrow with Danae."

Ninette continued to stare at the fire, not speaking straight away. "I just wish Pa was easier to live with. It would have been nice to spend a year as a warrior."

Mallory thought of her own father. "Some people can't change. Others can. Your brothers will grow up eventually and then you can go back to adventuring if you want."

Ninette nodded.

Chapter Thirty-Four

Before Mallory could say anything else to Ninette, Brodie and Callum returned, Brodie holding a basket that he swung back and forth as he walked.

"I better get another rock heated for that basket." Ninette rose to her feet, looking around the area until she found two suitable ones. A rock to have in the basket and one to heat for when it needed swapping out.

Brodie placed the basket beside the other two. "We got thirty arrows and the basket was five copper pieces." His expression fell. "But Ahron wanted thirty silver pieces for the arrows. We need to find a way to get more of them without spending so much money."

"What about the resources?" Ryan eyed Bobbi, the hide draped across her back. "I take it you couldn't sell the hide. What about the rest of it?"

"We traded a kilo of the meat for the basket. I think the weaver got the better deal," Brodie said. "Ahron took the other seven kilos of meat. He offered four silver pieces. I don't even know if that was a good or bad price. But at least we only had to pay twenty-six silver pieces for the arrows. And the hunter wasn't interested in anything."

Callum again shared out the arrows between himself, Ryan and Danae, so they had nineteen each in total. "Hopefully, we'll end up with more arrows after we go to Bard's Hollow."

"Do you have enough arrows to take it on?" Mallory asked.

Callum shrugged. "Possibly. Depends on what's in there. But we won't find more arrows around here. We'll have to travel to Wayholt if we want to buy more."

After the tiring fight, Mallory didn't want to travel to Wayholt and back before they could take on Bard's Hollow. All she wanted to do was have an early night and head to Bard's Hollow in the morning. "I suppose we could retreat if things become too much."

"That isn't always possible," Emica said. "What about the slings and slingshot in the chest? They could take them in case they run out of arrows."

The two slings were taken from the chest and given to Callum and Danae along with two bags of slingshot each, leaving a single bag in the chest.

Callum glanced around the group. "Bard's Hollow is a cave. It doesn't matter if we enter when it's day or night. It'll be dark either way. We could go after I've cleaned up and had something to eat."

Mallory groaned. "We can go in the morning. Haven't we done enough today?"

Ryan grinned. "Not according to Callum. We have plenty of time before the travelling bank is here. There's no need to rush. We're also sticking around this area until Ninette's younger brothers are fifteen. So definitely no hurry."

"If we get Bard's Hollow done, we might have time to go after the staff," Callum pointed out. "Then we'll have a home for Ninette and her brothers to go to."

"It's not the time we need," Mallory protested. "It's levels."

"We might get some levels doing Bard's Hollow," Ryan suggested.

"That's if we can complete it. Who knows what's in there. If it's as bad as the primordial crocodile, slingshot would be useless against it if you ran out of arrows," Mallory said.

"It'll be fine," Ryan assured her. "This is a low level area. There won't be anything too bad in there."

"Do you have to?" Brodie demanded. "Now there's sure to be something we can't beat."

Ryan grinned. "Guess we'll have to wait and see."

"Why don't we at least go down to the beach and see how we feel when we get there?" Callum suggested. "We can always fish if we decide not to enter the cave tonight."

Smudge made excited noises at the word fish and Fang joined in with a yip and running around in tight circles before turning and jumping up at Brodie.

Ryan laughed. "I think they made their vote." He glanced around the group. "Beach?"

The majority of them agreed and everyone helped pack the wagon. The campfire was left till last to put out so the rocks in the baskets could be replaced with ones that had been left in the fire, the cooler rocks being put in the wagon in preparation for heating at the end of their journey.

Danae drove the wagon while Ninette rode ahead on Dodger, planning to visit the tavern so she could leave a message with Ahron for her brothers. She rejoined them before they'd finished driving through Buckneth, coming alongside the wagon.

"Did you want me to drive?" Ninette offered.

Danae shook her head. "It's only an hour to the beach. Not far at all."

"Whose gathering resources?" Brodie asked.

"Emica has the lowest character level," Mallory said.

"Someone else can gather. We'll be in Shadhurst soon enough and I can use those XP vials," Emica said.

"Then Ninette, Brodie, Ryan and Danae are the lowest at two CAS points off character level five," Mallory said. "The four of you can take turns gathering. If there are resources around here."

There were no resources for the first twenty minutes of the journey and Brodie was adamant that no one should gather until there were resources, so the first one who gathered didn't miss out. The four of them ended up only getting the chance to gather resources for ten minutes each. While they gathered, Mallory wrote in her journal, not wanting to leave it until later in case they did enter Bard's Hollow. Not that she wanted to do anything other than sit on the beach and enjoy a campfire. Their earlier fight had taken way too long.

Mallory eyed the hessian bags of resources that had been added to the ones that were still in the wagon. There weren't as many as there'd been after their last journey. But there had been enough resources gathered to allow the four of them to gain a CAS point. Ninette put hers straight into smithing while the other three did nothing with theirs. Although Brodie had talked about putting his in brewer.

Mallory smiled, slowly shaking her head. Brewer wasn't at all practical while they were travelling around.

As they drew close to the beach, Jorgen and Esben ran ahead to light a fire so they could heat rocks as soon as they arrived, the ones in the baskets having only a little warmth left in them.

Emica, who was driving, glanced over her shoulder at Mallory, who rested a hand on one of the eggs. "We're not going to want to go far at a time until those eggs are hatched. After all the effort it took to take them, we don't want to lose any."

"Is there a way to tell how soon they'll hatch?" Mallory asked.

Emica shook her head, drawing the wagon up near the start of the beach, the campfire only metres away. "Not unless you saw the eggs laid."

Ninette took the three extra rocks and hurried to the campfire with them. "It shouldn't take too long to warm them."

Emica grabbed one of the baskets of drake eggs. "We'll take them closer to the fire while we wait for the rocks to heat."

Once warmed rocks had been added to the baskets, Callum asked, "Everyone up to entering Bard's Hollow?"

Mallory groaned. "Can't we wait until morning?"

"If we finish up here, we can take all the things we gain to Wayholt to sell. We could even stay there a bit longer and wait for the bank so Danae can visit her mum," Callum said. "Then be back in time for Ninette's brothers' birthdays. Or come back earlier and go after the staff."

"We could trade some of the stuff from the croc for things like water breathing potions, so we have enough for everyone," Brodie suggested. "That'll make it easier to go after the staff."

"We don't even know exactly where the house is that's being offered in exchange for the staff," Mallory pointed out. "It could be a long way out from Merrow."

"We could sell it if it's no good," Brodie said.

"Are we going to Bard's Hollow tonight?" Callum persisted.

Chapter Thirty-Five

Mallory sighed, not wanting to go to Bard's Hollow. "I guess we should vote on it." She sighed again when she saw she was outvoted. "Looks like we're going in."

Once they were certain Ninette was fine and had a lantern nearby in case she needed it, they walked along the beach towards Bard's Hollow. They heard it before they reached it. The wind whistled through the cave opening, making it sound like someone played a mournful instrument.

A shiver went through Mallory at the sound, her Magelight making it easier to see the area than the lantern they'd used last time they'd been here.

"I thought we'd never get to go in. It's been ages since we were here," Brodie said.

Ryan grinned. "Yeah, back when you took an arrow to the knee."

Mallory tried not to grin, but it was impossible.

Danae slowly shook her head. "I still don't get it."

Mallory wound her way through the scattering of rocks on the beach, headed towards the tumble of boulders that hid the cave entrance. The ocean wasn't far from the entrance, the remains of a campfire still in the cave. She couldn't help wondering if it was the same, or a different one. At the back of the entrance cave, which was three metres wide and two metres deep, a lengthy tunnel led down into the darkness.

"Should we be using Magelight?" Ryan asked. "What if it catches the attention of whoever is in here?"

"It's not like we can see in the dark," Mallory pointed out. "And we don't have many night vision potions left." She took out her wand.

"Stay at the rear of the group and it won't be as noticeable," Callum suggested.

"Did you want to make me invisible and I can go ahead and scout the place out?" Jorgen asked.

"It only lasts a minute," Mallory reminded him. "I doubt that'd be long enough for you to search the entire place."

"This isn't getting us any closer to the goblet." Ryan strode across the cave, heading for the tunnel at the back of it. "Time to get moving."

The tunnel was roughly a metre wide, causing them to walk single file, Mallory bringing up the rear. The rough walls of the tunnel had been smoothed out in places and Mallory assumed whoever had used it over the years had widened some sections to make it a more uniform size.

About four metres in, the tunnel branched off to the left as well as continuing straight ahead.

Mallory added everyone to their party, then cast Lightning Trap at a point a few steps into the tunnel on the left, the only method she could come up with to help them keep track of where they hadn't been. She just had to hope no one set it off.

They continued straight ahead for another eight metres where the tunnel turned to the left, a recessed area big enough to contain four barrels at the intersection of where it turned to the left. Another long corridor was ahead of them. This far into the cave, they could no longer hear the mournful sound of the wind in the cave entrance.

"Do you think we should have turned left at the previous one?" Danae asked.

Ryan shrugged. "We could split up."

"Absolutely not," Mallory said before turning to Brodie. "Leave those barrels alone. We can see what's in them on our way out."

"How are we going to get them back to the village if there ends up being as many barrels as the last cave we were in? We need another wagon." Brodie reluctantly stepped away from the barrels.

Once they were past the barrels, they walked another ten metres before coming to an intersection. Mallory tried to peer past everyone to see what lay ahead. When her magelight ran out, she was going to cast Tracking

Magelight on someone, so she didn't have to stay at the back of the group.

"There's light ahead and to the right. Only darkness to the left," Ryan said, keeping his voice low.

"Go left," Emica suggested. "See what's in the darkness first."

"Want me to scout ahead?" Jorgen asked.

After a short discussion, Vanish I was cast on Jorgen and Emica. Jorgen went to the right while Emica went to the left. She was back first.

"Seven beds set up in a cavern with all the beds full of sleeping bandits. There's a second entrance that leads to where you put the lightning trap. There's also another intersection before you reach that cavern, with one direction leading to more barrels and the other leading to another bed where a bandit is still awake sharpening his sword." Emica turned to Mallory. "Can I borrow the diplomat glasses so I can see what levels they are?"

Before Mallory could answer, Jorgen returned, going straight to her. "I didn't have enough time to check everywhere. I need you to cast Vanish I on me again."

"What did you see?" Callum asked.

"There's an empty cavern on the left with a fire burning low and some bench seats placed around it. Straight ahead of me was another cavern with a similar setup, also empty. There's another cavern to the right of that one where ten bandits are seated at tables eating dinner. I don't know what's to the left of the cavern that was straight ahead. I left before I became visible."

"So that's at least eighteen bandits," Ryan said. "That shouldn't be too bad."

"Depends on their levels," Emica said. "If I can use the glasses, I can check on that for you."

Mallory handed over the glasses, casting Vanish I on Emica. Before she could cast it on Jorgen, he shook his head.

"I'll wait until Emica is back so I can use the glasses. There is no guarantee they're all the same levels."

They waited silently, Mallory unable to stop looking in every direction, even though she couldn't see past everyone. How long would the bandits take to eat dinner? Would they head this way once they were finished?

Emica arrived back in the tunnel, handing the glasses to Jorgen when he held out his hand. "The lone bandit is on the move. Possibly in this direction. He's level three. There are two level threes in the cavern with the seven beds and the rest are level two."

Brodie drew a dagger. "Make me invisible and I'll get him."

"He has a lantern," Emica warned.

"How much health?" Ryan readied his bow.

Smudge made a soft warning cry.

"Looks like we're running out of time," Callum said. "What are we doing?"

"Forty-six health," Emica said.

Mallory wasn't sure what to suggest. All she knew was that she was glad there were only seconds left on her magelight.

"Take him out with arrows," Jorgen said. "Emica, Esben and I can attack in our animal forms. Between all of us, we should take him out before he can warn anyone."

Mallory cast Vanish I on Danae and Callum since they both had the highest attack with a bow. Everyone moved towards the oncoming light and Mallory was glad she hadn't recast Magelight when it ran out. They didn't need to warn the oncoming bandit they were there. He'd find out soon enough. Hurrying forward, she arrived too late to help.

Emica held a lantern, placing it on the ground with a grin. "I caught it before it could smash and alert anyone with the noise."

Chapter Thirty-Six

Mallory stared at the warrior lying on the ground, feeling a twinge of unease that there'd been so many of them and only one of him. It had hardly seemed like a fair fight. Then she remembered the bandits that had ambushed them on their recent journey to Wayholt. Straightening her shoulders, she took the five copper pieces Esben handed her from searching the warrior, the leather boots he'd taken having been given to Ryan to put in the backpack he carried.

"Who gets to go after the sleeping bandits?" Brodie asked. "I didn't get any XP from this one."

"Their health ranges from twenty-one for one of the rogues to forty-eight for one of the warriors," Emica said.

"Then we should take out the rogues first," Callum suggested.

Emica shook her head. "They're furthest from the entrance."

"Then first come first served," Ryan stated. "We need to get moving before any of them wake, or one of the ones from the other cavern comes this way."

"I'll see what else is in the other direction." Jorgen turned to Mallory. "If you want to make me invisible."

With a nod, Mallory did as Jorgen requested. She sighed. "I hate it when we go after sleeping people. It doesn't seem right."

"I doubt the bandits have the same problem with the tactics they use. They regularly attack under the cover of darkness. My father is often being called upon to send someone to investigate such attacks," Emica said. "Entire families wiped out in the night with no chance to fight back."

"We need to attack each bandit together," Callum said. "With enough damage that they can't warn anyone else we're here."

"We should have kept the glasses," Brodie said.

Callum drew out his spyglass. "We still have this."

"You won't be able to fight if you're watching their health and you do a lot of damage," Danae pointed out.

"If it's a warrior, assume they have forty-eight health. If it's a rogue, then expect twenty-four health," Emica suggested.

"Okay." Callum put the spyglass away. "Let's just all attack each bandit together with ranged weapons whenever possible."

"Start with the one on the left as we enter," Emica said. "Then on the right, before attacking those on the other side of the room."

Mallory followed at the back, not wanting to be at the front this time. The plan sounded terrible. There were too many things that could go wrong.

Emica placed the lantern well outside the cavern entrance, only a limited amount of light entering ahead of them. Jorgen arrived as they attacked the first bandit, a warrior. He didn't wake.

Mallory tried to remind herself the bandits wouldn't have had the same qualms she felt as she turned to the next bandit.

Jorgen came alongside her, returning the glasses as he whispered in her ear. "There's a level four hellion in one of the smaller caverns."

Fear rushed through her. "Is it Rass?"

"I didn't recognise him."

Jorgen's words didn't help push the fear away. But his warning that one of the bandits was a member of the dark forces helped her focus on the task ahead. The dark forces were the enemy of the guardians. They'd done many atrocious things. Images of how she'd first discovered Emica and Jorgen caged, and with very little health, ran through her mind, helping her take out the sleeping bandits. With everyone's help, it was done within minutes and they searched the cavern and bodies, having encountered no problems.

Mallory found an iron bar locked door in a tunnel leading out of one corner of the cavern. She cast Tracking Magelight on herself, not wanting to use Magelight since it lasted three times as long. The ball of white light lit up the tunnel on the other side of the door. Holding the bars, she shook it. The door was solid, not budging at all.

Jorgen joined her. "None of them had a key. The hellion probably has it. He's likely in charge of whatever is going on here."

She stared at the dark marks along the ground. "It looks like something that was bleeding has been dragged along the tunnel."

"Have a closer look." Jorgen pointed to scratch marks along the tunnel wall where it met the bars. "Whatever it is, wants out."

Mallory took a step back from the bars, feeling like she was too close with how deep the claw marks were. "Let's hope it doesn't get out." Turning her back on the barred tunnel, she returned to the middle of the cavern where an unlit brazier sat. "What did we end up getting?"

Brodie glared at Ryan. "No one will let me take the blankets. They can be washed."

Mallory glanced at the beds, not wanting to take any of the bloodstained bedding. "Forget the blankets. We're not going to be able to take everything. Focus on the more valuable items. So what did we get?"

"Two stilettos, a short sword, a belt pouch, fourteen silver and ten copper pieces." Callum handed the coins over to Mallory, who added them to her belt pouch.

Emica momentarily rested her hand on Brodie's shoulder. "Don't worry, Goblin Boy. There are five crates down a tunnel that circles around behind there and comes out on the other side." Emica pointed first in the direction of where Mallory had found the door made from iron bars and then to the corner across the cavern from it.

Brodie's expression brightened. "What's in them?"

"We can figure that out later." Mallory wondered if she should cast Tracking Magelight again or if they should make do with the lantern they'd taken from the warrior. Still trying to decide, she turned to Jorgen. "Are there any other bandits than the level four hellion you found?"

"Where's the hellion?" Brodie asked, glancing around as if he was hiding nearby.

"In the opposite direction to where the bandits were eating at the tables," Jorgen said. "Past another cavern with beds. None of them had anyone sleeping in them. I assume they have two rotations so there is always someone awake."

"Is there anyone else?" Ryan asked.

Both Jorgen and Emica shook their head, Emica the one to speak. "Unless there's someone in the area behind the iron bars. Either there's two entrances to it or there are two locked areas down this end of the caverns."

"There's another tunnel that has a door made from iron bars?" Mallory asked.

Emica nodded. "This way." She led the way along the tunnel that went in both directions past the door made from iron bars, having taken a right instead of a left at the door. At an intersection, she turned left, leading them past a single bed with a crate sitting beside it. Brodie had to be tugged away, protesting that it wouldn't hurt to check what was in it. Turning left again, they went three metres down the tunnel before their progress was halted by another door made from iron bars.

Mallory peered between the bars, casting Tracking Magelight on herself again. The tunnel only went another metre before opening up into a two metres by two metres cavern with a large hole in the ground. A roughly hewn tree trunk rested on the edge like a ramp leading into the darkness of the hole. There were dark stains on the ground and along the tree trunk, as if something bleeding had been dragged down there too. Off to the left of the cavern was a tunnel that it was impossible to see where it led.

Emica took the lantern from Callum, who currently held it. "I'll see if I can see your light from the other door." She was gone before anyone could agree or disagree.

Mallory couldn't drag her gaze away from the deep claw marks in the cavern wall near the iron bars. "I hope it is the same area. With how deep these claw marks are, I'd hate to think there were two of these creatures in Bard's Hollow."

"It doesn't matter," Callum said. "We're not in here hunting creatures. We're after a goblet."

Emica rejoined them. "It's the same cavern. It has two exits, both with locked doors made from iron bars. Whatever is in there, someone went to a lot of trouble to keep it from getting out."

"Well, whatever it is, it's not going anywhere," Ryan stated. "We need to focus on finding the goblet. The hellion first or the eating bandits?"

"It seems kind of mean to interrupt their meal," Brodie said.

Emica grinned. "If we interrupt their meal, there might be something left for you." She laughed when Brodie glanced in the direction Jorgen had taken earlier.

Brodie glared at Emica. "So what are we doing, then?"

"The group of bandits," Callum said. "We're better off taking out some of them so they can't come to the defence of the lone hellion. If they have similar stats to the ones we already took out, then we might have the chance to take two or three out before they can organise themselves."

"This way then." Jorgen led the way, the Tracking Magelight out by the time they reached the first cavern, which had a lit fire pit with bench stools set around the crackling fire. They went through it, stopping at the narrow entrance at the far end, peering into another cavern with a similar fire pit and bench seats. This one had two warriors and a rogue seated around it. Luckily, they had their backs to them.

"Where are the tables of food?" Brodie asked, keeping his voice low.

"There are two short tunnels on the right side of this cavern leading into another cavern. The tables are there. Any noise these ones make will be heard by those at the tables," Jorgen explained.

Chapter Thirty-Seven

Using her diplomat glasses, Mallory checked the health of the three bandits sitting by the fire. "Both the warriors have thirty-nine health while the rogue has twenty-one."

Callum turned to Mallory. "If Ryan, Brodie and Danae target the warrior on the left and you get two quick attacks in on the warrior on the right that I attack, they shouldn't be able to make a sound."

"What about the rogue?" Emica asked.

"Mallory can make Jorgen and Esben invisible and they can grab him. If she casts Lightning Trap behind him, they can drag him into it and keep him from making a noise until the rest of us have the chance to attack him," Callum suggested.

"Okay." Mallory cast Lightning Trap just behind the rogue, waiting until her mana was full before she cast Vanish I on Jorgen and Esben. She kept her wand ready, her gaze focused on the rogue. He was dragged backwards off the bench seat and she threw a fireball at the warrior

Callum attacked. Before he could do more than move his hand towards his sword, she'd cast Fireball again and he sprawled onto the ground.

"Don't forget the rogue," Callum reminded her.

Mallory faced the rogue, who was pinned to the ground, Jorgen and Esben still invisible. She threw fireballs at the bandit, about to lower her wand, when another rogue came out of one of the tunnels on the left of the cavern. "Bandit!" She attacked him, three arrows impaling him after she'd barely spoken.

"That'll make the next cavern a little easier." Ryan lowered his bow. "Let's get over there before more of them come out here and discover their mates."

"Maybe I need to put five levels in hunting so I can use a hunting bow for times like this. I didn't get a chance to attack anyone," Emica said.

"What about searching the bodies?" Brodie asked.

"Later," Ryan said. "Come on, before someone else comes in here. They certainly won't stop and ask questions when they spot the bodies."

"I'll make you invisible," Mallory said to Emica. "Give you a chance to get in close so you can help." When Emica nodded, she cast Vanish I on the kitsune.

Ryan grinned at Brodie. "Better hurry up before you miss out on some XP."

Mallory hurried forward, entering one of the short tunnels. She barely had time to take in the three tables where six warriors sat, meals mostly eaten, before she was spotted.

The largest warrior burst out of his seat, knocking the table over in the process. Plates and food went everywhere, causing Brodie to cry out in horror. Mallory automatically attacked the warrior, first with Fireball and then Poison Dart. She did the same to three other warriors before she started to go for the first bandit she'd attacked. He was down, arrows and throwing knives on the ground around him. She began to attack the second warrior she'd cast her spells on, but she was down too. The next one vanished and she hoped it was due to a revive rather than an invisibility potion or spell.

Glancing around, Mallory realised the fight was over already. She lowered her wand. "I was expecting it to be more difficult."

Ryan grinned. "You're not complaining, are you?"

She shook her head, smiling. "No. I was surprised. And relieved. We're making progress. It's not that long ago we would have found this fight difficult."

"Does that mean you think we can go after the staff?" Ryan asked.

"I don't know that we've made that much progress." Mallory emphasised the word 'that', laughing when she noticed her brother. "Stop mourning the food on the ground. We need to go after the hellion and get the goblet."

Brodie continued to slowly shake his head. "What a waste. It's full of broken crockery. Not even Fang can eat it." His gaze remained on the overturned tables, food and broken crockery scattered across the ground in front of them.

"Are we searching here first?" Jorgen asked.

Ryan shook his head. "If we only have one hellion left, we should take him out before we're distracted by anything else."

Mallory was halfway across the cavern where they'd taken out the bandits sitting at the fire pit, heading for a smaller adjoining cavern containing beds, when the hellion strode between the two rows of beds, freezing for a moment at the sight of her.

He drew a sword, his tattoo on his right hand marking him as a member of the hellions. He glanced around the group of them, not coming any closer. "What do you want?"

"The False Hope Goblet," Ryan said.

The hellion laughed. "Telling you won't help. You're not going to get past the guard."

"We've made it this far," Callum pointed out. "How hard can a guard be?"

"Great," Brodie muttered. "Not you too."

Mallory laughed at her brother's comment. "Stop going on every time someone says something like that."

The hellion laughed again. "I really wish I was going to be here to see how badly you fail. But don't worry. When I return, I'll have more than enough to get past the guard and take all of you out, too." He slipped his hand into his belt pouch and vanished.

Mallory stared at the spot where the hellion had been. "What just happened?"

"He must have had some sort of teleportation item." Danae lowered her bow. "In his belt pouch."

"How long until he returns?" Callum asked.

Danae shrugged. "Hours. Days. It depends."

"On what?" Mallory asked.

"The type of teleport he used, if there is some sort of teleport link here and how many he's planning on bringing back with him," Danae explained.

"He's only a level four warrior," Jorgen said. "It's probably safe to assume he'll be travelling back either on foot or horseback and bringing more people with him."

"He might use a ship and anchor out from here, using a rowboat to bring everyone to the beach," Danae suggested.

"What sort of guard would it be that the amount of people he had with him wasn't enough?" Callum asked.

"It might not be the amount of people with him that was the problem," Emica said. "It might have been the amount of people willing to face the guard due to how likely they were to die."

"And we're right back to what sort of guard it is." Ryan glanced around the cavern. "Actually, the question is probably where is the guard?"

Brodie's expression brightened. "Does that mean it's time to search the place?"

"No," Ryan stated. "All we're doing is looking for the guard. We'll split into three groups and meet back here once we've all done a check through. Shouldn't take more than five minutes if we move quickly."

Mallory, Ryan and Emica were in one group, Brodie, Danae and Esben in another and Callum and Jorgen in the last group. They all headed off in different directions once Mallory had cast Tracking Magelight on Brodie and Callum.

Mallory led the way to where the hellion had come from. There was a double bed at the end of the tunnel, which was two metres wide, the walls nearly smooth. Which meant there wasn't much room on either side of the bed. At the foot of the bed, a tunnel went to the left and they followed it to discover it led past the single bed and then onto the door made from iron bars. Circling back around, they checked the room with the tables.

Chapter Thirty-Eight

Meeting back up in the largest cavern, Mallory looked hopefully at the rest of her party, getting shakes of their head in answer to her unspoken question about the goblet.

"The only part we haven't checked is behind the locked doors," Danae said.

"How do we get past them?" Callum asked. "It's not like any of us can pick locks."

"I guess it's time to search for a key," Ryan said.

Brodie victory punched the air. "Hell yeah. Finally."

Ryan grabbed Brodie's shoulder, tugging him back to face him. "This isn't about raiding the place. We need to find a key. And we don't want to be weighed down by everything when we still have to find the goblet."

"I know that." Shrugging Ryan's hand off his shoulder, Brodie took a step towards the nearest bandit. "Where do we put the things we find?"

Mallory slowly shook her head. "That doesn't sound at all like you're focused on finding the key."

"Of course I am," Brodie protested. "But I might as well gather up everything else too, so we don't have to search twice."

Callum laughed softly. "That was a surprisingly good excuse."

Emica took the lantern. "Are we searching in groups or can we all look in separate areas since we now know the place is empty?"

"Either," Ryan said. "Whatever you prefer."

Finished searching one of the bodies, Brodie strode to the barrels at the other end of the cavern, opening one of them up. "There's rice in here. An entire barrel full." He put the lid back on. "Do you think it will fit in the wagon?"

Slowly shaking her head again, Mallory made her way to the crates in the corner, a single barrel amongst them.

It was Emica who found the key. It was in the crate next to the single bed around the corner from the door made from iron bars. In the time it took her to find it, Brodie had taken most of the barrels, crates and chests from the furthest end to the largest cavern.

Emica gave the key to Mallory. "It works. I tried it, but locked it again straight away. I didn't think we wanted to risk whatever is in there getting out without us knowing."

Mallory stared at the large, old-fashioned looking key. "How will we lure it out so we can find out what we face?"

"Throw some of the bodies in there," Jorgen suggested. "From the look of the dried blood in the caged area, it must be carnivorous."

"I don't know," Mallory said. "That seems wrong."

Esben hoisted one of the bodies over his shoulder. "It's one way to be certain no one can revive them so they can come after us. People tend to hunt down those who kill them."

"When you put it that way." Ryan grabbed another body. "We don't need anyone else after us. Rass is more than enough trouble." He strode across the cavern, glancing over his shoulder. "Let's go see what comes out of the hole in the ground."

When they reached the locked door, Ryan and Esben stepped to the side so Mallory could open it. She remained at the door, hand on the key as she watched Ryan and Esben toss the two bodies into the smaller cave before retreating. Closing the door, she turned the key, taking it out and dropping it into her belt pouch.

"How long will it take?" Brodie asked.

"Depends on how hungry it is," Danae said.

Danae had no sooner finished speaking, when an enormous black panther ambled gracefully up the tree trunk, stopping at the closest body to sniff it.

"That does not look good." Mallory took a step back from the bars. The panther would easily reach her through them, even where she was and she didn't know if she should retreat further when it glanced in her direction, or remain still.

"It doesn't seem like an ordinary guard," Callum said.

"I knew it," Brodie muttered. "I just knew it."

Ryan grinned. "No one jinxed it, Brodie."

Mallory drew in a sharp breath when the panther grabbed the body by the arm, its powerful jaws clamping down on it. With a quick movement, the panther jerked the body forward, so it dropped into the hole. "There's no way we can take that on."

"It's an ambush panther," Jorgen said. "They like high places from where they can ambush their prey. Such as trees."

"I've heard of them," Danae said. "Invisible and stealth type attacks don't work as they have a good sense of smell. They also have exceptional hearing and can see in the dark. They're very fast and dodge most attacks. They're also hard to track. But there shouldn't be any on Ruby Isle."

"Well, there's at least one here now." Jorgen nodded towards the hole. "And it's guarding the only place we haven't searched for the goblet."

"At least one." Mallory stared at the hole the creature had disappeared back into, repeating Jorgen's words. "Are you saying there could be more than one down there?"

"Oh great," Brodie muttered. "We're never going to get the goblet."

"I wonder why it didn't want the other body," Ryan said.

"It might be taking the first one to its lair," Emica said. "We don't know how big an area it is down there."

Ryan turned to Mallory. "You could put a lightning trap down for it."

"You should have checked its health," Brodie said. "We might have been able to take it out before it went back to the hole."

"They usually have about fifty health a level," Jorgen said.

Mallory put her diplomat glasses on. "What are we going to do if it doesn't come back out?" She really hoped the answer wasn't go in after it.

"We need to find a way to keep it up here. If it can't get down below, we can attack it through the bars," Ryan said.

"One of those large tables from the furthest cavern," Callum suggested. "We can remove the legs and push the log down. Then we can cover the hole with a table. It won't take much to remove the legs. One broke off when the warrior overturned one of the tables."

"You want to cover the hole while the panther is up here?" Mallory asked incredulously.

"Here it comes," Danae said.

Mallory watched the panther collect the second body, using the same method as last time, before returning down the log. "You can't really think being in there with that creature is a good idea. It has two hundred and fifty health."

"We'll bring two of the tables back," Ryan said. "Jorgen can help me. They're large enough that if we place them down next to each other, they should fill up most of the space in there. That way, the panther won't be able to push them out of the way to escape." He turned to Esben. "You grab another body and Mallory can unlock this gate and Emica and Danae can keep watch here so it doesn't get out." He turned to Mallory. "Let Esben into the other tunnel and yell when the panther grabs the body."

"This is a terrible plan," Mallory protested. Someone was certain to get hurt. Or die.

Ryan grinned. "Do you have a better one?"

She shook her head.

"Then let's get started. Cast Tracking Magelight on me." Ryan strode off the moment Mallory had cast the spell on him.

She cast it on Danae before she unlocked the door and headed around to the other locked door, her own magelight still in effect. Reaching the other door, she unlocked it, ready to open it when Esben arrived. Staring down the tunnel, she could see the other end, but part of the tunnel between her end and the area with the hole in the ground was in deep shadows.

"Open the door," Esben said as he approached.

Mallory swung the door open, keeping it open while Esben walked in a bit over a metre before dropping the body and retreating. She locked the door as soon as he was out. Not sure what else to do, she cast Lightning Trap next to the body, so she'd at least get one attack in.

"It's taking its time," Esben said.

"We don't even know if it'll come back out." Mallory wished she knew how much time had passed. It had to have been more than five minutes because the Tracking Magelight she'd cast on Emica had gone out, only the lantern casting limited light into the other end of the tunnel.

"Did you want me to go and see what they want to do?" Esben took a step away from Mallory.

"Wait up. They've only got the lantern. Tell them to send someone else back and I can put Tracking Magelight on them when it's nearly expired on you." She cast Tracking Magelight on Esben, watching as he changed forms and ran along the tunnel.

She was alone. Only the area close to her lit up. She couldn't help checking over her shoulder. Completely alone. A sound had her looking through the bars again. Was that the panther? There wasn't enough light. Then there was more light at the other end again, but the stretch of deep shadows were impossible to see into.

Chapter Thirty-Nine

Mallory nearly jumped when the panther stepped into the light, coming forward to grab the body. "It's here." She shouted as loud as possible, not sure if it was her calling out or the lightning trap that caused the creature to snarl. It had lost thirteen health. Unsure what else to do, she cast Poison Dart, grinning when it was a critical hit and the panther lost ten health.

It ran at the locked door, swiping at her through the bars, missing when she stumbled back out of reach. The damage over time effect of Poison Dart ran out and Mallory cast it again, following it up with Fireball.

Danae ran towards Mallory. "Is it still there?" She had her bow in one hand and an arrow in the other."

Again the ambush panther tried to attack through the bars. With a snarl, it turned away. Danae arrived in time to attack, the creature loping back towards the hole. An angry snarl echoed back to them.

"Sounds like they got the tables in place," Mallory said.

Danae kept her bow ready, her gaze fixed on the other end of the tunnel. "I left before they were finished. Emica will be here soon. You can cast Tracking Magelight on her. Callum said it'd be best to have us at each entrance since we don't know what it'll do."

"I'm here," Emica said as she arrived and changed into her human form.

Mallory cast the spell on the kitsune. "Did everyone get out of the area in time?" She couldn't see the journal details for Emica, Jorgen or Esben. Everyone else had all their health.

Emica nodded. "I better get back before they run out of light." Becoming a fox again, she darted off.

"It's coming back," Danae warned.

Once it was close enough, Mallory attacked with Fireball, following it up with Poison Dart. Danae managed to attack twice before it retreated.

"It only has thirty-nine health. It avoided one of your attacks. The others should take it out easily." Mallory waited for the experience points that would tell her the creature had been killed. They didn't come. "What are they doing?"

"Did you want me to check?" Danae asked.

Esben joined them. "It's staying just out of reach. None of us can get it."

"I can't see it clearly enough to attack," Danae said. "I'd only be wasting arrows."

"It has thirty-nine health left," Mallory said. "At least two attacks and there's no guarantee we'll hit the first time."

"What about casting Beacon in there?" Danae asked. "It should light up all the shadowy areas."

"I didn't think of that." Mallory cast Beacon at the furthest point she could see along the tunnel. It lit up the entire area.

"That's better." Danae released an arrow. The panther dodged out of the way.

"I really need some throwing knives," Esben said. "I can't do anything if I can't get up close."

Mallory cast Fireball, hitting the panther. "I don't think it can dodge magic. Just weapons." She studied the creature for a moment, then placed Lightning Trap to the left and right of it. "Attack it again, Danni."

Danae released an arrow. The panther again dodged, howling when it set off the lightning trap. It instantly went to the other side, setting off the other one before retreating around the corner.

Mallory gained six experience points, grinning at Danae. "Looks like we did it."

Danae glanced in the direction she'd come from. "We should join everyone else. We still need to find the goblet."

They met Ryan halfway. He carried the lantern, grinning when he spotted them. He came to a stop. "You all ready to go down and see what we can find?"

"Getting down isn't a problem, but how do you plan to get us out of there now the tree trunk is at the bottom of the hole?" Esben asked.

As he spoke, Ryan led the way back to where everyone else waited. "Brodie found rope in one of the crates. It's long enough we can tie it to one of the bars of the door. That's providing the hole isn't more than six metres deep."

They arrived back to find the rope had been tied and the tables moved to the side of the cave. The ambush panther had been skinned, so they now had a glossy black pelt and Callum had gained five claws.

"This is taking forever," Brodie complained. "When are we going to check the rest of the crates and barrels?"

Ryan took out his pocket watch. "It's a little after nine. We've only been in Bard's Hollow a couple of hours. Not long at all, considering the size of it." He put the pocket watch away. "We'll check the rest of the things after we've found the goblet." He made his way over to the hole in the ground. "Who wants to go down first?"

Brodie stepped forward.

Before he could speak, Mallory stepped in front of him. "There's sure to be something dangerous down there."

"Because Goblin Boy wants to go down there first?" Emica asked.

Callum laughed. "Obviously."

Brodie glared at all of them. "None of you are funny."

"I wasn't trying to be funny," Mallory protested. "But you have to admit there's a good chance there's something dangerous down there. We don't even know if that was the only panther."

Jorgen strode towards the hole, staring down at it. "Make me invisible. I'll go down."

Mallory hurried after him. "Just because you've got the highest character level out of all of us, it doesn't mean it's any less dangerous for you to see what's down there."

Jorgen smiled briefly. "No, but I don't mind retreating if things are beyond my capabilities. I can also use my abilities stealth and dodge to help me escape if it comes to it."

Mallory held his gaze. "Be careful and don't take any risks. Retreat the moment you see trouble."

"As a wolf, I'll notice it well before it can reach me." Jorgen shifted into his crystalline wolf form, the snowy coat with its crystal blue tinge vividly bright in the small area.

Mallory cast Vanish I on Jorgen and assumed he'd jumped into the hole. He was as silent as ever. She cast Locate Party, but it only showed the location of the first people she'd added to her group, since the group was currently too large for it to show everyone. She'd hoped there'd be an option to choose who it showed. There was none.

Wanting to keep track of all her party members, and see them at a greater distance, Mallory added five CAS points to the spell, bringing it up to level five. She could now see ten party members within a ten kilometre radius of herself. The spell also lasted fifteen minutes and had a four-minute cooldown and only cost twelve mana now. It also showed where Jorgen was. It looked like he was on the way back to them. Mallory grinned. The spell was far more useful than she'd originally thought it would be.

"What's so funny?" Brodie asked.

"I can follow where Jorgen is. He's nearly back at the hole," Mallory said.

"It's not fair that levels take so long. What if someone wants to be all the classes?" Brodie asked.

Danae smiled. "There are some people who are. It just takes a lot of years."

Jorgen appeared beside them in human form, causing Brodie to jump back.

"You could have said something," Brodie muttered.

"It's safe to enter," Jorgen said. "There's a chest down there. I thought you all might like to be there when it's opened." He glanced back at the hole. "I also tied the rope around the end of the tree trunk if you want to pull it up to make it easier to get in and out of the hole."

They dragged the tree trunk back into place before going down, arguing over whether someone should remain behind to guard the entrances, so they didn't get locked in if someone came wandering into Bard's Hollow.

Jorgen volunteered since he'd already been down there, describing where they needed to go. "Just keep your noise down as you approach the chest."

"Why?" Mallory asked. "I thought you said there was nothing down there."

Jorgen smiled fleetingly. "I said it's safe to enter. Not that there isn't anything down there."

"What's down there?" Brodie asked.

Again Jorgen smiled fleetingly. "I wouldn't want to ruin the surprise." He strode to the entrance of the short tunnel.

Chapter Forty

Mallory laughed at her brother's disgruntled expression. "Come on. Whatever's down there can't be too bad, or he would have warned us." She cast Tracking Magelight on Brodie and Magelight on herself.

Entering the hole by the tree trunk wasn't as easy a process as Mallory had hoped. But she reached the ground without a mishap and turned to face the direction Jorgen had taken. The smell of rotting meat came from that direction and she made a face. "I hope the stench isn't the surprise."

Ryan chuckled, walking beside her when she strode towards the other side of the large, shadowy cavern. "Not with how amused he was. I'm expecting a pleasant surprise."

Mallory had nearly reached the chest when she realised what Jorgen hadn't told them. She came to a stop, unable to resist smiling.

Callum came to a stop beside her, exclaiming, "Baby tree kitties."

"We're not keeping them," Brodie stated.

"They're not the sort of companion animal that's welcome in most places," Danae said. "They don't have a good reputation. Nor do their owners."

Ryan moved slowly forward. "We don't want to hurt you."

Two ambush panther kittens crouched at the side of the chest, backs arched as they hissed and spit at Ryan.

"Come on," Ryan said softly. "We can't leave the two of you here. You wouldn't survive."

One of the kittens swiped at his hand, blood welling up along the claw marks left behind.

Ryan drew his hand back. "That was unexpected."

Mallory checked his stats. "Five health! Stay back Ryan." She healed him until his health was full again. "How are we meant to get them out of here? And what are we meant to do with them?"

"We could sell them," Danae suggested.

"They're the sort of companion animal rogues like," Emica said. "The type of rogue that likes to set traps."

"I could go back up and get a couple of blankets," Esben offered. "Just don't open the chest before I get back."

"We'll wait," Mallory assured him. She studied the kittens while he was gone. "They are cute."

"Most villages don't treat those that have them as companion animals in a friendly manner," Danae warned. "They really do have a terrible reputation."

Esben returned with two blankets and tried to toss them over the kittens, who dodged out of the way.

In the end, they had to collect more blankets and slowly close in on each of the kittens to capture them. The kittens got in a few swipes during the process so that Mallory needed to heal most of the group.

Mallory stared at the two bundles of wriggling blankets the kittens were in, several layers needed to keep them in due to some of the holes they'd put in the blankets. "We can't leave them in the blankets too long. I wonder if the hunter has a cage we can put them in."

Esben glanced towards the chest. "Before we worry about them, are we going to check the chest to see if the goblet is in there?"

Callum was the one to open it, taking out a rather plain looking silver goblet that had demonic runes engraved in a band around the middle. "It looks exactly like the picture Goswin showed us."

Brodie looked from the goblet to the blankets, which were currently still. "I wonder if Goswin knows anyone who wants two ambush panthers."

"Do you think they're okay in there?" Mallory studied the blankets, relieved when they moved a fraction.

"How about we take everything we want back to where Ninette is camped and work out how to get it all to Buckneth," Ryan suggested.

"We should take everything," Brodie said.

"Some of those barrels don't have much in them," Callum pointed out.

"So?" Brodie demanded. "That doesn't mean we should leave them behind. Most of them have cooking ingredients."

Mallory helped Ryan carry the kittens to the hole, the two of them needing to tie the rope around each bundle since the kittens made it impossible for them to carry them up the tree trunk.

Callum and Brodie came out of the hole, both still arguing about Brodie's need to take everything. Brodie finally said, "If we leave anything behind, the hellion will only use it for whatever the dark forces have planned."

"That's actually a good point," Callum said.

Mallory slowly shook her head, trying to mentally count how many barrels, crates and chests they'd come across. There had to have been at least thirty in total. She had no idea how they were going to deal with everything. Maybe seeing it altogether in one place would change Brodie's mind about keeping it. "Let's get this over with, then." She cast Tracking Magelight on Ryan and Callum and Magelight on herself.

Once everything was back at their camp, they counted seventeen barrels, sixteen crates and seven chests. They'd also found on the bandits three brown trousers, a pale blue shirt, a leather belt, a throwing knives belt, a short sword, twenty silver pieces, forty-one copper pieces and a tooth regrow potion. They also kept the lantern they'd taken from the first bandit they'd taken out.

Callum laughed softly when he held out the potion. "We should keep it with how accident prone Brodie is."

Brodie glared at Callum. "I am not." After a few seconds, he added, "Not anymore."

Not wanting to listen to another argument, Mallory turned to Ninette. "Did anything happen while we were gone?"

"I took out two giant mud crabs and caught three fish. I ended up with the shells from the mud crabs and a couple of kilos of crab meat." Ninette glanced at Brodie. "I didn't cook any of it."

Jorgen joined them. "How do we plan to get all this back to Buckneth? There's no way it'll all fit in the wagon. We'd need a second wagon. One that's empty."

"I could ask the wagoner if he wants to collect it," Ninette offered. "I'm sure he'd do it for a fee. Probably a percentage of the sale price."

"But we're not selling all of it," Brodie protested. "We want some of the cooking ingredients in the barrels."

"We can't keep all of the barrels," Mallory said. "We don't have the space. We also need to do something about the kittens as soon as possible." She glanced towards the two bundles that moved occasionally. "We can't leave them wrapped in blankets forever."

"The hunter would have a cage we can borrow," Ninette said. "We're also going to need a couple of cages to keep the drakes in when they're hatched. Did you want me to ride back to Buckneth and organise everything?"

"Not on your own," Mallory protested.

"I'd offer to go, but I only have three arrows left," Danae said.

"More than I have," Ryan said. "I only have two."

"I have the same as Danae," Callum said before turning to Ninette. "You also might want to enter Bard's Hollow and get your location XP before you go."

In the end, Jorgen and Esben went with Ninette, who rode Dodger, first having entered Bard's Hollow and given directions on what needed to be done with the eggs.

Mallory settled down by the fire to finish writing in her journal once Ninette and the crystalline wolves had left. She managed not to smile when she noticed her brother started cooking after having raided some of the ingredients from the barrels and prepared the fish Ninette had caught. He'd also shared the crab meat out between Smudge and Fang. The smell of fish fritters and smoky honey sauce cooking made Mallory's mouth water even though she hadn't felt at all hungry before Brodie had started making food.

It was after midnight when Mallory thought it might be a good idea to get some sleep. Before she did, she took two of the health potions from the chest Rodina had given them and slipped them into her satchel. She'd see if anyone else needed any in the morning, but she was too tired to stay awake any longer. She curled up amongst the resources in the back of the wagon, too exhausted to set up a tent.

Chapter Forty-One

The sound of a wagon arriving woke Mallory and she disturbed Ryan, who was lying next to her. "Who's on guard?" She blinked, trying to focus on what was happening as she looked out the back of the wagon.

"Callum and Brodie. Can you cast Magelight so I can check the time?" Ryan asked.

Mallory did as he'd asked, squinting at the sudden increase in light. "That was a terrible idea."

Ryan chuckled, putting away the pocket watch. "It's one-thirty. So much for getting a decent amount of sleep."

Stumbling out of the wagon, Mallory spotted Ninette, Jorgen and Esben standing beside a wagon with the Buckneth wagoner sitting on the seat.

Ninette grabbed a cage out of the back of the wagon, Jorgen grabbing a second one, both of them heading for the now quiet kittens.

Mallory looked between the kittens and the wagoner, eventually deciding she should help with the kittens rather than risk them escaping. After being clawed twice while trying to put the kittens into a single cage, she began to wonder if helping had been the right choice. Locking the cage door, she stared at the hissing kittens. "You'd think they'd be happy to get out of the blankets."

"I'll get them some food and water." Ninette hurried away.

Jorgen, who'd placed the second cage near the baskets of eggs, joined Mallory. "You might want to ask Ninette about her brother."

Mallory frowned, trying to make sense of his words. "What do you mean?"

"Just ask her." Jorgen joined Brodie, who was talking to the wagoner.

Mallory sighed, wishing she could return to sleep. Instead, she waited until Ninette had returned and helped her put the food and water in the cage. "Jorgen said something about your brother."

Ninette nodded. "Pa kicked him out. Wouldn't let him take any of his things, either. He said he'll sneak back in tomorrow when Pa is working with the sheep and take his things. He'll also check on our brothers."

"Where's he staying? Did he want to travel with us?" Mallory asked.

Ninette shook her head. "He doesn't want to leave the area until our brothers can leave, too. In case they need him. I paid for him to stay at the tavern until the end of the month. Ahron only charged me for five nights. But that was still twenty-five copper pieces. I'm going to need to get more money from the bank than I thought."

Mallory took two silver and five copper pieces from the group money in her belt pouch, holding them out to Ninette. "You helped earn this money, too. It's to pay for group expenses."

"Osbert isn't part of your group."

Mallory smiled. "He is now." She pressed the coins into Ninette's hand when she didn't take them. "We'll pay for the ship fare to Merrow for the four of you out of the group money, too."

"We can't expect that of you," Ninette protested.

Mallory tried not to think about how dangerous going after the staff would be. "Of course you can. Aren't you going to look after the house we'll get in exchange for the staff?"

Ninette smiled. "I thought you said it was too dangerous to go after it."

"We'll get more water breathing potions so the majority of us can go after it." Mallory hoped they could find the potions and they weren't overly expensive.

Brodie joined them, grinning. "The wagoner said we can load everything up on his wagon that won't fit in ours and he can take it all to Surith for five percent of the sale. He also doesn't mind us picking out the things we want, including some of the cooking ingredients. I told him the tree kitties aren't included because they're going to Goswin."

"You don't know if he'll want them," Mallory said.

Brodie shrugged. "No, but I bet he does. They seem like the kind of thing he'd want."

"Do you think we can leave some food with Osbert so he doesn't have to buy any of the tavern meals?" Ninette asked. "And did you want me to stay there too so I can keep the eggs warm without needing you to stop regularly so I can heat up the rocks?"

"Of course we'd leave food with him," Brodie said before Mallory could do little more than open her mouth to speak. "I made a heap of fish fritters and smoky honey sauce to dip them in." He frowned. "They won't keep long. Maybe I should make some adventurer's savoury biscuits. Or nutty oat bars. I could also make flatbread and leave honey to put on them." Brodie wandered towards the campfire, muttering under his breath about the different options and how food storage was more complicated without a fridge.

Mallory somehow managed not to laugh at her brother. She turned to Ninette. "Guess that's sorted. And if it'll be easier for you to look after the eggs at the tavern, you're welcome to stay. Did you want me to leave extra money with you in case anything happens?"

Ninette shook her head. "I have enough money to cover anything that might come up. Besides, I'm sure you won't be gone long. The wagoner said he'd only go if it was a trip straight there and back."

When an argument broke out near the campfire between Brodie and Callum, Mallory nodded towards them. "I better see what's going on." She arrived in time to hear Callum speak.

"They're useful patterns. Ones for clothes, shoes and furniture."

Brodie snorted. "Not for you, they aren't. Not unless you use some CAS points."

"They'll give me the option to make those things if I decide to put points in any of those abilities," Callum said.

"What are you arguing over?" Mallory asked.

Callum pointed towards an open crate. "It's filled with patterns."

Mallory eyed the crate, which wasn't exactly small. "Where would we store it?"

"See," Brodie said triumphantly. "Told you we didn't need them."

"That's not what I said," Mallory protested. "I asked where we'd store them. Our wagon is always on the full side lately. We only have so much space in our chest at the guild, so where would we store them if we kept them?"

Callum sighed. "We really need a house."

"That'd only help if we didn't travel far from it or had a portal to it," Ryan said, joining them. He gestured towards the crate. "Add this one to the ones to be sold?"

"I suppose so." Callum put the lid back on the crate.

"I've taken the ingredients we need from the barrels, checked what's in the crates and looked at most of the chests. There's only two left to search." Brodie gestured towards two chests set off by themselves. "But I've got to make food before we leave."

"Anything worth keeping in the crates and chests?" Ryan asked.

Brodie shook his head. "Clothes, cloth, leather, wool and stuff like that. A lot of things for making stuff."

Mallory made her way to the chests Brodie hadn't searched, finding blankets in the first one. They were only average quality, so she closed the chest again and turned to the second one, opening it. "I think this one is someone's travelling chest."

"Why do you say that?" Callum joined her to peer into the chest.

"A couple of sets of clothes, a blanket, an empty leather notebook, nib pen, ink, lantern, lantern oil, waterskin, flint and steel, seven rations, crockery and cutlery for one, a small hanging pot, a deck of cards, a hand mirror and a hairbrush." Mallory picked up the hand mirror, nearly dropping it when she saw a man's face instead of her own. "What sort of mirror is this?"

"Who are you?" the man demanded.

Again Mallory nearly dropped the mirror. "It spoke."

Danae came over and took the mirror from Mallory, studying the man in it. "Who are you?"

"I believe I've already asked that question," the man said. "Where's my son?"

Danae shared a look with Mallory before speaking. "I don't know. We took a chest of items out of Bard's Hollow and the mirror was in it. Let me show you." She turned the mirror so he could see into the chest.

"That belongs to my son," the man said.

Danae turned the mirror so she could see the man again. "Bandits were in Bard's Hollow."

"Oh." The man remained silent a moment. "I haven't heard of that place. Where is it?"

"About an hour from Buckneth," Danae said. "Along the beach."

"That's a long way from home."

"Where's home?" Mallory asked.

"Shadhurst." Again the man was silent a moment. "I need to know if my son is well. Could I convince you to travel to Shadhurst?"

Chapter Forty-Two

"Not until next month," Mallory regretfully told the man in the mirror.

"What is the date?" the man asked. "I'm afraid I've lost track of time."

"Early in the morning of the twenty-fifth day of the second month." Mallory checked the journal notification as she spoke, seeing it was a quest.

Missing Son: A father requests that you travel to Shadhurst to see if his son is well.

"I can't believe so much time has passed. Are you certain you can't travel to Shadhurst sooner?" the man asked. "I'm sure my son would reward you handsomely."

"It's not the reward money," Mallory said. "We need to wait so we can escort some people to that side of the island."

"Would they be willing to leave earlier?" the man asked.

Mallory shook her head. "They can't. They turn fifteen on the last day of the month."

"Oh." The man was quiet long enough Mallory began to think he wouldn't speak again. "Will you talk to me occasionally? Let me know what's happening? Tell me what day it is?"

Mallory tried to see his surroundings, but there was very little light wherever he was and he held the mirror too close to his face for much else to be seen. "Are you okay?"

"I just need to see my son."

His words had been guarded, so Mallory didn't push for more information. "Okay. I'll have to put the mirror away for now. We're getting ready to leave this location. But I'll regularly let you know where we are while you wait for us to travel to Shadhurst."

"Thank you."

About to put the mirror back in the chest, Mallory stopped. "I'm Mallory."

The man hesitated. "Morth Helden."

"I'll talk to you later." Mallory returned the mirror to the chest and she and Danae put it on their wagon, needing to shift around some of the bags of resources to fit it in. She stared at the trunk. "Will he be able to hear us?"

Danae shook her head. "Not as long as the lid is closed."

"What is the mirror? Is he trapped in it?" Callum asked, having come close when Mallory had begun to talk to the mirror.

Again, Danae shook her head. "There will be two mirrors. They're linked together so the two people can talk to each other while they're apart. Usually they set a time for the next conversation since there isn't any way to leave messages. Only talk in person."

Brodie, who still cooked at the campfire, was close enough to hear. "Could we get them to talk to you?"

"Not in any of the villages around here," Danae said. "You could buy them in Shadhurst though."

"I assume they'll be expensive?" Callum asked.

Ryan, who'd come over to grab another crate to put on the wagoner's wagon, grinned. "Isn't everything?"

By the time the wagon was loaded and the rocks for the baskets heated, Brodie had finished cooking. He'd made all the recipes he'd suggested, having to wrap them in calico cloths since the baskets were in use.

The majority of them slept on the way to Buckneth, only Jorgen and the wagoner remaining awake to drive. When they reached the village, they remained long enough to help Ninette take some of the food Brodie had cooked, her gear, the baskets of eggs and the spare cage into the tavern.

Mallory drifted back to sleep as Emica swapped places with Jorgen and drove out of the village, headed towards Surith.

It was a two and a half-hour trip to Surith, the journey uneventful. They pulled up not far from the travelling bank, a line already in front of it even though it was only a quarter to seven.

Mallory, Ryan, Brodie, Callum and Danae lined up at the bank while everyone else except Esben slept. He was left to guard the two wagons until they returned. As always, Fang and Smudge were with them and when Brodie drew a nutty oat bar out of his belt pouch, chewing on it as they waited, the companion animals begged for their share. The cage of kittens rested on the ground beside them, one of the damaged blankets draped over the cage in the hope the kittens would remain asleep. Mallory carried the goblet in her satchel while Brodie had put the gold ring they'd gained in his belt pouch in case they could find out if it had an enchantment.

Considering the length of the line, it took them longer than expected to reach the start of it. Just over two hours. Stepping up to the counter, Mallory said, "We need to visit Goswin. We have an item he's waiting for."

"Who will pay the fee to travel to the vault?" the bank clerk asked.

Mallory had no idea what to say and was relieved when Danae answered.

"Goswin. He'll either pay the costs himself or take it from what he owes us and pay it out of that."

"Leave your weapons behind and move to the compass rose," the clerk said.

One of the guards stepped forward. "If you're taking the cage with you, we need to see what it contains."

Mallory drew the blanket back, causing the kittens to hiss. When the guard's hand went to the hilt of his sword, she feared he'd tell them to leave it behind.

"I'll follow you through and bring the cage." The guard drew the blanket back over the kittens. "If you will all move to the compass rose."

Relieved, Mallory stood on the compass rose, standing close to the rest of those with her so they could all fit. She supposed it was a good thing the guard was bringing the kittens since the five of them barely had room to stand there together.

As soon as they arrived, the guard who'd followed them through led them to Goswin's vault, carrying the cage for them. Upon reaching the vault, they were admitted by a nephilim, the guard leaving the cage with them and returning outside the vault to stand at the door.

"What business do you have with Goswin?" the nephilim asked.

"We have the False Hope Goblet," Ryan said.

"And two ambush panther kittens. If he wants them," Brodie added.

The nephilim inclined his head. "Wait a moment and I will inform him." He sat at the desk, taking out a piece of paper that was half filled with handwriting and adding another sentence to it. A moment later, he rose from the desk, a line of writing having appeared on the paper.

Mallory wished she'd been close enough to have read what had appeared on the paper, but assumed it would be bad manners to move closer so she could see.

"Goswin won't be long if you're willing to wait," the nephilim said.

Mallory nodded.

Goswin arrived ten minutes later, looking like he'd been woken from sleep. He sat behind his desk, the nephilim having put the paper away. "I've been told by the guard outside my vault that I need to pay your travel costs." He glanced at the nephilim. "And I've also been informed you have the False Hope Goblet I've been waiting for."

"We told the bank clerk you'd either pay the costs or take them from what you owe us," Danae said.

Ryan stepped forward and placed the cage on the desk, drawing off the blanket. "We have more than just the False Hope Goblet."

There was a flicker of excitement in Goswin's eyes before it was masked. "You're interested in selling the two of them? I don't trade many animals, but these are fairly rare to come by at this age that I could find a buyer reasonably quick."

Chapter Forty-Three

Mallory nodded in answer to Goswin's question. "We're also interested in going after the Staff Of Imp's Fury and we have a lead on a unicorn. We were told it's aggressive, so I don't know how we'd get it to you." She placed the False Hope Goblet on the desk beside the cage, the kittens hissing again, backs arching and claws striking the bars of the cage.

Brodie drew out the gold ring. "I don't suppose you can tell if this has an enchantment on it. And would you have birthday cake recipes?"

"Birthday cake?" Goswin momentarily looked confused. "Ahh, yes. I have a few cake recipes. What sort would you prefer?"

Brodie shrugged. "Something like chocolate cake, I guess."

"That I can do. As well as wildberry, strawberry, honey or spice."

At the look of excitement in her brother's eyes, Mallory hastily said, "Only one recipe."

"Aw, come on, Mal. They all sound good. What if she wants something other than chocolate?" Brodie asked.

"She loves chocolate," Mallory said, remembering the story she'd been told about Ninette pestering her father to buy her chocolate. "Besides, we're probably going to need more water breathing potions if we're going to get the staff."

"What level spell can you cast?" Goswin asked.

"Level four."

Goswin looked over to the nephilim who'd let them into the vault. "Bring me the book of level four spells." He faced Mallory again. "Where is the unicorn?"

Callum came forward. He took out the map he carried in his belt pouch, unfolded it and placed it on the desk. "There." He pressed a finger to the location.

Goswin inclined his head. "I can offer you a potion of complacency that will last long enough to get you to Eastvale, with twenty minutes to spare, as long as you promise to bring the unicorn to me to broker the deal."

Callum folded the map and returned it to his belt pouch. "What does the potion do?"

At the same time as Callum spoke, Brodie asked, "There are other treasure brokers?"

Goswin took the leather bound book from the nephilim with a nod of thanks, his gaze returning to Brodie. "I'm the only broker who can do the deal with the person offering the property near Merrow in exchange for the staff." He held Brodie's gaze a moment longer before he looked at the book in front of him, flicking through the pages until he eventually stopped on one. "Level four spell. Breath Of The Merfolk. Unlevelled it allows the person or companion animal it is cast on to breathe underwater for ten minutes. Costs fifteen mana and has a cooldown of twenty seconds."

"How much?" Brodie asked.

"Twelve hundred gold pieces, but I will offer you fifteen hundred gold for the two kittens and include the costs of travel here and assessment of the ring," Goswin said.

"You never said what the potion does that you want us to give to the unicorn," Callum said. "Will it hurt it?"

"It will make it happy and satisfied with itself and willing to be led where you wish to lead it, remaining oblivious to all dangers. It will be up to you to protect it," Goswin warned.

"And the person wanting the unicorn," Callum said. "How do we know they'll take care of it?"

"They're a reputable collector who takes great care of all their animals. I always make sure any animals I trade go to those who will value and care for them." Goswin glanced towards the kittens. "Just like I will do for these two. I have a reputation to maintain as well."

"How much would we get for the unicorn?" Brodie asked.

"After my fee is removed, five thousand and two hundred gold pieces," Goswin said.

"That's more than the goblet," Brodie exclaimed.

"A unicorn can use its horn to purify water as well as neutralise minor poisons in all liquids," Danae explained. "The only problem is that it also removes alcohol from liquids, too."

"Who would want to do that?" Brodie asked.

Ryan grinned. "Someone who's more worried about dying than getting drunk."

"What about the cake recipe? How much is it? And will you include the cost of the travel here if we bring the staff and the unicorn?" Brodie asked.

"That depends. I can sell you a basic chocolate cake for a gold piece all the way up to divine chocolate cake for ten gold pieces," Goswin said. "If you bring the staff and unicorn to me, I'll cover the cost of portal here for two of you. More than that isn't necessary."

Brodie turned to Mallory. "I need the divine chocolate cake recipe. That sounds perfect for a birthday cake. Who wants basic for a birthday? Besides, you're getting a spell."

"I didn't agree to the spell," Mallory protested. "And you don't even know if you have the level to cook any of the cakes."

"Oh." Brodie turned back to Goswin. "What level is the divine chocolate cake recipe?"

"Level eighteen. You'll also need access to an oven."

"I wonder if the Buckneth baker will let me use hers. Or Ahron. Maybe he won't mind if I use his oven once they've finished cooking meals for the day," Brodie said. "I can test it out for Ninette's brothers first. See how well it works."

"Does divine refer to the quality of the cake?" Callum asked.

Goswin shook his head. "It's a descriptor only. Although it could easily refer to how good it tastes."

"What about the ingredients?" Callum asked. "Will they be difficult to find?"

Again Goswin shook his head. "Most towns would stock them. Villages might be another matter, though."

"So what's the plan?" Ryan asked. "We sell the kittens and goblet and buy the spell and recipe. We get the ring assessed, are given a potion and agree to bring the staff and unicorn here. Did I miss anything?"

"The spell is expensive. We'll have to spend most of what we'll gain for the kittens," Mallory protested. "Maybe we should just get a couple of water breathing potions instead."

"The spell will help us go after the staff. We'd be crazy not to get it," Ryan said. "So, did I miss anything?"

"What about a book to unlock the crafter class for Osbert?" Callum asked. "Is that a thing?"

Goswin inclined his head. "A hundred gold pieces. One use only, but as long as the book is held and the first paragraph read by all those holding it, the book can be used to unlock the class for more than a single person."

Mallory sighed. "I better not be the one in the middle this time."

"That's a lot of money," Brodie protested. "Is the class worth it?"

Danae nodded. "It's very useful if you plan to focus on crafting abilities rather than a combat class. Even some combat classes choose to unlock the crafter class because of some of the skills like decoy and disinterest, which give you the chance to run from a dangerous situation."

"Besides," Mallory said. "With all Ninette has done for us, helping her brother unlock the crafter class might help him get settled quicker and allow Ninette to return to adventuring sooner."

Callum smiled. "And it'll be good to learn more about the class ourselves."

Ryan chuckled. "You sure it's not just the idea of getting your hands on another book?"

Callum's smile widened into a grin. "Once the book has been used to unlock the class, he might not have any use for it."

Ryan chuckled again before asking, "Is that everything now?"

293

Chapter Forty-Four

Mallory thought back over what Ryan had said, eventually nodding. "That sounds like all of it." She was tempted to ask if there was a better healing spell, but they'd already spent too much.

"Do you agree to the quests and prices?" Goswin asked. They all nodded.

Goswin took a black tile from his desk drawer and placed it on the desk, looking towards Mallory. "If you place your hand on the tile, it'll activate the quests for you."

Mallory did as Goswin said, this time not surprised that she gained a journal notification. What did surprise her, when she checked the notification, was to find both quests in her journal.

Treasure Seeker II: The treasure broker Goswin will broker a deal for a property near Merrow in exchange for the Staff Of Imp's Fury and pay the portal for two members of your group to travel to the vault with the staff. The last known location of the staff was in the waters off Ruby Isle.

Treasure Seeker III: The treasure broker Goswin will pay five thousand and two hundred gold pieces for a unicorn. He has provided a potion to assist with bringing the unicorn to him and will pay the portal for two members of your group to travel to the vault with the unicorn.

While Mallory had been reading over the quests, Goswin had asked the nephilim to fetch the potion and recipe and he'd removed the spell from the book, placing it on the desk. The nephilim placed the potion and recipe with the spell.

Goswin held out his hand. "If you want to give me the ring, you wish to have appraised?"

Brodie placed the ring in Goswin's hand, clasping his hands together.

Goswin studied the ring before handing it back. "There is one enchantment. When in water, you use fifty percent less stamina." He handed the ring back to Brodie.

"Can you also use the animal speak amulet on the unicorn when we bring it here? We need to find out why it's being so aggressive to complete the quest we have for it."

Goswin inclined his head. "Was that all? You can't keep adding things to the deal."

Brodie frowned. "I think so. I only thought of it when we got those new quests."

"I'll write a note to the bank for the amount of four thousand six hundred and ninety gold pieces to be drawn from my funds and paid to you." Goswin took a piece of paper from the desk drawer, writing the note to the bank, signing it with a flourish and dipping a seal in red wax to press against it. He handed the folded letter to Mallory.

"Thank you." Mallory put the letter, along with the potion and spell in her satchel, grinning when Brodie grabbed the recipe and Callum took the book.

As they were led back to a portal by the guard, Mallory checked the journal notification that had appeared when she'd taken the letter from Goswin.

Treasure Seeker I: Your party was paid for locating and retrieving the False Hope Goblet. You also earned two experience points each.

Mallory couldn't help wondering if everyone would gain the two experience points since she hadn't taken them out of the party. She'd kept them in the party in case she'd needed to find them with her Locate Party spell.

Arriving back at the travelling bank in Surith, the guard coming through after them, Mallory took her weapons, asking to have the money listed in the note from Goswin paid into everyone's bank accounts. Five hundred and twenty-one gold and one silver piece went to each person and the left over silver piece went into Mallory's belt pouch that contained some of the group money. Mallory,

Ryan, Callum and Brodie's share went into their joint account.

Finished dealing with the money, Mallory headed outside. The rest of her party followed her outside, having collected their weapons, too. In the time they'd been gone, the line of people waiting for the bank had grown to four times the length and Mallory was relieved they'd arrived so early.

The wagoner came towards them, nodding to where the shops were in Surith. "Did you want me to see what I can get for your resources now?"

"I'll come with you," Brodie said.

Mallory tried not to grin at her brother's comment, but was unsuccessful. She was certain her brother would be unable to resist helping with the bartering.

"Don't forget we need arrows," Callum said.

"And try to sell all the resources in our wagon," Mallory added. "We need the space back."

"Thanks for leaving me in the party for the quest XP," Emica said to Mallory when Brodie was out of sight. "Even though it wasn't much, every bit is appreciated."

Mallory smiled. "With my new spell, it seemed pointless removing anyone from the party in case something happened and we had to find one of you."

Emica grinned. "Thanks anyway." She glanced in the direction Brodie had taken. "I might go and see what Goblin Boy is doing. He gets really involved in bartering.

It can be rather entertaining." With another grin, Emica headed off, Jorgen and Esben joining her.

Mallory climbed into the wagon, shifting a hessian bag of vegetables so she could sit in the back. Yawning, she closed her eyes for a moment, not realising she'd fallen asleep until her brother disturbed her by taking the hessian bag she was leaning on. "Did you sell all of them?"

"Only half of them." Brodie shoved a hessian bag of resources at Mallory. "We tried everywhere. Not just this place. Even the ships. This is the only one we have left to deliver resources too, though. We did the rest of them while you were sleeping. But you can help bring this lot in since you're awake."

"How much did we make from selling everything?" Mallory hopped out of the wagon, grabbing a second bag of resources.

"Those patterns sold for a good amount. The chests too. As well as what we got from the ambush panther and primordial crocodile," Brodie said. "Everyone has twenty arrows each again and we still earned four hundred and seventy-seven gold and nine silver pieces. And that was after the wagoner's fee was taken out. And we have the ingredients for two divine chocolate cakes." Brodie frowned. "Maybe I should have got twice that amount. One cake isn't going to be enough with how many of us there are." His frown vanished. "We'll be somewhere we can buy more by the time it's Ninette's birthday. Anyway,

Danae is at the travelling bank, putting the money in everyone's accounts. Jorgen and Esben went and waited in line earlier, so we wouldn't have a long wait once all the trading was done."

Mallory slowly shook her head, trying to take in everything her brother was saying as she struggled to dispel the fogginess from her unplanned nap. Maybe falling asleep hadn't been the best idea. "What are we going to do with the rest of the resources? They won't last forever."

Brodie shrugged as he entered the shop, waiting behind the woman the trader was serving. Ryan, Callum and Emica were already in the shop, each holding two hessian bags.

"What am I meant to do?" the woman asked, running a hand through her short, dark hair. "What you donated last week barely provided enough food for the shelter. This week we have more staying there."

"Have you tried elsewhere?" the trader asked. "I can't afford to donate more than I do. I have a family to support."

The woman sighed, nodding her head, shoulders slumping. "Everyone says the same. I appreciate the help you give, but the last ship had half a dozen injured sailors on board whose ship had been sunk in an attack. They're homeless, destitute and unable to fend for themselves.

They were dropped here because it was the closest port to where they were rescued."

"Sea attacks seem to be getting more frequent," the trader said.

The woman nodded, taking a step towards the door. "I'll be back on the usual day, but if you have any ingredients you can spare before then, I'd appreciate it." She continued towards the door.

"Mal." Brodie looked at his sister. "People shouldn't have to go hungry. It's an awful feeling when you've got nothing to eat. It feels like your stomach is eating you from the inside." He dumped what he was carrying on the counter, turning back to his sister. "We have resources we don't need."

"It'd be nice to have all our space back in the wagon," Mallory said.

Brodie hurried after the woman, who was stepping out the door. "Wait." He grinned at her when she turned to face him, still in the doorway. "We have a heap of veggies and herbs left over. And some berries. I can even cook a stew with them for you. I got a new recipe recently and it doesn't need meat. It actually tastes pretty good." Brodie ushered the woman outside as he spoke. "Did you want us to take them to your place?"

Emica stared at the doorway Brodie and the woman had gone through. "Goblin Boy is always surprising me."

Chapter Forty-Five

Mallory smiled at Emica. "Brodie loves food. But that also means he thinks everyone should be fed. Not just him." She didn't bother mentioning the amount of times their father had punished her brother by making him go without food. He knew what it was like to go hungry. And she'd never managed to sneak much food to him during his punishments since their father watched for that after having caught her once.

"Is this all the resources?" The trader made a sweeping motion with his hand, indicating the hessian bags they carried and the ones that had been dumped on the counter.

Ryan stepped forward. "Where would you like us to put them?"

It didn't take long to offload the resources and they returned to the wagon with their empty hessian bags to find Brodie talking animatedly to the woman from the shelter.

Brodie grinned at his sister when she reached his side. "This is Lialanore. I told her you have level fifty apothecary."

"With how many have broken bones, it's a pity you don't have level fifty-five. Strong rapid mend would have helped them greatly," Lialanore said. "But I do appreciate the willingness to help when you're not even from Surith."

Mallory grinned, not at all surprised her brother had volunteered her help. "That's okay." She glanced over her stats, weighing up if she should use most of her six CAS points on apothecary. She wasn't far off earning another CAS point, so she wouldn't be down to a single point for long. Drawing in a steady breath, she hoped she wasn't making a mistake. "I'll add five points to apothecary. I now have the ability to use strong rapid mend on broken bones."

Lialanore clasped Mallory's hands between hers, meeting her gaze. "Thank you ever so much. May good fortune always follow you."

"Where is the shelter?" Callum asked.

While Lialanore explained the location to Callum, Mallory turned to Ryan. "Where is the wagoner and his wagon?" She couldn't believe she hadn't noticed until now.

Ryan grinned. "At the tavern. He headed over there as soon as he'd unloaded, telling us to fetch him once we'd finished with the bank."

"Should someone tell Jorgen, Esben and Danae where we're heading?" Mallory cast her Locate Party spell and checked her journal map. "Actually, don't worry about it. They're headed this way."

Ryan grinned. "Looks like that spell is going to get a lot of use."

Mallory laughed. "And not just to keep track of Brodie."

As soon as Danae and the travellers arrived back, they all headed towards the shelter. Emica offering to return to the tavern once they'd arrived so as to let the wagoner know where they were in case he went looking for them. She wasn't gone long, having used her fox form to get there and back quicker.

While Mallory healed and Danae made herbal teas, the rest prepared food, peeling and cutting while leaving the main cooking to Brodie so it would turn out well. Mallory and Danae ended up treating nearly all fifteen residents, with the newest ones being those that needed the most tending.

It took two hours to heal everyone as much as possible, leave herbal teas and instructions for each patient and cook enough meals that would store well so as to feed the residents over the next couple of days.

Lialanore stood at the front door of the house, that looked like it needed more than a few repairs. She clasped Brodie's hands between hers, smiling at him. "You have a good heart."

Brodie, looking thoroughly uncomfortable, glanced away. "We should go. We have to get back to Buckneth."

"You're welcome to stay here the night," Lialanore offered.

Taking pity on her brother, Mallory stepped forward. "Thanks, but we left someone in Buckneth and they'd worry if we didn't return today."

Lialanore released Brodie's hands to clasp Mallory's. "Any time you're back this way, feel free to drop in and visit."

Mallory smiled and, with a nod, drew her hands away from Lialanore. "We'll call in if we're in the area again. But we're not sure which road we'll take when we head to Shadhurst."

"Safe travels no matter the road you take." Lialanore waved to them from her front door as they drove the wagon back towards the waterfront, taking a right when they reached the road that stretched along the coastline.

Ryan headed in to collect the wagoner, Brodie left behind to complain that he could have gone in. That he wouldn't have bought anything. His protests resulted in laughter.

Brodie's complaints ended with him blurting out, "We gained a reputation point for Surith. Cool. I didn't expect that."

The wagoner came outside, striding ahead of Ryan. "I was wondering if I should come fetch you. We won't get back to Buckneth until four-thirty at the earliest. Providing we run into nothing."

"Sorry about that," Mallory said. "Everything took us longer than expected."

"I'm not complaining. You saved me a trip on my own next week. I was able to collect all the items everyone in Buckneth wanted as well as sell some balls of wool," the wagoner said. "The roads are a little quieter lately, but not completely safe, so it was good to have company."

It didn't take the wagoner long to get ready and they headed out of the village. The wagoner was accurate in his prediction and they arrived in Buckneth at four-thirty, leaving the wagoner at his house to continue driving through the scattering of trees behind it until the village was just in sight.

They set up camp first, planning to let Ninette and Osbert know they were back once they were finished. The tents were up and a stew set to cook, but no one had the chance to leave camp. Smudge made a high-pitched warning cry.

Mallory took out her wand, scanning the area. Six people came towards them, a mix of warriors and archers as well as a mage and a rogue. One of them was Rass, a familiar skull tattoo on his left cheek. Fear raced through Mallory and her grip tightened on her wand. Zorla wasn't with him, but she didn't know if that was good or bad.

"Rass!" Danae readied her bow.

Emica hurried to Mallory's side. "Make me invisible. I have a score to settle with him."

Mallory did as Emica requested before turning to Jorgen, who had come along her other side. At his nod, she cast Vanish I on him. Before she had the chance to do anything else, she was struck by an arrow. Pain shot through her and her health dropped to thirteen, fear quickly following on the heels of the pain. Removing the arrow from her leg, she healed herself, taking out the diplomat glasses. She needed to know what they faced. She couldn't afford to lose another thirty-two health. Not until she healed the first lot she'd lost.

Spotting another archer aiming an arrow at her, she moved towards the wagon, ducking behind it. There was no way she'd survive another attack yet. Her health wasn't full. The majority of her party joined her behind the wagon as she peered around the edge of it, drawing in a sharp breath. "Rass is now level six."

"We should have expected that," Ryan said.

Brodie popped up to one side to throw one of his knives, ducking straight back down again, knife not thrown. "There aren't enough trees in this area for decent cover."

"That's more of a disadvantage for them than us," Callum said. "We have the wagon for cover." He rose, stepped to the side, aimed and released his arrow, dropping back in behind the wagon seconds before an arrow went through the spot where he'd been.

"Make me invisible so I can help Jorgen and Emica," Esben said.

Mallory did as he asked before peering around the side and checking what was happening on the other side of the wagon. She dropped back down before she had a chance to do anything, the archer who'd attacked her before having released an arrow the moment he'd seen her.

"Great," Brodie muttered. "Now we've got them behind us."

Chapter Forty-Six

Mallory turned to face the other direction, seeing only two warriors. "We take these two out, then focus on the ones on the other side of the wagon." She cast the Locate Party spell, wanting to know where everyone was. "Then we take out the archer with the longbow. He does a lot of damage." While she spoke, Ryan, Callum, Danae and Brodie attacked the approaching warriors, the two of them breaking into a run.

The warriors came towards them, rather than retreating. Mallory cast Fireball at each warrior. The level four warrior dropped before he reached them while the level five attacked Ryan, who'd dropped his bow, taken several steps away from the wagon and drawn his sword in time to block.

The warrior vanished, the archer on the other side of the wagon getting an attack in on Ryan while he was defending himself. Ryan retreated to the side of the wagon, most of his health gone.

"We can't stay here all day," Brodie muttered. "Make me invisible and I'll go after them."

"Leave Fang in the wagon," Mallory said. "I can't cast it on both of you. I need to heal Ryan."

Brodie protested.

Callum cut him off. "We might outnumber them, but we're not in an easily defended location."

Emica came running around the side in her fox form, stopping in front of Mallory to paw at her leg.

Assuming Emica wanted to be invisible again, Mallory healed the kitsune twice before she cast Vanish I on her.

"What about me?" Brodie demanded.

Ryan grinned. "Should have put Fang in the wagon when you had the chance."

"Make Danae invisible," Callum suggested. "She has the highest attack." He slipped off his silver ring. "Here. You can borrow this. It'll give you a plus two on your bow attacks."

Danae slipped the ring on just before Mallory cast Vanish I on her.

"I need more mana," Mallory said. "There's never enough." At least not when they were in combat.

"Then focus on levelling mage." Brodie peered around the edge of the wagon, drawing back straight away. "We need to get rid of the mage too. What was his health?"

Before Mallory could speak, a rogue came around one end of the wagon while a warrior came around from the other end. Mallory attacked the rogue, retreating as she did to avoid the swiftly moving stiletto. The rogue drove her away from the cover of the wagon and an arrow barely missed her. Then the rogue vanished and she threw herself back into cover just in time, casting a fireball at the warrior as she did.

Danae reappeared behind the wagon with them. "Can you make me invisible again? I tried to get the archer with the longbow, but the mage got in the way. He must have had a revive because he vanished. Jorgen and Esben took out the archer with the short bow. She vanished too."

Mallory cast Vanish I on Danae before she finished healing Ryan. "Are we all ready to go out there? There should only be two left."

Ryan grinned. "Lets get rid of another one of Rass' revives."

Laughing, Mallory stood, striding around the side of the wagon in time to see the last archer vanish.

Rass attacked Emica, who was again visible, Jorgen and Esben joining in. Rass broke away, running towards Mallory, Ryan, Brodie and Callum.

"You can't beat us." Ryan readied his sword. "You're outnumbered."

Rass ran around them, stopping to face them when they were all behind him. "I don't need to beat you today. Just out level you." He threw a vial in the middle of their group, vanishing before the object smashed against the ground, mist rising from it.

Assuming Rass had teleported away to avoid what he'd thrown at them, Mallory staggered back from the mist, covering her mouth and nose with her arm. Everyone else backed away too. "What is it?" She checked her health. It seemed unchanged. The only difference she noticed was she'd gained a CAS point during the fight.

Danae, who was visible again, stopped retreating. "Check your buffs and negative stats." She slipped off the ring, handing it to Callum, who stood not far from her.

"Experience points blocker," Brodie said. "What does that mean? And why does it say a hundred and seventy-four days next to it?"

"That until we get rid of the debuff, or it ends in a hundred and seventy-four days, we won't gain any XP," Emica stated.

"What?" Brodie demanded. "No! How are we going to get rid of it? A hundred and seventy-four days is forever."

"Only half a year on Inadon," Callum pointed out.

"Exactly," Brodie said. "Forever."

"Usually, a potion is used," Emica said. "There's also a high level spell that gets rid of negative stats, but you'll be lucky to find a mage on Ruby Isle with that spell. Some enchantments can do the same too, but they're usually a single use enchantment and likely to be more expensive than a potion. So a potion is probably our cheapest option."

"How cheap?" Brodie asked.

Emica shrugged. "I don't know. I've only heard of them, not bought them."

"Probably a few thousand for each potion," Danae said.

"Great," Brodie muttered. "There goes all our money."

"We might not have enough money," Danae said. "There are eight of us that need the potion."

"If we don't have enough money, who gets the potions first?" Brodie asked.

"No one," Mallory stated. "We either all get rid of the negative stat or no one does."

"Where do we buy the potion?" Callum asked.

"Shadhurst," Emica said at the same time as Danae spoke.

"Goswin might sell it."

"Will we still be able to unlock crafter with the book we bought for Osbert?" Callum asked.

Danae nodded. "That's different to gaining XP."

"What about my character level I got during the fight?" Brodie asked. "Can I sort it out or will I lose the attributes if I use them now?"

"You can do anything except earn new XP," Danae said. "Including XP gained from potions. If you were to drink one now, the XP would be wasted."

"Should we return to Surith and use the travelling bank to visit Goswin?" Jorgen asked. "Esben and I need to keep levelling up if we hope to rescue our family. Not that we have enough money if the potion is three thousand gold pieces."

"They'll be in Mer Point on the twenty-sixth," Callum said. "Then they'll be in Buckneth on the twenty-seventh. But they didn't say what time they leave or arrive at each place. Only what day they'll be there." He turned to Mallory. "Rass was after us."

Mallory nodded, knowing exactly what Callum was getting at. "It's our fault Rass was here. We can't expect you to spend your money on getting rid of the negative stat."

Jorgen shook his head, a smile briefly appearing. "We escaped and helped ruin his plans. He'll want us to suffer too. We'll help pay for the potions. The sooner we get rid of the XP blocker, the better."

"Lucky Ninette and Osbert weren't here when he attacked," Danae said. "At least they can earn XP."

"We should let them know we're here," Ryan said.

"We should figure out how to get rid of the blocker," Brodie protested.

"Ninette and Osbert first," Mallory stated. "Then we'll figure out what to do next."

Muttering under his breath, Brodie checked on the food while Jorgen and Esben volunteered to bring Ninette and Osbert back to their camp.

When Ninette and Osbert arrived, having been told what had happened, Ninette glanced around at each of them. "Is there anything I can help you with? Did you want the money in my account?"

"No," Mallory said. "You and your brothers will need it when you travel to Merrow." She tried not to think about how much that would cost. She wasn't about to make Ninette pay travel costs after telling her they'd pay for it. Once again, they desperately needed to earn money. "We'll go after more treasures if we need to. Goswin has a book filled with them."

"Where are the eggs?" Brodie asked. "Have they hatched yet? We could sell them if they have."

Chapter Forty-Seven

Some of Mallory's worries eased. She'd forgotten about the eggs. Her hopes were dashed when Ninette shook her head. "At least when they do hatch, we can earn back some of what we have to spend on potions."

"If we have enough money for them," Brodie muttered.

"We need to find out as soon as possible what they'll cost us," Ryan said. "So we can plan our next move."

"We could use the horses," Callum suggested. "Some of us could stay here and watch the wagon while the rest ride to Surith or Mer Point if they've already left Surith."

"What if you need money from the account of someone who isn't there?" Emica asked.

"If Ninette, Ryan, Brodie and Callum remain behind, we'll have everyone we need to access all the bank accounts," Mallory said.

"Why should you get to go?" Brodie demanded. "Scorch doesn't like being ridden by anyone other than me."

"He has a point," Ryan said.

Mallory stared at Ryan in disbelief. "You want to send Brodie."

Ryan grinned. "Not particularly, but Scorch doesn't like to be ridden by anyone else."

"What's wrong with sending me?" Brodie asked.

"I'm surprised you have to ask, Goblin Boy," Emica said.

"Ninette and Osbert should go. They could gain some location XP," Callum said.

"We don't have enough horses," Ryan pointed out.

"We could borrow two from the wagoner," Ninette said. "He'd probably want a silver piece or two, though. And someone would have to look after the eggs. I reheated the rocks before I left the tavern, but the heat won't last all night."

"How will Danae, Ninette and Osbert see to find their way without Mallory's magelight?" Ryan asked.

"They'll have to use lanterns. Or wait until morning," Callum said. "No option will be perfect."

"Did you want me to borrow the horses?" Ninette asked.

Mallory thought of the crafter book, but they could deal with it later. Fixing their negative buff problem had to be their priority. She took two silver pieces from her belt pouch. "Organise the horses." She dropped the coins into Ninette's hand, casting Tracking Magelight on her since there was very little light left in the day. "You might want to take a lantern with you." She turned to Callum. "Did you want to take care of the eggs while I get the group money from the chest?" When Callum nodded, she cast Tracking Magelight on him too.

It took longer for them to get ready than Mallory had expected, as Brodie had insisted they eat before leaving. Callum brought the eggs back to the camp and Mallory put all the money from the chest into her belt pouch since it had a weight reducing enchantment on it, removing her own coins. There was two hundred and twenty-two gold, seventy-six silver and one hundred and six copper pieces. She hoped they helped.

Emica grinned when Mallory handed her the belt pouch. "Don't you trust Goblin Boy with it?"

Mallory returned the kitsune's grin. "Something like that." She ignored her brother's mutterings.

It was nearly seven by the time everyone had eaten and were ready to leave. Mallory watched them go, standing arm in arm with Ryan. "They'll be okay, won't they?" Casting Locate Party, she brought up her journal when they were no longer in sight. She wouldn't be able to see them the entire way to Surith, let alone Mer Point. Maybe putting more points into Locate Party would be a good idea. When she had a few more CAS points, that was. And didn't have anything preventing her from earning experience points.

"We should have returned to the beach so we could fish while we waited," Callum said.

Smudge, looking over the edge of the sling Callum wore, chattered excitedly.

Ryan patted Smudge on the head. "Sorry. Too late now. We have no horses to pull the wagon."

After checking her journal map once more, Mallory said, "I should probably write in my journal."

"I'll clean the dishes," Callum said. "With how long the waits usually are at the travelling bank, I'd be surprised if they returned before morning."

Mallory found herself checking her journal map regularly, unable to see them once they were more than ten kilometres away. Judging from what she'd seen as their markers had moved across her map, they were mostly trotting, dropping back to a fast walk every now and then. When they were no longer visible on her map, she kept an eye on their stats, noticing her brother had done his character level at some point.

He'd put a point in dexterity, constitution, luck, charisma and wisdom. She had no idea why he'd put a point in wisdom. He didn't need mana for anything. His health was now forty-two, stamina seventy and mana thirty. And he'd added the class point to rogue. Everything he'd done made sense except for the point in wisdom. Knowing her brother, he'd probably have some strange reason that she wouldn't have a chance at guessing.

Mallory fell asleep by the fire, having tried to remain awake as she waited for everyone to return, leaning against Ryan, who had his arm around her.

They were woken in the early hours of the morning by their returning party members, Callum still awake and taking care of the eggs.

Mallory struggled to sit up, untangling herself from Ryan. "What time is it?" She cast Magelight, wincing at the brightness and wondering if a dimmer light would be useful after all.

Ryan took out the pocket watch. "Half two."

Callum, yawning, came over to them. "One of you two can take care of the eggs for a bit. I'm off to bed as soon as someone tells me the news."

Brodie dismounted. "There are no other treasures in this area. They're either up on the north east side of the island, on top of the mountain near the mines or south of the capital."

Joining him, Emica slowly shook her head. "You should have started with the cost of the potions. They're three thousand gold each and we're about three thousand three hundred and thirty-three gold short. Give or take a handful of coins. We had to pay twenty gold pieces for Brodie to travel to the vault. He won the dice roll. We'll also need an extra twenty gold for one of us to travel to the bank vault to collect the potions."

Mallory momentarily closed her eyes, trying to ignore the dreadful feeling that washed over her. What if it took them ages to gain the money and Rass out levelled them to the point of making him impossible to face?

"I suggested contacting my father," Emica said. "But Jorgen thinks that's a terrible idea. He thinks Rass might find out we're close to getting rid of the problem and come up with another plan to cause problems for us."

"I agree with Jorgen," Danae said. "It'd be better if Rass doesn't find out what we're trying to do. I've heard it's hard to keep a secret in the capital. There are too many spies."

"I also suggested Danae, Ninette and her brothers travel to Merrow incognito," Jorgen said. "Change the colour of Augusta and their looks with potions or temporary spells. We don't want Rass following any of us to the mainland."

"The XP blocker might turn out to be a good thing to have happened," Danae said. "Rass might leave us alone for a bit. At least until he gains a few levels."

Mallory wasn't sure she'd go that far, but keeping their plans from getting back to Rass was a good idea. "So we need enough money for potions, disguises and transport to the mainland." Mallory tried to focus on the positives, but it was hard with the expenses piling up. They had the majority of the money needed. They'd earn enough by completing the unicorn quest. She checked her journal. It was still available. No one had done it yet. Things certainly could have been worse. At least Ninette and Osbert hadn't been with them. That would have cost an extra six thousand gold pieces.

"What's the plan?" Brodie asked.

"Sleep," Callum said. "We'll figure it out when we wake later this morning. I can't think clearly with how tired I am."

"I had some sleep while we were waiting to use the bank," Brodie protested.

Ryan grinned. "Good. Then you can look after the eggs while I get more sleep."

Mallory laughed at her brother's expression, that quickly went from stunned to annoyance.

"That wasn't what I meant," Brodie protested.

"Keep them warm," Ryan ordered.

"But-"

Ryan interrupted Brodie. "We'll need every egg to hatch if we're to gain back some of the money Rass has cost us."

Mallory was still smiling when she crawled into the tent she shared with Ryan. Her smile vanished as she settled in beside him. "Do you think he'll look after them? What if he falls asleep?"

"And risk losing money?" Ryan asked.

Mallory smiled again. "I suppose." Her smile faded. "What are we going to do about Rass?"

"He has too many revives. Our only option is to see him caught and incarcerated," Ryan said.

"Like in a Guardian jail? Or somewhere else?" Mallory asked.

Ryan shrugged. "I don't know. We'll have to figure out what's the best option. But first we deal with the XP blocker. Without letting Rass know."

Mallory snuggled in beside Ryan, her magelight going out. "I thought we were making progress, but we're going backwards again."

Ryan's arms tightened around her. "No, we're not. It's a step sideways. We're still moving forward. Now we know he's still focused on us. And that we need to make sure he doesn't find out where we go next."

Mallory couldn't help thinking about how she thought she'd seen Rass while they were back home. No wonder she was seeing him everywhere. If he continued to hound them like this, she'd be jumping at shadows.

Chapter Forty-Eight

It was eight when Mallory finally dragged herself out of the tent, having slept longer than she'd planned, her sleep disturbed by bad dreams. They needed to figure out their next move, not sleep the morning away.

After a quick trip to the Adventurers Guild to use the bathroom, Mallory joined Brodie at the campfire where he was cooking blueberry pancakes, the scent making her mouth water. "Did you get any sleep?"

Brodie nodded. "I've had a few hours. Ninette took over looking after the eggs." He glanced to where the young warrior was checking the contents of the baskets, pressing her hand against each of the cloth wrapped rocks in the middle of the eggs. "That was after she rode down to the beach and caught two fish for Smudge and Fang to have for breakfast. It's a lot quicker to ride than use the wagon." This time he glanced to where the companion animals were happily eating their meal.

"Where did you find the travelling bank?" Mallory asked.

"We missed it in Surith by about an hour. Then we had to wait ages for all the people who lined up the moment it arrived in Mer Point. It took forever."

Mallory hid a grin at her brother's comment. It obviously hadn't taken forever. They were only gone seven and a half hours and part of that was travel. "What about the money I sent with Emica?" She glanced around, spotting only Ninette, Ryan and Callum. "And where is everyone?"

"At the tavern." Callum joined them at the fire. "Danae said that's the best place to hear all the gossip of any town or village. She wants to find out if anyone has seen Rass or if he's completely left the area."

Mallory turned to Brodie. "And the money?" She'd been too tired when everyone had returned to even think about asking.

"Emica said I should put most of it in the bank. I kept out ten gold, twenty silver and fifty copper pieces." Brodie frowned. "Should I have put more in?"

Mallory shook her head. "The bank will be here tomorrow, anyway. But we probably shouldn't keep so much on us. We shouldn't need to buy anything all that expensive for a while once we can afford the potions. And by then, we'll be on the side of the island that has a few places with banks in them."

"She put the belt pouch in the chest you normally keep the money in, since you'd gone to bed by the time she remembered to give it to you," Brodie said.

Mallory collected the belt pouch from the chest, leaving the ten gold as well as thirty copper pieces behind in the chest. She returned to the campfire when Brodie called out that breakfast was ready.

He handed her a plate of blueberry pancakes. "When can I get enchanted leather armour? I can use it now I'm level five rogue."

"Not for ages. The potions are going to set us back a lot," Mallory said. "Besides, why do you need armour when you have the demonic mask?"

Brodie shrugged. "Actual armour might have better stats."

Being reminded of stats, Mallory asked, "Why did you put a point in wisdom? You thinking of being a rogue mage?"

Brodie handed out plates of food as everyone returned from the tavern. "So I can visit Drohgolrik on my own. It took fifteen minutes for my mana to come back before I put a point in wisdom. Now it takes less than twelve minutes, so I can leave more than three minutes earlier now."

"Three minutes and twenty seconds earlier," Callum corrected.

Ryan grinned. "Can't forget those twenty seconds."

Brodie glared at Ryan. "It's not like I want to spend that long waiting to leave if I only go there for a few minutes." His expression brightened and he turned to his sister. "I could borrow your mana regen jewellery."

"Not likely," Mallory stated. "We can't afford to replace them." Ignoring her brother's pleas to borrow the jewellery, she turned to Danae. "Did you hear anything interesting at the tavern?"

Danae shook her head, having just taken a bite of her food.

Emica spoke instead. "No one has seen anyone new around here. Ninette also asked the person where the wagoner's horses are kept. They haven't seen anyone since Darwil and his group got rid of the ones hanging around waiting for us."

"We're going to need another tent. Four people can't sleep comfortably in the wagon," Brodie blurted out.

"Ninette's brothers might have to sleep under the wagon for now," Ryan said. "We can't afford another tent."

"You don't need to spend any money on us," Osbert assured them. "We're just glad you're helping us leave the village."

Ryan grinned. "Too late. We got something you might like." Setting his now empty plate aside, he fetched the crafter class book.

Osbert's mouth hung open as he stared at the leather bound book.

"We were told that as long as we all hold it and read the opening paragraph, we can all unlock the class," Callum said.

It took some effort to position all ten of them so everyone could hold the book and read the words aloud together. Mallory made sure she wasn't in the middle this time and let go of the book, stepping away from the crowd as soon as the class was unlocked. It was listed under class, like warrior and mage, and was level zero. She checked her notification that had appeared when she'd read the first paragraph aloud.

You have unlocked the crafter class. You now earn two times the experience points from using crafting abilities.

"Like that's going to help for now," Brodie muttered. "What are we going to do about getting rid of the XP blocker?"

Mallory assumed her brother had read his journal notification. "At least when we can gather resources again we'll get one XP instead of half an XP like we have been earning."

"Maybe we should have waited until Ninette's younger brothers could have unlocked the class, too," Callum said.

"We struggled to have as many of us hold it as we did," Ryan pointed out. "I doubt they could have joined in."

"What about the XP blocker?" Brodie demanded again. "What are we going to do about it?"

"Go after the staff so we can travel to the other side of the island as soon as Farlie and Martie are old enough to leave home." Mallory tried to ignore the worry her words caused to form. They had to give it a try. A house near Merrow would save them a lot of money. She thought of the spell still in her satchel that she hadn't learned yet. She'd need to learn it before they went after the staff.

"We're going to lose all that XP," Brodie complained.

"Who says we would have earned any?" Mallory asked. "I want to get out there, grab the staff and get back to shore as quick as possible. I have no plans to focus on gaining XP." An image of the undine came to mind, her enticing song drawing them all towards her. The last thing she wanted to do was stay in the water any longer than necessary.

"Are you going to ask the merfolk for help?" Danae asked.

Mallory nodded. "I also want to tell them what Rass has been up to and see what ideas they have about dealing with him. What we're doing isn't working." It had only caused them more problems.

"We need to head to the beach then," Ryan said.

Mallory again nodded, this time not speaking, worried she might blurt out that she'd changed her mind. It was madness going after the staff. She'd hoped to gain another character level first. Her next level was only three CAS points away. The fear was replaced with anger at Rass. What did he expect when he was the one capturing people and causing problems? That everyone would let him go ahead with his nefarious plans?

"Anyone need to do anything in Buckneth before we head to the beach?" Ryan asked.

"I'd rather stay at the tavern in case Farlie or Martie need me," Osbert said.

"You should have put in a request years ago to leave your father," Emica said. "Asked for an apprenticeship that took you away from here before you gained your journal."

"He wasn't always like this," Osbert said.

"Pa became angrier the more time passed after our Ma's death," Ninette added.

Osbert nodded. "He just kept getting worse after Ninette left. A lot worse."

Ninette glanced around the group. "I'll help you get the staff. Osbert can look after the eggs. He knows how to do it. I showed him while we waited for you to return with the wagoner."

"I made more of the nutty oat bars. Do you need any of them?" Brodie asked Osbert.

"I've still got some of the food you left with us yesterday," Osbert said. "More than enough for a couple of days."

Mallory hoped they weren't gone that long. Before she could comment, Ryan spoke.

"We need to try to be back tomorrow so we can use the travelling bank to hand the staff over to Goswin. I don't want to be going far with something everyone wants. That's just asking for trouble."

"If it takes us two days, at least Wayholt isn't far from Buckneth and we can use the travelling bank when it reaches there," Callum pointed out.

"I'll help Osbert take the eggs back to the tavern." Ninette strode over to the baskets of eggs before anyone had a chance to comment.

"Guess we better pack up camp and get moving," Ryan said.

By the time Ninette returned, they were ready to leave for the beach. Mallory climbed into the back of the wagon, getting comfortable for the journey ahead. She had no idea if the merfolk would help them, or if they could even find the staff, but she refused to let Rass ruin all their plans. No wonder she'd thought she'd seen him back in her world. With how many times they'd encountered him, she was surprised she wasn't seeing him everywhere she looked.

Pushing aside thoughts of Rass, she focused on all they had achieved. They were making progress. Rass wouldn't keep them from continuing to progress. They'd get past this setback and find a way to deal with him.

She just wasn't sure how. But they had time to figure that out. In the meantime, they'd go after the staff. And if they were lucky, they'd find it and gain a home near Merrow. Not long now and they'd be travelling to the mainland and progressing even further. She couldn't wait. Was the mainland anything like Ruby Isle? Would they make new friends over there? She couldn't prevent a stream of questions from filling her mind. Questions without answers.

The one thing she did know was that whatever awaited them on the mainland, she was certain it included plenty of adventures. She smiled. Adventures and new places to explore. And hopefully, Rass wouldn't be able to find them there. She couldn't wait. First, though, they had a staff to find and money to earn. She wasn't about to let Rass win.

Final Stats

Character weight does not include any backpacks, satchels, their contents or items carried by livestock.

Mallory

Character Level: 6
Health: 45
Stamina: 75
Mana: 70
Weight: 6kg 226g/90kg

CAS XP: 2/165
Available CAS Points: 2
Available Class Points: 0
Level Progress: 6:7/10

Attributes

Strength: 9
Constitution: 15
Intelligence: 14
Wisdom: 14

Dexterity: 5
Charisma: 5
Luck: 6

Class

Mage: 3
Warrior: 3
Crafter: 0

Class Skills
None

Spells

Fireball: 0
Health I: 0
Vanish I: 0
Locate Party: 5

(Expand For More Details)

Weapon and Armour Affinity

Wand: 1 (+1% damage)
Cloth Armour: 0
Short Sword: 0

(Expand For More Details)

Crafting

Alchemy: 1
Apothecary: 55
Wheelwright: 1

(Expand For More Details)

Reputation

Global: 0
Local Areas:
Ruby Isle
(Expand For More Details)

Buffs and Negative Stats

Necklace: doubles healing done
Silver bracelet: +1 mana every 15 secs
(Expand For More Details)

Available Revives 5

Spells Expanded

*All attack spells have +43% damage to base attacks.

Level 0

Fireball: 0
Mana cost: 3
Cooldown: 2 seconds
Damage: low 3, normal 5, critical 7
Duration: Instant

Flame: 0
Mana cost: 5
Cooldown: 3 seconds
Damage: low 4, normal 6, critical 8
Damage Over Time: 4 every 2 seconds
Duration: Non-flammable materials 6 secs,
flammable materials until runs out of fuel

Ice Shard: 0
Mana cost: 3
Cooldown: 2 seconds
Damage: low 3, normal 5, critical 7
Duration: Instant

Lightning Strike: 0
Mana cost: 3
Cooldown: 2 seconds
Damage: low 3, normal 5, critical 7
Duration: Instant

Mend I: 0
Mana Cost: 17
Cooldown: 5 seconds
Area Of Effect: 1cm2
Duration: Instant

Level 1

Beacon: 0
Mana Cost: 15
Cooldown: 5 seconds
Area Of Effect: to be cast on a
solid surface
Duration: 10 mins

Health I: 0
Restores health to target
Mana Cost: 6
Cooldown: 3 seconds
Area Of Effect: +1HP to target within 2m
Duration: Instant

Poison Dart I: 0
Mana Cost: 6
Cooldown: 3 seconds
Damage: low 4, normal 6, crit 8
Damage Over Time: 5 every 3
seconds
Duration: 3 secs

Spells Expanded 2

Level 2

Lightning Trap: 0
Mana Cost: 10
Cooldown: 5 seconds
Damage: 10
Duration: damage on contact

Nightfall: 0
Causes the target's vision to go black.
Mana Cost: 20
Cooldown: 60 seconds
Targets Effected: 1
Duration: 5 seconds
Range: 2 metres

Shrink I: 0
Mana Cost: 20
Cooldown: 10 seconds
Area Of Effect: cast on the object,
living creature or sentient being
the castor wishes to shrink
Duration: Permanent.

Shrink Reversal: 0
Returns an object, living creature or
sentient being, that has been shrunk,
back to normal size.
Mana Cost: 25
Cooldown: 30 seconds
Range: Touch
Duration: Permanent
Target: unenchanted objects and
creatures up to level 10
Quantity Effected: 1

Slow Target: 0
Slows target.
Mana Cost: 10
Cooldown: 30 seconds
Targets Effected: 1
Duration: 120 seconds
Range: 2 metres
Target Slowed: 10%

Vanish I: 0
Mana Cost: 25
Cooldown: 5 seconds
Area Of Effect: causes target, within
a 2m range, to vanish
Duration: 1 min

Water Manipulation: 0
Mana Cost: 12
Cooldown: 5 seconds
Area Of Effect: relocate up to five
litres of water up to a distance of
five metres
Duration: Instant

Spells Expanded 3

Level 3

Locate Party: 5
Shows location of party members
and their companions on your
journal map.
Mana Cost: 12
Cooldown: 4 minutes
Targets Effected: 10
Duration: 15 minutes
Range: 10 kilometres

Magelight: 0
Mana Cost: 20
Cooldown: 10 seconds
Area Of Effect: creates a ball of light
near caster
Duration: 15 mins

Spellbound Shield: 0
Mana Cost: 35
Cooldown: 120 seconds
Duration: 10 minutes
Size: Small
Target: Warrior
Defence: -2 damage

Teleportation Link I: 0
Mana Cost: 30
Cooldown: 1 minute
Initial Area Of Effect: Cast at a location
the castor wishes to return to
Initial Duration: Instant
Delayed Area Of Effect: Recast to
return to the initial location,
transporting the castor, companion
animal and gear worn or carried by
the castor
Delayed Duration: 1 hour

Weak Reanimate: 0
Mana Cost: 20
Cooldown: 5 seconds
Area Of Effect: reanimate one of the
dead level 3
Range: 2m
Duration: 1 min

Level 4

Tracking Magelight: 0
Creates a ball of white light that trails
a fraction behind the target above
head height
Mana Cost: 25
Cooldown: 20 seconds
Targets Effected: create a ball of light
that follows 1 target
Duration: 5 minutes
Range: target within 5 metres
Target Type: sentient race

Weapon and Armour Affinity Expanded

Dagger (and enchanted): 1 (+1% damage)
Wand (and enchanted): 1 (+1% damage)
Cloth Armour: 0
Unarmed: 0

Chain Mail Armour: 0
Short Sword (and enchanted): 0
Shield (and enchanted): 0
Dual Swords (and enchanted): 0

Crafting Expanded

Alchemy: 1
Apothecary: 55
Artist: 1
Bard: 0
Bartering: 0
Brewer: 0
Cobbler: 0

Cooking: 0
Diplomacy: 0
Enchanting: 0
Farming: 0
Fishing: 0
Glassblowing: 0
Hunting: 0

Husbandry: 0
Languages: 0
Mason: 0
Potter: 0
Sailing: 0
Scribe: 0
Sculptor: 0

Shipwright: 0
Smithing: 0
Thatcher: 0
Weaver: 0
Wheelwright: 1
Woodcutter: 0

Reputation Expanded

Ruby Isle:
Buckneth 22
Coastview 0
Cutthroat Harbour -17
Delten 2
Eastvale 1
Estwater 0
Jenlea 0

Donris Island:
Drohgolrik 0

Lilica 0
Longmeadow 0
Mer Point 10
Ransted 4
Seacoast 2
Simria 0
South Peak Mine 5
South Point 2

Surith 6
Ursen 0
Valley Of Wandering Souls 10
Velkden 42
Wayholt 10
Wildebay 10
Wrentville 1

Guilds And Factions

Adventurers Guild: Rank 0

Buffs And Negative Stats Expanded

Necklace: doubles healing done
Silver bracelet: +1 mana every 15 secs
Mage cloth armour hooded jacket: -1 dam when attacked, +1 mana every 5 secs
Gold ring: +1 mana every 10 secs
Gold ring, single jewel: +5 mana/1 min
Gold ring, single jewel: +5 mana/1 min
Silver bracelet, single jewel: +10 mana/1 min
Gold ring, blue jewel: +8 mana/1 min
Experience points blocker: 174 days

Ryan

Character Level: 4
Health: 45
Stamina: 75
Mana: 20
Weight: 10kg 660g/150kg

CAS XP: 76/147
Available CAS Points: 5
Available Class Points: 0
Level Progress: 4:9/10

Attributes

Strength: 15
Constitution: 15
Intelligence: 5
Wisdom: 4

Dexterity: 8
Charisma: 5
Luck: 6

Class

Warrior: 4
Crafter: 0

Class Skills
None

Spells

None

Weapon and Armour Affinity

Chain Mail Armour: 0
Dual Swords (and enchanted): 0
Longsword: 30

(Expand For More Details)

Crafting

Artist: 1
Hunting: 10
Wheelwright: 1

(Expand For More Details)

Reputation

Global: 0
Local Areas:
Ruby Isle
(Expand For More Details)

Buffs and Negative Stats

Experience points blocker: 174 days

Available Revives 5

Ryan

Weapon and Armour Affinity Expanded

Chain Mail Armour: 0
Short Sword (and enchanted): 1
Shield (and enchanted): 1

Dual Swords (and enchanted): 0
Longsword: 30

Crafting Expanded

Alchemy: 0
Apothecary: 0
Artist: 1
Bard: 0
Bartering: 0
Brewer: 0
Cobbler: 0

Cooking: 0
Diplomacy: 0
Enchanting: 0
Farming: 0
Fishing: 0
Glassblowing: 0
Hunting: 10

Husbandry: 0
Languages: 0Mason: 0
Potter: 0
Sailing: 0
Scribe: 0
Sculptor: 0

Shipwright: 0
Smithing: 0
Thatcher: 0
Weaver: 0
Wheelwright: 1
Woodcutter: 0

Reputation Expanded

Ruby Isle:
Buckneth 22
Coastview 0
Cutthroat Harbour -17
Delten 2
Eastvale 1
Estwater 0
Jenlea 0

Donris Island:
Drohgolrik 0

Lilica 0
Longmeadow 0
Mer Point 10
Ransted 4
Seacoast 2
Simria 0
South Peak Mine 5
South Point 2

Surith 6
Ursen: 0
Valley Of Wandering Souls 10
Velkden 42
Wayholt 10
Wildebay 10
Wrentville 1

Guilds And Factions

Adventurers Guild: Rank 0

Brodie

Character Level: 5
Health: 42
Stamina: 70
Mana: 30
Weight: 6kg 789g/70kg

CAS XP: 16/148
Available CAS Points: 5
Available Class Points: 0
Level Progress: 5:0/10

Attributes

Strength: 7
Constitution: 14
Intelligence: 5
Wisdom: 6

Dexterity: 12
Charisma: 10
Luck: 9

Class

Archer: 5
Crafter: 0

Class Skills
Stealth: 0 (30 seconds, 1 hr cooldown)
(Expand For More Details)

Spells

None

Weapon and Armour Affinity

Stiletto (and enchanted): 1 (+1% damage)
Throwing Knives (and enchanted): 2 (+2% damage)
Leather Armour (and enchanted): 0

Crafting

Bartering: 20
Cooking: 20
Wheelwright: 1

(Expand For More Details)

Reputation

Global: 0
Local Areas:
Ruby Isle
(Expand For More Details)

Buffs and Negative Stats

Experience points blocker: 174 days

Available Revives 3

Class Skills Expanded

Stealth: 0 (30 seconds, 1 hr cooldown)
Sleight of hand: 0 (take low value small object unnoticed, cooldown 6 hours)

Crafting Expanded

Alchemy: 0	Cooking: 20	Husbandry: 0	Shipwright: 0
Apothecary: 0	Diplomacy: 0	Languages: 0	Smithing: 0
Artist: 1	Enchanting: 0	Mason: 0	Thatcher: 0
Bard: 0	Farming: 0	Potter: 0	Weaver: 0
Bartering: 20	Fishing: 0	Sailing: 0	Wheelwright: 1
Brewer: 0	Glassblowing: 0	Scribe: 0	Woodcutter: 0
Cobbler: 0	Hunting: 0	Sculptor: 0	

Reputation Expanded

Ruby Isle:
Buckneth 22
Coastview 0
Cutthroat Harbour -17
Delten 2
Eastvale 1
Estwater 0
Jenlea 0

Lilica 0
Longmeadow 0
Mer Point 10
Ransted 4
Seacoast 2
Simria 0
South Peak Mine 5
South Point 2

Surith 6
Ursen: 0
Valley Of Wandering Souls 10
Velkden 42
Wayholt 10
Wildebay 10
Wrentville 1

Donris Island:
Drohgolrik 0

Guilds And Factions

Adventurers Guild: Rank 0

Callum

Character Level: 4
Health: 33
Stamina: 55
Mana: 25
Weight: 8kg 186g/90kg

CAS XP: 116/147
Available CAS Points: 45
Available Class Points: 0
Level Progress: 4:9/10

Attributes

Strength: 9
Constitution: 11
Intelligence: 5
Wisdom: 5

Dexterity: 14
Charisma: 5
Luck: 9

Class

Archer: 4
Crafter: 0

Class Skills
None

Spells

None

Weapon and Armour Affinity

Hunting Knife: 1 (+1% damage)
Studded Leather Armour: 0
Longbow: 0

(Expand For More Details)

Crafting

Artist: 1
Wheelwright: 1

(Expand For More Details)

Reputation

Global: 0
Local Areas:
Ruby Isle
(Expand For More Details)

Buffs and Negative Stats

Silver Ring: +2 damage to bow attacks
Experience points blocker: 174 days

Available Revives 4

Weapon and Armour Affinity Expanded

Short Bow (and enchanted): 1 (+1% damage)
Hunting Knife: 1 (+1% damage)
Studded Leather Armour: 0

Sling (and enchanted): 0
Slingshot (and enchanted)
Enchanted Arrows
Longbow: 0

Crafting Expanded

Alchemy: 0
Apothecary: 0
Artist: 1
Bard: 0
Bartering: 0
Brewer: 0
Cobbler: 0

Cooking: 0
Diplomacy: 0
Enchanting: 0
Farming: 0
Fishing: 0
Glassblowing: 0
Hunting: 0

Husbandry: 0
Languages: 0
Mason: 0
Potter: 0
Sailing: 0
Scribe: 0
Sculptor: 0

Shipwright: 0Smithing: 0
Thatcher: 0
Weaver: 0
Wheelwright: 1
Woodcutter: 0

Reputation Expanded

Ruby Isle:
Buckneth 22
Coastview 0
Cutthroat Harbour -17
Delten 2
Eastvale 1
Estwater 0
Jenlea 0

Donris Island:
Drohgolrik 0

Lilica 0
Longmeadow 0
Mer Point 10
Ransted 4
Seacoast 2
Simria 0
South Peak Mine 5
South Point 2

Surith 6
Ursen 0
Valley Of Wandering Souls 10
Velkden 42
Wayholt 10
Wildebay 10
Wrentville 1

Guilds And Factions

Adventurers Guild: Rank 0

Danae

Character Level: 4	CAS XP: 110/147
Health: 39	Available CAS Points: 28
Stamina: 65	Available Class Points: 0
Mana: 25	Level Progress: 4:9/10
Weight: 7kg 612g/80kg	

Attributes

Strength: 8	Dexterity: 14
Constitution: 13	Charisma: 5
Intelligence: 5	Luck: 8
Wisdom: 5	

Class / Spells

Class	Spells
Archer: 4 Crafter: 0 Class Skills None	None

Weapon and Armour Affinity / Crafting

Weapon and Armour Affinity	Crafting
Hunting Knife: 1 (+1% damage) Studded Leather Armour: 0 Longbow: 0 (Expand For More Details)	Alchemy: 9 Bartering: 1 Cooking: 1 Glassblowing: 5 (Expand For More Details)

Reputation / Buffs and Negative Stats

Reputation	Buffs and Negative Stats
Global: 0 Local Areas: Ruby Isle (Expand For More Details)	Experience points blocker: 174 days

Racial Bonus

Racial Bonus	
Archer +10% damage Mage capable of using spells one level above class level	Available Revives 3

Danae

Weapon and Armour Affinity Expanded

Short Bow (and enchanted): 1 (+1% damage)
Hunting Knife: 1 (+1% damage)
Studded Leather Armour: 0
Sling (and enchanted): 0

Slingshot (and enchanted): 0
Enchanted Arrows: 0
Longbow: 0
Unarmed: 1 (+1% damage)

Crafting Expanded

Alchemy: 9	Cooking: 1	Languages: 0	Smithing: 0
Apothecary: 0	Diplomacy: 0	Mason: 0	Thatcher: 0
Artist: 1	Enchanting: 0	Potter: 0	Weaver: 0
Bartering: 1	Farming: 0	Sailing: 0	Wheelwright: 1
Brewer: 0	Fishing: 0	Scribe: 0	Woodcutter: 0
Clothier: 0	Glassblowing: 5	Sculptor: 0	
Cobbler: 0	Husbandry: 0	Shipwright: 0	

Reputation Expanded

Ruby Isle:
Buckneth 4
Coastview 0
Cutthroat Harbour -17
Delten 2
Eastvale 1
Estwater 0
Jenlea 0

Donris Island:
Drohgolrik 0

Lilica 0
Longmeadow 0
Mer Point 10
Ransted 4
Seacoast 2
Simria 22
South Peak Mine 5
South Point 2

Surith 6
Ursen 0
Valley Of Wandering Souls 10
Velkden 42
Wayholt 18
Wildebay 10
Wrentville 1

Guilds And Factions

Adventurers Guild: Rank 0

Companion Animals' Final Stats

Smudge 8HP (Callum)

5427XP/6000XP

Level: 5

Items: None

Wearing: Jewelled bracelet (tiny colourful jewels creating a bright band).

Abilities: +25% movement speed, increased ability to forage or hunt for food, +25% increased agility, +25% attack damage.

Fang 6HP (Brodie)

5619XP/6000XP

Level: 5

Items: None

Wearing: leather collar (made from belt) with revive ring tied to it (plain gold band)

Abilities: +25% movement speed, increased ability to forage or hunt for food, +25% increased strength, +25% attack damage.

Free Ebook

Subscribe to Avril's newsletter and receive a free ebook. This ebook is exclusive to those on her mailing list. To find out more about this offer visit:

https://www.avrilsabine.com/free-ebook

*

We value your privacy and will not sell, rent, exchange or loan your email address to third parties. Your information is confidential and you are under no obligation to remain on the mailing list and can unsubscribe at any time.

Acknowledgements

As always, our thanks go to our usual crew, who helped make this book possible.

To The Reader

If you enjoyed this book, why not consider leaving a review to help other readers discover it too? Reader engagement is one of the few ways that lets an author know readers want more books in a particular series or genre. So leave a review and tell friends, not only about this book but also about other ones you've enjoyed, so you can continue to enjoy books by your favourite authors for years to come.

Dreams are meant to be lived,
Avril, Storm and Rhys.

About The Authors

Avril is an Australian author who lives with her family on acreage in South East Queensland. She writes mostly young adult and children's speculative fiction, but has been known to dabble in other genres. You can find more information about her at https://www.avrilsabine.com where you can also subscribe to her newsletter to be kept informed about new releases, current projects, blog posts and exclusive news.

Storm has a wide range of interests from gaming and blacksmithing to cooking and sewing. It's not unusual to find him cooking at any hour of the day or night, particularly after a long gaming session.

Rhys loves books and gaming and has thoroughly enjoyed combining two of his favourite things. He has been running tabletop gaming sessions for the past few years and enjoys creating characters and doing in depth worldbuilding.

Titles By Avril Sabine

Stories about strong characters and characters who discover their strengths.

Series

Assassins Of The Dead- Young Adult Fantasy/Paranormal

Book 1: Dark Blade

Book 2: Dragon Touched

Book 3: Society Against Vampires

Book 4: King's Request

Book 5: Duke's Courier

Dragon Blood- Young Adult Urban Fantasy (with elements of romance)

(5 book series)

Book 1: Pliethin

Book 2: Wyvern

Book 3: Surety
Book 4: Knight
Book 5: Mage

Dragon Mage- Young Adult Urban Fantasy (with elements of romance)

(Series two of Dragon Blood series)
Book 1: Promise
Book 2: Pact

Dragon Blood Chronicles- Young Adult Urban Fantasy (with elements of romance)

(Companion stand alone series to Dragon Blood)
Book 1: Oath
Book 2: Betrayed

Guardians Of The Round Table- Young Adult Fantasy LitRPG (Co-written with Storm and Rhys Petersen)

Book 1: Dexterity Fail
Book 2: Goblin Boots
Book 3: Singed Feathers

Book 4: Frog Mage
Book 5: Crystal Mine
Book 6: Cursed Harp
Book 7: Treasure Seeker
Book 8: Bard's Hollow

Set in the same world as Guardians Of The Round Table Series

Tales Of Inadon 1: The Disc (short story in Game On! Anthology)

Rosie's Rangers- Young Adult Western Steampunk

(6 book series)
Book 1: Justice
Book 2: Vengeance
Book 3: Treachery
Book 4: Accused
Book 5: Wanted
Book 6: Corruption

Mark Of Kings- Children's Fantasy

(Upper middle grade/preteen)
(4 book series)
Book 1: The Arena

Book 2: The Island

Book 3: The Assassin

Book 4: The King

Stand Alone Series

Demon Hunters- Young Adult Urban Fantasy/Horror (with elements of romance)

Book 1: Blood Sacrifice

Book 2: Retribution

Book 3: Tainted

Book 4: Premonition

Book 5: Cursed

Book 6: Feud

Book 7: Extrication

Plea Of The Damned- Young Adult Urban Fantasy/Paranormal

(6 book series)

Book 1: Forgive Me Lucy

Book 2: Forgive Me Aiden

Book 3: Forgive Me Jena

Book 4: Forgive Me Kobe

Book 5: Forgive Me Marti

Book 6: Forgive Me Dawson

Realms Of The Fae- Young Adult Urban Fantasy (with elements of romance)

The Sword (short story)

Call Forth The Wild Hunt (Short story in Summer Solstice Shenanigans Anthology)

Heart Of Stone

Book 1: A Debt Owed

Book 2: Marked By The Hunt

Book 3: The Magic Collector

Book 4: An Unexpected Betrayal

Book 5: Imprisoned By Iron

Book 6: Woven From Dreams

Fairytales Retold (Short Stories)

Snow-White And Rose-Red

The Twelve Brothers

The Light Princess

Beauty And The Beast

Sleeping Beauty

Aschenputtel

The Golden Bird

The Frog Prince

The Death Of Koshchei The Deathless

Myths And Legends Retold (Short Stories)

Ion, Son Of Apollo

Sir Gawain And The Maid With The Narrow Sleeves

Princess Ilse, The Giant's Daughter

Young Adult Novels

Young Adult Fantasy (with elements of romance)

Elf Sight

Earth Bound

Young Adult Urban Fantasy

Stone Warrior (with elements of romance)

The Jungle Inside

Young Adult Contemporary (with elements of romance)

Through Your Eyes

The Ugly Stepsister

Perfect Little Princess

Young Adult Contemporary/Paranormal

Whispers In The Dark (with elements of romance)

Over Too Soon (with elements of romance)

Young Adult Sci-Fi

Experiment X-One-Six (Urban Sci-Fi/Superheroes)

An Endless Dawn (Post Apocalyptic Sci-Fi)

Children's Books

Dragon Lord (Preteen/early teens) (Fantasy)

The Irish Wizard (Upper middle grade) (Urban Fantasy)

Short Stories

Urban Fantasy

Eternally Late

Dealings With Joe

Glimpses (short story in That Moment When Anthology)

Contemporary

The Brat Next Door

Post Apocalyptic Sci-Fi

Compulsive Directive

Nonfiction

A Year Of Weekly Writing Exercises (Creative Writing)

Cooking For Families With Allergies (Cooking) (Co-written with Storm Petersen)

Tell Me A Story, Grandma (Memoir)

Overview Of Independently Publishing A Book (How To)

For the most up to date details on available titles visit: www.avrilsabine.com/books/bibliography

Guardians Of The Round

Table Series

To learn more about this series visit:
www.avrilsabine.com/series/gotrt
Find maps, stats and details about the various books.

Books available in the series
Book 1: Dexterity Fail
Book 2: Goblin Boots
Book 3: Singed Feathers
Book 4: Frog Mage
Book 5: Crystal Mine
Book 6: Cursed Harp
Book 7: Treasure Seeker
Book 8: Bard's Hollow

Books set in the same world as the Guardians Of The Round Table Series

Tales Of Inadon 1: The Disc

Lore books related to Guardians Of The Round Table Series

Adventurers Guild Handbook

Legend Of The Ancestral King

Lost And Powerful: Myths Of Misplaced Staves

Returners Guild Handbook

Crafting Abilities series of books

Classes Of Inadon series of books

For the full list of available lore books visit:

www.avrilsabine.com/series/gotrt/lore-books

Disclaimer

This is a work of fiction. Names, characters, businesses, places, events and incidents are either the products of the author's imagination or used in a fictitious manner. Any resemblance to actual persons, living or dead, or actual events is purely coincidental. The opinions expressed or beliefs held are those of the characters and should not be assumed to be the opinions or beliefs of the author.